2020 Vision- The Wisdom of Hindsight

Claire Suyen Grace

Published by Suyen Talken-Sinclair, 2020.

2020 VISION- THE WISDOM OF HINDSIGHT

First edition. November 13, 2020.

ISBN: 978-1393442073

Written by Claire Suyen Grace.

Table of Contents

To the Past and all the Wise behind me,

To the Future, and all the Enlightened before me,

To my Family and Friends, for making my NOW so
blessed.

I have just finished the book. I thought it was very good. A compelling read- so much so I did it in one sitting. I hope it won't be the last one you write.

Absolutely outstanding: thought-provoking, compelling, enlightening, deeply sad and also hopeful. I cried and laughed many times over. An honest story from an amazing woman who has many life lessons to share. An absolute must read in these difficult times. Thank you

A thought-provoking and compelling read from start to end.

One woman's brave reflections on choices made. Shocking and beautiful. A story spanning time and place, written from the heart. I thoroughly enjoyed it

My mind marvels at how soul-sisters are soul sisters not through shared time experiences but because of a far deeper and longer history of knowing and recognition.

Such eclectic and exotic experiences.

A marvellous saga unleashed in quarantine.

Heart-stoppingly honest.

I find myself inspired to travel down roads of profound thought, and to see things from a different perspective.

What can I say other than I loved them? When reading it felt like I was shifting in and out of an ethereal dancing dream, skipping about through a lifetime of journeys. During post Covid times, adventures like these seem like distant history. Really enjoyed them and look forward to reading more on paper.

Bugger
  I've started your book.....
  I NEED TO SLEEP
  The two are clearly incompatible

Just finished reading your book Suyen and loved it. It evokes time and place, people and events so clearly that we're there with you. You bring us a whole life of love, care and an amazing family with moving truth and honesty.

  What a life you've lived and allowed us to share. Thank you and hope we can meet if fate allows.

For me it was a very painful read...If a measure of a writer's success is whether s/he moves emotions, mine were certainly moved.....For me the messages are mixed but perhaps that's life?

  Your 'moving our feet thought' reminded me of Mandella – 'judge me by how many times I fell down and got up again'.

  Your story moved me and you write elegantly and with a lot of style.

2020 Vision - The Wisdom of Hindsight

By

Claire Suyen Grace

"Enlightenment is a destructive process. It has nothing to do with becoming better or being happier. Enlightenment is the crumbling away of untruth. It's seeing through the facade of pretence. It's the complete eradication of everything we imagined to be true."

Adyashanti

DAY NINE

Clarity

November 2020.

As I sit here having finished writing, the election in America is in its final spasms, we do not yet know the result. We all fear the worst and predict a future with worrying levels of governmental control and a lack of conscience, a void of plain old-fashioned goodness.

On this side of the Atlantic the country is coming to terms with the idea of a four-week lockdown due to the Covid-19 virus, and is struggling to maintain a positive mental attitude when all we really feel is exhaustion and despondency.

We seem to have forgotten all about Brexit and the monumental changes that it brings to our everyday interaction with our European relations.

My own personal friends are fighting off various stages of depression and the feeling of inevitable impotency, uncertain of whom to believe and how to respond in order to stay safe. To survive.

When I first sat down to write a short story six months ago based on the then new C-19 global pandemic, I had no inkling that I would feel inspired to write about not just one, but several days out of my life. The structure soon created itself- the repetitive nature of our lives that is inherent to a twenty-four hour period, but within which we all travel backwards and forwards through Time, remembering, reliving, re-evaluating, and learning. Making choices based on our own internalised collective consciousness.

I soon realised that it is those Life Lessons, not just our own, but also those of our family and our ancestors, that make each of us into who we are, and who we are decides what choices we make throughout our lives. The Lessons we learn come to us via many means, and seem destined to be repeated time and time again until we change our reactions to them, thus causing not a cyclical pattern of life but a spiral created by the minutiae of change that occurs around us as we walk what we think to be a straight line through history.

So it is that 2020 Vision came to be.

Part diary, part adventure story, mainly fact, one fiction. The stories move in Time across all but two continents- I will need to have somewhere new to travel next- and span at least two centuries of memory. I have been more than fortunate in my life, which is now into its sixth decade, having laughed with Royalty, supped with Witch Doctors, rescued lions and slept with panthers.

I have worn the very best diamonds and limped along tarmac with holes in my shoes. I have enjoyed the best champagne and lived for several weeks on nothing but tinned sardines and black tea. I have owned the acres that led to the sea where once Arthur was said to roam, and I have slept cold and wet in an empty room, filled with sadness and despair.

Through it all I remember that we are only here for the tiniest of moments in Time and that if we are really lucky, we get to Be the good that we hope for in the world around us.

The world now grapples with Covid-19 and the profound changes being forced upon it both in the everyday realities that affect us all, and the even deeper changes that each individual is experiencing within themselves and their values and priorities. This is a time of great change, and true change is never birthed easily or without pain. We can only hope that each and every one of us has the strength to look at the mirror of our soul and create within it a future that nurtures and sustains the best aspects of Humanity.

It is a noble aspiration for us all.

Suyen.

IF

If you can keep your head when all about you
    Are losing theirs and blaming it on you;
    If you can trust yourself when all men doubt you,
    But make allowance for their doubting too;
    If you can wait and not be tired by waiting,
    Or, being lied about, don't deal in lies,
    Or, being hated, don't give way to hating,
    And yet don't look too good, nor talk too wise;
    If you can dream—and not make dreams your master;
    If you can think—and not make thoughts your aim;
    If you can meet with triumph and disaster
    And treat those two impostors just the same;
    If you can bear to hear the truth you've spoken
    Twisted by knaves to make a trap for fools,
    Or watch the things you gave your life to broken,
    And stoop and build 'em up with worn out tools;
    If you can make one heap of all your winnings
    And risk it on one turn of pitch-and-toss,
    And lose, and start again at your beginnings
    And never breathe a word about your loss;
    If you can force your heart and nerve and sinew
    To serve your turn long after they are gone,
    And so hold on when there is nothing in you
    Except the will which says to them: "Hold on";
    If you can talk with crowds and keep your virtue,
    Or walk with kings—nor lose the common touch;
    If neither foes nor loving friends can hurt you;

If all men count with you, but none too much;
If you can fill the unforgiving minute
With sixty seconds' worth of distance run—
Yours is the Earth and everything that's in it...........
Rudyard Kipling
1865-1936

DAY ONE
Another Bloody Beautiful Day

I wake up to the sound of Bailey tapping on the windowpane, impatient to get out. The sun has cleared the rooftop next door, and the light streams in to show up the water stains on the outside of the glass and the dust on the inside on the sill. Bailey taps again. It's all of five thirty according to the travel clock, bought for less than a pound at Ikea- my daughter had been most amused by my parsimony. Bailey begins to scratch at the window frame in earnest, while outside the small songbirds flit from feeder to feeder in the relative safe dawn hours before I liberate my three cats. Piri and Yoda, hearing their feline companion, dart into the bedroom and jump up beside him on the sill.

Outside on the patio the birds are busy. A pair of woodpeckers peck nervously at the fat balls, conscious of even the slightest indoor movement, and a magpie cocks his head while he debates whether to fly down from next door's guttering and take deep beakfulls of seed or lard. The little people, the finches, tits, blackbirds, robins and nuthatches, all hop or fly from one seed holder to another, having grown brave with the confidence which comes with familiarity.

Bailey never catches a bird, he is far too heavy now in middle age and never much inclined to be a hunter. Piri and Yoda, just out of kittenhood, are both intrigued by the movements of flying machines, but it is the small wild rodent population that is suffering from the kittens' recent liberation from house arrest, not my avian friends. Many a tiny shrew has already ended up on my bedroom carpet, with me frantically trying to catch it- "Please don't die, please don't die" my desperate whispered mantra to stop it dying from shock.

I clamber out of bed, top up the cats' dry food and open the windows. Looking down the short passage outside my bedroom door, I notice my son's trainers are outside his partially closed door, and a flood of relief fills my heart and mind.

The Devonshire summer sunlight streams across my bed and throws rainbows onto the white wall, bouncing through a crystal lightcatcher given to me decades ago at university in Canada. Outside the view is of verdant woodland and green fields on undulating hills, charming thatched cottages and beautiful gardens.

"It's another bloody beautiful day in Paradise."

Sarah Miles, in that incisive film, White Mischief, utters those immortal lines.

They sum up the total ennui that beleaguered the privileged expats of 1930's Kenya. She stands on her huge balcony, looking out over the natural beauty of East Africa, lost in the repetition and dreamlike quality of her existence, unfettered by working to survive or having to have a raison d'etre, overwhelming with irony.

It is an isolation of a kind, being locked into a privileged position, where you cannot escape into the real world that surrounds you. Sarah Miles' character escapes into alcohol, drugs, sexual promiscuity and eventually, voluntary death. Most don't have that type of freedom. Most of us are fettered by the years of conditioning that takes place from the nanosecond of our conception and lead us to each pinprick of our day.

My day has begun.

Day whatever it is of Covid-19 Lockdown.

I walk quietly past the spare room, where my son lies deep in sleep. The tiny door is kept open by the towel hanging over it, and I have no wish to wake him. It was a tough night. Only a few hours earlier I'd had the police knocking at my door at half past one asking me if I knew the whereabouts of my son as they were concerned about his state of mind. Cue euphemism for suicide risk.

There's something surreal about standing in your kitchen looking out into the night over the top of a stable door at a policeman who is telling you that your adult son could be wanting to kill himself. The polite veneer of remaining calm and civilised, of asking the officers if they want a cup of coffee, of explaining to them that you have absolutely no idea where your child is even though he is under your roof living with you at the present time. The light humour, interspersed by the black and threatening spectre of horror, heartbreak and despair.

Eventually they leave, promising to search in all the favourite haunts, and you collapse onto the spare bed, screaming inside, sobbing, thinking of all the times you've crossed thoughts, words and swords with this man of your blood, this child of your loins, the boy made flesh, now tortured, heartbroken and deep in the depths of complete emotional destruction.

I cried for hours, praying out loud for him to simply "be safe", to not be fathoms deep under the cold, black heartless sea that he loves or wrapped in a metallic mess of blood, gore and steel in a ditch somewhere. Then I decided to sleep, to wait for the morning as there was nothing I could change by crying, and now I wake up and find him back in my house, in his room, alive.

I tread softly down the stairs.

The dogs look up as I open the child gate and go into the kitchen. MJ, the old, almost blind Jack Russell wags her tail enthusiastically and snuffles her way around the kitchen trying to find her way past Emma the labrador who is lying flat out in their basket. Ellisar, the borzoi, is curled up in a ridiculously compact position on an old reclining chair. The one my ex-lover gave me, before he screwed one of my closest friends and tossed me onto the pile of unwanted complications in his life.

Ten years of devotion and love flipped over like a dried-out frog skeleton squashed on the road by passing traffic. Only in this case the traffic was someone I had trusted and supported for longer than I'd had the lover- someone who saw an opportunity when I went to work overseas and snapped at it, lying and cheating her way all the way into our bed.

Sweating and moaning all over our memory-foam mattress and goose down duvet, clamping on so tight that no amount of pleading or prostration could loosen her grip, could prise apart the combination of need, want, guilt and fear which surrounds so many mid-life crises. Or to put it more succinctly, she lied, he listened, they fucked. I crumpled.

She laughed. He complied. I writhed and fell.

Love doth make fools of us all.

I snap the dogs' collars on and take them out for their early morning wee. MJ walks loose as we're only going across the lane to my parking area. Emma and Ellisar know the routine and so no one gets to see me in my dressing gown and slippers- or bare feet if the temperature is warm. Like it is today. That's one of the perks of living in a small village, although it is apparently the longest village in the country, we can saunter about in the early hours of the day in our PJs and bare feet without having to worry about the neighbours casting aspersions on our morality or our social finesses. My grandmother would have been appalled.

My elderly neighbour waves from her kneeling position by the emerging dahlias. Years ago she wrestled with the local council and won the right to commandeer the land below her house and cultivate it. Now it's famous, pictures of her garden adorn postcards and magazines, and in the tourist season small bottlenecks occur outside our homes as visitors stop and gaze in amazement at the plethora of blooms which are festooned outside her house.

I wave back. I'm allowed to use her outside tap to water my plants, and I'm grateful. Her water supply isn't metered, and since I have several pots and planters outside the cottage and on my patio, watering in the summer is a necessity. I also take the opportunity to water the plants of the neighbour whose cottage fits snuggly in between the two of us.

She sold him the property several years ago, before she knew that he was homosexual- a transgression from the norm that she simply cannot accept- and from time to time her extreme prejudices cannot help but make themselves heard. It's not pretty. So I water his plants when I water mine, daring her to object out loud to my face, to own her appalling biase and simple bad manners and lack of compassion. She never does, he says it's because she is afraid of me, but I think it's because I've already told her that I have several gay friends and that they are all wonderful, kind, compassionate people.

Once back indoors I feed the dogs their mixture of raw meat and dry food. I've learnt much in the last couple of years about raw feeding of carnivores, makes such sense really. Think wolf. More so after my vet told me how much sugar is put into processed pet food just to addict cats and dogs to certain products. Who knew?! The two now no longer kittens Yoda and PiriPiri jump up on an old kitchen chair that used to grace my grandmother's dining table and wait for their pilchards in tomato sauce. Tomato sauce is good for animals, full of lycopene, and both the dogs and the cats love the fish.

Food and nutrition has become something of a hobby horse of mine over the last decade... before that I had no idea what an alkaline diet was, or a Keto meal plan, or a hundred and one other bits of information that I can now spew forth to support my choice to eat more plant based nutrition. Hard when I have to confess to still really enjoying the flavour of cooked dead animal parts. Just as well I'm no longer having to earn my rent as a chef and am now working as part of Children's Services instead.

The phrase "lambs to the slaughter" comes to mind for both worlds, no doubt as a result of the disillusionment I feel in my professional role after recently witnessing first hand the appalling bad practise that can contribute to the destruction and total devastation of the very families we are supposed to be helping. My deep set fury starts to bubble up again, and I close my eyes and sigh. One of those long, deep, meditative sighs, the ones that are used to ground all the detritus that floats across our vision every day and blocks out the sun. My eyes fly open, it's a curse sometimes, twenty twenty vision.

Picking up the cat and dog bowls, I place them into the sink and wash them out with hot water to kill the fishy smell. Then I tell the dogs to wait and I go outside to fill up the bird feeders. For some reason the birds are eating their way through at least ten fat balls a day this year. A small fortune in suet, millet, sunflower seed and mealworms. My guilty pleasure. One of the robins is very tame, and when I moved into the cottage I had to keep the kitchen top door closed to stop her flying inside as she had been used to do. Mind you, it wasn't too difficult for me as I moved in on the 20th of December, just three days before my daughter was scheduled to arrive with her family for Christmas.

The cottage is supposedly 17th Century, so low beamed ceilings, two foot thick outer walls and small windows. The master bedroom is the piece de resistance, with its high vaulted ceiling and two six-foot windows that allow the morning sun to shine in unhindered from the east. Finding somewhere to rent in this village had been more challenging than finding a true black Thoroughbred over 16 hands high, but fate had intervened after keeping me on the hop for four months, and the previous tenants had decided to move out and offered it to me. Eureka.

On the day I moved in I froze in stunned horror. It was so tiny! How could I have even imagined I would be able to fit everything I owned into it? And that was after having had to give away almost all of my furniture a year earlier when the property owner from hell well and truly screwed me over-telling me she had changed her mind about me living in her coach house, and would I please remove myself within the next twenty-four hours.

My friends were all stunned, but I was in shock, homeless and without any financial safety net. I had three dogs and twice as many cats, and a house full of goods and chattels. That night I lay on the floor with my dogs and wept in despair, really wondering how I could salvage this mess. Then I remembered a small pebble I had found several weeks earlier, a pink stone with the word Faith cut into it.

I had picked it up off of the pavement and put it into my purse, from whence I took it out now. Faith. I remembered my father's voice saying, "This too will pass," and I thought, I must have faith that this is all for the best, that something better will happen to take its place. The next morning a friend of mine overseas offered to pay for a week's AirBnB for me to catch my breath, and I was allowed to go there with my dogs. Another friend looked after my cats. My daughter started looking for a house that I could rent, and two weeks later we had found one.

Faith, it moves mountains.

That was the property before this one, and although I did lose a couple of hundred of my books when I moved in there, thanks to one of my granddaughters turning on a bathroom tap and flooding all the bags of books I had stored in the tub, it had been large enough to accommodate all of my belongings. The Cottage seemed minute in comparison, and it is. Nonetheless, it is quite magical and just like the Tardis, everything fitted in eventually.

Having fed all of the homebased furred and feathered, I grab a bag of carrots out of the fridge and pick up my car keys. The fobs are medals from World War Two, commemorations for social loss and personal suffering. Words of solace etched into the highly polished silver and bronze, but no amount of polish can remove the blood stains and spilt guts on a battlefield.

My parents weren't in the war, both born just a little too late and at a far distance from the guns of Navarone. Instead my father cycled from Johannesburg to London in his early twenties, sans money, weapons or a Channel 4 back up vehicle, while from the age of six my mother raised eleven half siblings after her own mother had died from pneumonia. One of my father's cousins was awarded the DFC- Distinguished Flying Cross- for shooting down an extraordinary number of German aircraft in one day; my father remembered his cousin as the child who would knock the heads off of his precious lead soldiers when they played together as children. Battles come in many forms.

When my son's best friend came to me towards the end of sixth form and told me that he was considering joining the army I asked him only one question:

"You may be prepared to die for your country, that's easy, but are you prepared to kill for it?"

I added that to kill under orders one has to have implicit trust and faith in the people who are in the positions of power and control. He went on to become an excellent skiing instructor, his only casualties the odd pupil who took a bend too fast.

The horses have been moved recently and are now a mere five minutes drive from where I live. I moved them a couple of months after the death of my foundation stallion, a real soul partner that had been with me for three decades. Tarac was a stunning grey Arab that put me on the map in the showring and stayed with me through all the ups and downs of my life.

Tarac navigated with me the many hardships and challenges that can accompany a person when they choose to leave a comfortable marriage with their two children and no financial security. It was a bone of contention for not a few of my friends- my determination to hold on to my horses when I was lurching month end to month end in penury. They felt, possibly justifiably, that I should be content in a small flat somewhere, particularly once my children had left home, and not keep on insisting that my home be somewhere beautiful and rural and make me feel content. I've had a few discussions about that. As the ex-lover once said, "It's not fair for you to expect other people to help you out of debt if you won't get rid of all the things that you don't need."

He was right of course, and his comment made me look at my life and find myself wanting. Nowadays I work full time and I rent my home, and I have next to no disposable income after everything is paid, but at least these days I am working on getting all the debts and loans paid off, and if I can maintain that then what I choose to feel as necessary in my life is my choice, and I pay for that choice. Literally. So, I still have two horses, both of whom needed to be rehomed, three cats- pure frivolity- and three dogs, only one of which I actually wanted in an active sense but all three of whom needed to be with me.

Once at the new horsey place, I park my car in the shade of an old oak tree and climb over the five-bar gate. Sparkle, a twenty-one year old sports horse and Darcy, a two year old Arab gelding, are grazing quietly in the sun in the middle of two acres of old meadow grass. Perfect. Huge improvement on my last place which, although a godsend when I found it proved to not be ideal in the longer run, mainly due to the lack of grass. Horses need grass- at least they do if one wants them to live as near to naturally as possible. Which I do.

Tarac was blessed in that. So many showing stallions spend their lives cooped up in an artificial hell of confinement and solitude, hardly ever being allowed to roam freely or in a herd. Horses are social animals and need other horses with them to be complete. No wonder so many modern competition animals now suffer from gastric ulcers, while their owners look outwards with worry and concern instead of observing internally all their own motivations and how those impact upon their steeds.

I amble over to my two and break off chunks of carrot to treat them with. Darcy has been here only two months and is slowly settling into a relationship of trust with me. Sparkle has been with me for a handful of years, and it is only now that her eye has softened and that she no longer squeals in anxious fear at the world around her. It's been a long journey, teaching her that it is okay for her to just be a horse, to just Be.

When Tarac died, Sparkle stood over him until he was driven away, and I could sense her palpable grief, so Darcy joined us. Horses grieve. Sparkle grieved for years over the foals she had lost to sloppy husbandry in her past, and it was Tarac who healed her. Day in, day out, he simply kept her company, never asking, never demanding, and then one day, she saved his life in return.

It was lambing season, I remember that because the farmer I called for help was busy lambing and couldn't come. Tarac was upside down in a ditch and stuck. The ditch was deep and on the wrong side of a ten-acre field. I ran- ever try running across a muddy field? Murder!- up the drive to the land owner and called out, "Can your Volvo get across the field in the mud?"

He assured me it could, but it couldn't, 4x4 notwithstanding.

So he ran too. With mountaineering ropes and two body boards. He is a tree surgeon, hence ropes.

"Will Sparkle pull him out?" I was asked.

"I have no idea, but if she bolts, we are all screwed."

We managed to pass the ropes under Tarac's body and tie them, then a makeshift rope harness was tied around Sparkle. I prayed that she wouldn't panic once she started to feel the weight of Tarac pulling her backwards, and I really prayed that she wouldn't panic and take off with Tarac being pulled along behind her. I took hold of her head collar and asked her to walk on, slowly, one step at a time. Over half a tonne of slightly unmanageable horseflesh being asked to do the unthinkable- to pull and not overreact when the body of weight behind her started to slither in the mud.

Sparkle saved Tarac's life that day, and I told him she'd never let him forget it. My tree surgeon friend saved all of us too of course, with his quick thinking and knowledge of quick release knots. Tarac was in his late twenties by then, so the odds against him surviving a night in a ditch upside down were very high indeed, but he did, and we both went on to fight other dragons on other days, until the cardiac dragon claimed him.

Even then, his death saved another, and Darcy came to live with me.

By the time I get back home, my son is awake and cleaning his car. It's a good sign.

I throw a salad together- greens, tomatoes, cucumber, avocado, nuts, my own chilli sauce and salad dressing. I've been mainly vegan for a year or so now and like it. Bacon and cheese, the two foods that tempt like Sirens many vegetarian and vegan wannabes. What is it about bacon? Some things can't be unseen though, and for me I've seen too many images of slaughterhouses and animal transportation methods and just outright cruelty aimed at animals that are eventually part of the human food chain. It's all about choices really, choices around what type of person I want to be, and what I choose to subscribe to.

Cheese I thought would be the real problem as I love cheese, especially soft gooey smelly cheese that runs off the plate and nestles happily against a cracker or oozes over warm vegetables. My paternal great grandfather used to like his Stilton literally walking off his plate. It happened to me only once, when I left a French unpasteurised cheese on top of the fridge in the warm for too long and later found it moving with tiny white creatures...unlike my relative, I fed mine to the outside. Now I hardly think about cheese at all, which just goes to prove that change is possible if it's important enough to us. It's all about Choice.

Lunch is on the patio, my oasis of flowers and birds and small water feature, aka plastic baby bath hidden by planted hostas. I've ordered a tiny solar powered fountain to enhance the effect, although I suspect that it's main effect will be me wanting to have a wee more often! I do my video clips outside as well, weather permitting.

A wasp is buzzing around me, attracted perhaps by the smell of honey in my tea. Back in 2012, while in Lutz with the animal charity Four Paws caring for a rescued bear cub, I inadvertently attracted a whole plethora of wasps into the large jar of honey I had purchased as part of Nastia's breakfast.

Two inches deep, the struggling insects were literally drowning in delight. I was horrified, since the last thing I would choose would be to kill unsuspecting creatures without a good reason. Frantic, I tried to think of a way to save so many when they were all covered in honey, submerged completely in a sticky grave. Unsure of whether any would survive, I tipped the jar with its writhing contents onto a large tray and flushed it with water- they'd either survive or drown. The water washed the honey off the black and yellow army, and very soon the sun had dried off their wings. They spent several minutes preening before flying off. Amazingly, not one died.

The sky is a pale cornflower blue, and the sun has been shining for enough days to make me think the plants need rain. I'm busy emptying the reserves in the rainbutt but I can hear the water pressure fading. My water is metered, so gardening is a luxury at times. I'm grateful for my tiny patio and the pots of plants that bask in front of the south-facing wall of my cottage entrance.

Birds twitter and chimes occasionally ring out in the breeze- big improvement on the clattering and crashing two days ago when the sunny reverie was interrupted by the staccato bursts of stone on metal and bamboo pipes clanking in the winds. I tied them together in the end, nothing at all serene arising from the clatter and crashing.

Today I sit and drink tea. The smoky aroma of Lapsang. Work meeting in thirty via the internet to touch base with internal management and my area team. These are shaken times- our targets are short and our service deemed non-essential by this particular council... how long will we continue to be able to play our role? Ironic when we have just won a national award for being the best Social Work team.

Alternative revenue is becoming a target in its own right.

Yesterday I treated myself to buying my feathered entertainers a large bag of seed and some fat-balls, truly an extravagance, but they are rewarding me with their company, even though I sit only a few feet away. They even ignore Bailey, this huge ginger cat curled up in a wicker basket on a chair in the sun beside me. He stopped hunting them long ago. He meows now for attention, and I stop typing to give him a cuddle and put him back in the sun. We're very lucky.

Looking around, the plants that have survived the Spring cold and rain are all starting to overflow the boundaries of their pots.

I have thyme and marjoram and oregano, troopers all, that I nibble at every morning to combat any nasties hoping to latch onto me. Great antivirals. Lilies are standing tall in bud but sadly yesterday in my enthusiasm of cleaning I neatly lopped off the shoots of two of my favourites. No idea if they will survive and bear blooms after all.

Four miniature pink rose plants that came out of one pot which a close friend gave me last autumn are now each established in their own right and have been planted into Strider's burial pot for the summer. Miniature roses that are sold in pots are usually four separate plants, just in case anyone wants to split them. The large roses that I planted months ago are now starting to bloom and I think I have finally managed to create some robust growth on the spindly purple one.

A bumble bee is buzzing loudly behind me, I think it's tapping into sheep's nettle, and our resident robin Jackie- or her mate- is watching me in that quizzical way that robins have when they tilt their heads. A chaffinch has just dive bombed me, taking a closer look to ensure that Bailey is washing himself and not stalking, and that I am indeed harmless. He goes now to sample the seeds I filled the feeders with yesterday and is quickly joined by others.

I have rigged up a trellis on my patio that the feeders hang from and which can be seen by anyone walking up the lane from the church outside my house. I am told by several people that they take pleasure from just watching the birds as they themselves amble past. It's a privilege to share the joy. The birds are singing all around me and often provide the musical accompaniment to my video clips.

The hover-flies seem to have appeared all of a sudden, eager to aspire to their honey-producing very distant relatives.... I personally hope their ruse fails and lots of birds second guess them, but that's because I really dislike flies. I mean, if God had to create something to do all the nastiness couldn't the species have been a beautiful one? I make no bones about it, if I see a fly I ask it to get lost before I assist it on its karmic way- after all, I'm doing it a favour, maybe it will rebirth as a kingfisher. Flies are psychic (ever noticed how quickly they scarper once you pick up a rolled newspaper?!) so any I have in the house tend to fly out the window as requested pdq - pretty damn quick.

Sunshine means that people are busy mowing their lawns so the quiet isn't, as it were. Still, no cars, which on any other sunny afternoon simply wouldn't be the case. Last weekend it was like bloody Grand Central Station here, as literally dozens if not hundreds of visitors flocked to the seaside.

Which brings to mind a post on our village Facebook page.

Several weeks ago, when the nation was just getting used to the idea of social isolation, one of the villagers was taking her morning exercise down to the sea when she saw an elderly couple sitting on the beach who were not local. When she asked them about ignoring the government guidelines to not travel unnecessarily out of area she was told "We can go anywhere we want!"

I think this illustrates two things, one is the inherent arrogance cushioned within their attitude and response and two, it's not just young people who can behave like prats. There was also someone getting his parking ticket who didn't live here, he had apparently driven here because he "knew it would be quiet and no one would be here."

No, just the locals. In a place where the vast majority of houses stand empty for most of the year, being the holiday retreats or tax evading second or third or fourth homes of a certain stratum of society, maybe locals are "No one" after all.

It's my granddaughter's birthday soon and of course I can't celebrate it with her as I normally would. She is only five but can understand about sickness and that it will be a very quiet birthday for her. Normally I would be going to see her, or the whole family would come to me for the day, but such plans are now cancelled. Thank goodness for FaceTime- we have all had to become techno savvy these days, regardless of our age.

During the time I'm having to stay home-based I've set up two groups on social media, one based on Chinese cooking and the other on the development of Darcy's training. The cooking one resulted from me not being able to hold classes in my home, but still wanting to reach out to people, and the Darcy page is a way to share horse stories and animal tales. Doing weekly video clips is a good way of keeping people engaged, and no doubt somewhat amused at the foibles of my life. There are many.

This afternoon I decide to do a short video explaining the dishes that I intend to showcase at some point this weekend. Making a video out on the patio is easy, all I have to watch out for is that I'm not squinting into the sun and that I don't have a telegraph pole growing out of my head. Making a video inside my kitchen is a whole different ballgame.

First, positioning the iPad so that both myself and the wok are in frame has proved nigh on impossible. I have tried everything. Stacked the iPad on a collection of coffee jars, saucepans, bowls and tea caddies. Angled the iPad high, low, looking up, looking down, even hanging over the rustic kitchen shelf that runs along the wall above my stove... all only relatively successful, as in better than no video at all...maybe.

My good friend in Chile, herself an accomplished film maker and traveller extraordinaire, assures me that audiences want to see ME, not some old wok, but I'm not convinced; I think that people need to see the food cooking in order to understand what I mean, since I teach with neither measurements nor precise timings. So this weekend I am planning to cook sweet and sour something with stir-fried something to go with it, I will decide on the details later.

Now I spend about ten minutes addressing my happy band of warriors, just touching base and hopefully keeping their imaginations engaged. It is fun, and somewhat gratifying in these times of isolation, to know that almost two hundred people may take the opportunity to learn how to fry rice!

Cooking I learnt from my Chinese mother. She was herself a remarkable woman, one of true grit tempered with romance and an unlimited capacity to love. She met my father in Trinidad when he was managing a sugar plantation in the mid 1950's and followed him back to the UK on the first banana boat she could find. She left a ruptured marriage behind her, her husband married his mistress of seven years and my mother cast her fortune to the wind.

My parents' lives together were spent mostly in Africa, with the occasional four month road trip and visit back to England, but they never could really fit in here, this country with its damp cold weather and inherent stoic behaviour that often masks social injustice. My father was a white South African, as they were known then, and left the land of his birth for over three decades, returning only after the end of apartheid.

After that he worked in several of the southern countries as a newspaper editor until, in the grandest of ironies, he realised that he would never be able to escape the colour of his skin in the eyes of the people around him, and he returned to England to care for his aging mother.

I myself was born here in London, and later I returned here from Liberia to go to boarding school which I loved. Domestic Science was not on my timetable, but I was at university before my seventeenth birthday enrolled in veterinary science. I loved uni as well, although the lessons I learnt there had nothing to do with the degree I eventually graduated with, which wasn't a qualification in veterinary science but instead a mixed one combining the arts and sciences- always a Renaissance Woman, even then. Is University ever really about getting a Degree? What I did learn whilst there was about survival, resilience, discipline, ingenuity and integrity.

Which is why I am now teaching people how to cook online instead of in my kitchen.

The High Street is almost deserted. A few couples walking together, some with their dogs, and a few solitary folk walking briskly as if self-conscious about their individual status. The shops are closed, except for a few food based stores, and the chemists. The Post Office is open, which is just as well since I have driven into town to post a Cheetah skin off to a taxidermist. It's an old skin, made into a rug just before my father was born and left languishing on its bais of brown felt ever since. Nowadays very non PC. Times change.

Back when this particular cheetah was roaming the plains of East Africa, my Godfather was growing up to become one of the last Great White Hunters in Tanganyika, and my own father, while on safari, had to help track down and shoot an elephant that was terrorising local villagers. The photograph of my father sitting on the dead carcass of a young male elephant, its belly starting to bloat with gas, rifle casually slung over his shoulder, fills me with sadness now but back then my father referred to the picture as the "definitive shot". The one everyone would remember from the trip, and it is a definitive shot in many ways, just not in the ways my father imagined at that time.

A few years ago my son-in-law's mother had felt quite ill at ease to see a dead animal's pelt hanging over the back of my sofa, even if that skin was several decades old. When I mentioned the rug on a social media page i was practically lynched, so much so that I soon deleted my post and disappeared into the anonymity of cyberspace. Thankfully, a local taxidermist had no such squeamish reaction and offered to take it off of my hands. Since neither of my children want the rug I happily agreed to send it to him.

The skin shows signs of age, and wear and tear- literally. Mydas, my panther, used to practise his stalking skills with it when a cub and pounce onto the head from several feet away, a practise that's resulted in poor old Cheetah losing most of his ears. Cheetah has more recently been prey to PiriPiri's sharp claws, as her Bengal instincts have led her to scamper up and over the skin as it lay balanced on the top of the balustrade in the cottage. So I'm very grateful that the Post Office is open, and that I can post the rug off to a different future which doesn't include me.

Besides, Cheetah has sad eyes, and maybe this taxidermist can make him look happy again.

In Cheetah's heyday the skin was draped over the Chinze settee in my Grandmother's parents' gracious home. Later it settled onto the back of her own two-seater sofa in a less salacious Welsh farm worker's cottage that had neither running hot water nor indoor bath. The walls were three-foot-thick and the pervasive damp meant that we had to use at least three hot water bottles on the feather mattresses all year long.

My Grandmother exchanged the easy luxury of the colonial East African life for years of drudgery in a tiny hamlet on the Wales- England border. She looked after her bedridden misogynistic mother-in-law for years after the love of her life left the Kenya Police after Mau Mau and returned to work for the Ministry of Defense in Whitehall.

Love again, making fools of us all. No wonder Cheetah looks sad.

By the time I return to the cottage, my son has gone out. He's in his early thirties now so i don't even try to keep tabs on him, especially since he tends to resent any such solicitous behaviour on my part at the moment. We all lash out at those nearest to us, because we know that we are safe doing so, and right now I'm closest and right in the line of fire. It's not a comfortable place to be, and it hurts deeply, but that's what Mothers do for the children they love- they take the pain and run with it until the course is done. Of course I'm worrying, but that too is something that I just have to accept, accept not being in charge, not being in control, not being able to make things any easier for someone I love.

There's a scene in Mel Gibson's The Passion where Christ falls down as a child- I think it comes when Mary is watching him carry the cross to Calvary, but I'm not a hundred per cent certain- and Mary bends down to help him up and comfort him. That memory tore my heart out at the time. The juxtaposition of Christ the Child with Christ the Messiah, and the love of his mother totally and completely powerless to stop her child's suffering.

Motherhood. No one sets out to become a bad mother, or a bad child. Life just happens and all those innocent hopes and beliefs get skewed to fit into the places which we find easy to access within ourselves. I like to think of Life like a map- we are born into a certain section of the map, but then our genes and our experiences decide which roads we follow, and which directions we take when we are faced with a choice of pathway. We all make different choices, but it's still the same map.

Families share the section of the map but can often move across it in completely different ways. Children are the arrows that parents shoot out into the Cosmos, as Kalil Gibran describes so beautifully in The Prophet. We parents are neither their anchor nor their taskmaster, but simply a safe haven to which they should feel always welcome to return.

A good friend of mine, now deceased, used to refer to this part of the world as Paradise. Every Friday he would post a photo of a beach somewhere and comment wistfully about his lifelong dream to buy a home overlooking the Channel. He died with a bladder tumour the size of a football that had gone untreated, having spent the last thirty years providing a roof over the head of his only child. In hindsight it was an unappreciated gesture, and I regret never being able to convince him to let his child follow a path of their own choosing, albeit a more risky one without a financial safety-net.

We all choose our own prisons, as my friends have heard me say often, and Freedom comes at a price, no doubt about it.

We all have to choose how much we are prepared to pay in order to obtain the freedoms we strive to have.

My own freedoms have always cost me very dear indeed.

This Time, NOW, with whole countries immobilised as their citizens stay locked into their homes, is a time when many people are being forced- whether through their own fear, or the consent to conform, or the belief that they are doing what must be done- to stay with themselves, to take a look at who, and what they are, who they perpetuate by their choice of actions, and what they choose to align with- both inside and outside of their Self.

These are tricky portals to navigate.

I find myself wondering about how best to go forward from here, how to balance my true Self with the limiting practicalities of survival in a material world.

I have no partner or government subsidies to keep me housed, so I work full time to exchange my energy for the aspects of reality I want to enjoy, but it's a tough game, and I'd like to move the parameters if I can. This then is the challenge facing so many of us once our imposed isolation comes to an end- who will we choose to be? And how can we create that reality?

In the words of Primo Levi,

If I am not for myself, who will be for me?

If not now, when?

It's eight o clock on a Thursday evening and my neighbour is knocking on my door. She has appointed herself the conscience of the terrace and sees it as her civic duty to remind me that we should all be outside hammering on pots or whistling or clapping, or letting off fireworks to show our support for the NHS. The noise startles the dogs, so they're doing their bit to show their appreciation too... I can't help but think to myself that our whole amazing national health service is actually going to the dogs now one way or another. My daughter's a paediatrician so I feel justified in having an opinion.

A couple of months ago, when we were only just starting to hear regularly about Covid-19 I had a chat with my daughter who lives five hours drive away and works in a large city hospital. She had just finished a night shift and told me how a mother of a twenty-two month old child had posted a completely erroneous story online about her son having the C-19 virus. The story was picked up by MSM -mainstream media- and within minutes had been shared over twenty thousand times. The mother claimed she hadn't posted the original story as she shared her account with her partner, but the story was now out there causing huge panic and concerns. The hospital had to contact the newspaper (think galactic central star) and the story was removed immediately, but not before it had been shared over twenty-two thousand times. Such is the speed of our new internet viral spread.

The phone rings and it's a friend I've known since just before my return from Jordan eight years ago. Hopefully all those nurses and carers will forgive me for not adding my applause to the cacophony of cheering outside... It's a small village, so maybe cacophony is a slight exaggeration, although the fireworks exploding on the beach at the bottom of the cliffs opposite to me could lead you to think otherwise. Guy Fawkes would be thrilled, the local livestock are less so.

Jordan was a gift from the Gods. A personal invitation to go out and work with an NGO (non-government organisation- God, I hate acronyms) set up by HRH Princess Alia of Jordan. On the turn of a card I left my life here in Devon and flew out to the Middle East to create an equine therapy program for children on the autistic spectrum. I named it Growing Together, and thanks to the Princess Alia Foundation, the project is still running a decade after it was established.

Those were days of "small miracles" as I referred to them- and the phrase was eventually used as a book title about PAF- when children suddenly began to speak after years of no verbal communication and parents heard the words " I love you" after a lifetime of only shrieks and frustrated anguish. Those were very special years for me, and now I am once again scheduled to return and reboot the program, just as soon as the international air carriers start to operate again and I can fly out to Amman without the restrictions at present imposed upon countries around the globe as a pandemic calls the shots.

The day I welcomed the first group of six special needs children we had the Press present, along with Princess Alia of course, and her cousin, the CEO of the Foundation. Everyone had cameras at the ready. This was ground-breaking stuff after all back in 2010, with only a handful of initiatives operating around the world.

A little boy of about seven years of age was brought forward to me by his teacher. He was on the autistic spectrum and had never spoken. His teacher, who spoke no English- and I spoke no Arabic- looked at me as if I was out of my mind. The idea was to take the child into the pen with a small group of horses, we had picked out six of the retired Arabs from the Royal Stud and allow a horse to choose to "work" with the child. The horses were loose and wore no tack and were all completely without any special training.

Everyone held their breath, even me, as the little boy wandered vaguely from one horse to another as they ate their burseem- the local word for dried alfalfa.

Not one horse showed the slightest interest in the boy and seemed far more focused on the hay. The cameras rolled, the silence from the crowd watching was palpable. After ten minutes I gestured to the child to follow me out of the pen. No one said a word. I looked around for the next child and was able to hold her hand as we went into the horses. The cameras kept rolling. This time things went to plan.

When I came out of the pen I noticed that the CEO was in tears, as were several of the journalists and the teaching staff. My heart lurched. What could have happened in ten minutes to cause such distress? I need not have worried. After the first little boy had left the pen he had wandered about the area and picked up a handful of burseem and then gone back to the netting which enclosed the horses' area.

"Come horse, come," he said.

His teacher later told me, "In twenty minutes you have done more for him than we have done in seven years."

Sometimes, God listens and small miracles happen.

My friend is a trained nurse and zoopharmacologist, retired as the former years ago before training as the latter. I have been fortunate to learn many things about the uses for essential oils for animals' treatments, with Sparkle owing no small thanks to the power of woodland violet for grief. Tarac was also once offered some essential oils to choose from, but he literally turned up his nose at all of them and walked away.

A few months later when my friend tried Tarac again with a wider range of oils he eventually picked one out but, as she heard quite loudly in her head, it wasn't for him, it was for her, as she needed it far more than he did. That was the last time we asked Tarac if he needed any Healing.

It's after eleven by the time I hang up the phone. The night outside is still and warm, and I am trying to decide whether to walk the hounds now or wait until after midnight. More than likely I shall walk down to the sea, about a twenty-minute amble both ways. Sometimes I cut through using the National Trust footpath and sometimes I stay on the tarmac lanes, going up and down hill as opposed to the level pathway cut out for pushchair and wheelchair accessibility.

When the moon is full the walk needs no extra torchlight, and Emma, Ellisar and myself can enjoy the quiet of a village softly snoozing under a clear star-covered sky. MJ stays at home in comfort, neither her eyesight nor her legs up to the three miles or so of distance. The dogs know the routine well, and as soon as I pick up the leads both hounds are springing into action and by the door. Yoda wants to come too but the beach is too far, so I have to make certain he cannot escape through any of the windows. Bailey often walks with us at night but not on the seaside route, only the shorter one that takes us up to the primary school and back. Piri has other fish that she fries and explores the fields up on the hill behind my house.

Tonight I choose to walk to the beach via the lanes. It is warm and the breeze only slightly cooling. The sky is a plethora of dying suns and the moonlight is just starting to crest the wave of hedgerows that surround our patchwork fields. It's a world ripe for magik. A stag barks in the woods and the screech of owls sends little furry folk scuttling into the undergrowth. I can smell badgers, and in the silver-grey light of the rising moon families of rabbits nibble their way around grazing flocks of sheep and cudding cows. I live in an Amanda Clark painting.

As we walk towards the sea my mind tumbles into thoughts of how fortunate I am, having experienced enough hardship to keep me grounded and empathetic to the difficulties other people have to endure, yet so blessed to have tenaciously been able to live my life without too many compromises. I'm still not in that prudent bedsit or studio flat.

And then my thoughts slither onto more philosophical matters, around the hubris that allows us to believe that any of us really matter in the greater scheme of things, at all.

And then the Zen.. if none of it matters, if the goal is total non- attachment, then Everything matters, because each moment is all there is.

And so we go full circle.

Hubris indeed.

The sea is quiet, just a muffled rumble, muted by the shelves of shingle going out to a very low tide. I can smell the seaweed.

Dawn isn't thundering from across the bay, Kipling style, it's more like a languid stretching across the sky, and the wind is gentle upon my cheek. The hounds pad beside me as we stroll, Emma on the lead so that she won't hurt her cruciate trying to swim the Channel, and Ellisar off lead for the first time in months while the beach stretches ahead deserted. I realise I have cracked the timing- the horrid security lights that literally blind me at night are off, which means that I don't have to walk intrepid into the unknown darkness as per usual.

Homeward, I choose the cinder path that goes through a few hundred yards of woodland. Blue smudges are just starting to shyly appear from between the puffs of silver cloud. The birds are singing their morning exultation, and I wish I had the

expertise to identify the many different sounds, but blackbirds I do recognise, and there are a few.

No doubt due to the recent summer temperatures, the wildflowers festoon the banks and hedges, campions, hawthorn, forget-me-nots, parsleys, dandelions already seeded and casting wishes to the winds, and where garden hedges back onto wildness, japonica, lilac, forsythia and roses in bud.

It is almost six when we walk past the church, and pink wisps stretch out across the sky.

A robin chatters an alarm.

Bailey comes down the patio steps to greet us, and MJ barks a hello.

Morning has broken.

I see that my son's car is parked next to mine.

I can hear MJ in the kitchen addressing one of her imaginary intruders- it's a soft, quiet, repetitive bark that makes me wonder if she is slowly losing her marbles...or maybe she has already lost them and just wants me to know where they are. She will stand and stare for hours at a blank wall if not redirected to somewhere more comfortable. Bailey walks inside as soon as I open the kitchen door, Yoda is asleep in his basket in front of the Welsh Dresser, and we are home.

I wake up to the sound of Bailey trying to scratch his way out through the double glazing in my bedroom. Piri and Yoda are sitting on the sill mesmerised by the two large ravens strutting around on the picnic table outside on my patio. Nothing has munched through the delphiniums for yet another night, and their electric blue flowers are already attracting a very large bumblebee. The sun shines through onto my bed and I reach for the cat food.

Another bloody beautiful day in Paradise.

You start dying slowly

if you do not travel,
    if you do not read,
    If you do not listen to the sounds of life,
    If you do not appreciate yourself.
    You start dying slowly
    When you kill your self-esteem;
    When you do not let others help you.
    You start dying slowly
    If you become a slave of your habits,
    Walking everyday on the same paths...
    If you do not change your routine,
    If you do not wear different colours
    Or you do not speak to those you don't know.
    You start dying slowly
    If you avoid to feel passion
    And their turbulent emotions;
    Those which make your eyes glisten
    And your heart beat fast.
    You start dying slowly
    If you do not change your life when you are not satisfied
with your job, or with your love,
    If you do not risk what is safe for the uncertain,
    If you do not go after a dream,
    If you do not allow yourself,
    At least once in your lifetime,
    To run away from sensible advice.
    Pablo Neruda.

DAY TWO

Yet Another Bloody Beautiful Day

It's another beautiful day in Paradise, the sky is blue, the birds are singing, the sun is shining, and some bastard is using a strimmer at seven o'clock on a Sunday morning. Joy.

I'm lying in bed contemplating my plan of action for the day and watching the cats Piri and Yoda trying to escape through the locked double-glazing...I try and give the birds outside a few hours of peace around dawn before letting slip the dogs of war, or in this case, the cats from Hell.

Piri is quarter Bengal, an F2, which sounds like an old time bomber letting loose death and destruction from on high. In Piri's case, that's not too far off the mark. She came to me almost totally feral, by which I mean that I ignored the advice to only have F3 Bengals as pets. F2 refers to how watered down their wild side is, or in Piris case, isn't, and reflects in how often and how badly you get scratched while trying to do really ambitious things with your new kitten-like stroke it. Don't even think about worming for at least a year.

Now though, after nine months, I am able to pick her up with something akin to a great pincer movement from the sky, scooping down on her with my hands like Poseidon catching fish, and plonk her onto my lap without her trying to eviscerate my wrists and belt hell for leather to the nearest safe space. All things come to he who waits.

She even purrs when I rub her neck and closes her eyes. I am not fooled however, I KNOW she is simply waiting for the first opportunity to surprise me.

Yoda, her travel companion and alter ego, is a big, fluffy, so laid back as to be almost horizontal Ragdoll Maine Coon cross. He oozes sensuality, and complete at oneness with his world. The most energetic action I ever see from Yoda is him sprinting down the lane for all of ten yards, before bouncing up onto the church wall, and then lying down fully stretched out in the sun. For him great exertion not necessary is.

The irritating zzzzzzzzzzz of the strimmer cuts through any thoughts of having a later start to the day and I clamber out of bed and open the windows. Better be on the lookout now birds, all bets are off.

Dressed, I go downstairs and start the morning routine. MJ, my decrepit Jack Russel, is still alive -dammit- and snoring loudly in her basket. She lifts her head briefly and the light reflects off the opaque centres of her eyes, her world grown small through lack of sight.

MJ is fifteen now, not really old for her breed, but an attack of pancreatitis last year scuppered her old age and turned her into a snuffling, foul breathed, semi- incontinent liability, and there are times I wonder about the morality of keeping her alive in her twilight world of almost constant hunger pangs and restricted movement.

We have "the pouvoir" as my friend Chris likes to say. We do indeed. It would be an easy decision if I thought MJ was in pain, but she isn't. She's just a nuisance- especially when I don't get to her quickly enough after she wakes up and she nonchalantly wees all over the carpet- but how can I kill her just because she's a nuisance? Well, I can't, and so I create my own frustration.

Kathleen is in her mid-eighties now and lies before me in her own twilight. The carer tells me that Kathleen hasn't eaten for the last week and that they are administering liquids via a straw. On no account must I try and help her to drink as she will choke. The carer leaves and I put down my bag with the moisturiser, air freshener and bunches of yellow roses in it. It also has a box of Innocent juices hidden between the necessities and the small portable radio I've brought in with me.

In a different reality Kathleen would have been my mother-in-law, but even after a decade her son never asked me whether I wanted to live under his roof and so he found someone else who took it from him instead. Now Kathleen lies inert and unresponsive in a nursing home, her skin more delicate than rice paper and just as translucent. I see her two or three times a week, my love for her born out of my love for her son, and just as never ending.

When I first started visiting Kathleen she could still move independently and sit for hours on end bored out of her wits in an overheated room full of other semi-comatose residents. We would talk then, her reality drifting in time, of her mother and childhood, of her brother and the war, of Roland her husband - who had already passed- and how he and she would romance to the music in the skating hall once a week.

She would tell me how she loved forget-me-nots, and baking, and how she had always hoped for grandchildren. Now, I am the only one who sits by her and interacts. Her son, always dutiful to a fault, comes once a week on Sunday evenings and watches as his mother fades away not speaking, and he plays solitaire on his phone until his guilt is assuaged enough for him to leave. He was devoted to her, until his father's aging peaceful character inflamed all of Kathleen's buried frustrations and she lashed out in fury. Keith never could understand why, but he moved his father out of harm's way and Roland died in peace.

Kathleen looks as if she is asleep. I brush her hair and smooth cream over her face and arms and legs, there are some marks I am suspicious about and I will have to let Keith know about them. Also, the nails on her feet could compete with Howard Hughes' and I will ask him to mention that to the Manager. He won't like it, Keith never likes to make a fuss.

Kathleen opens her eyes and looks at me. Does she know who I am? Does that matter?

I open a carton of juice and place the straw on her lips. She drinks greedily, gulping down the heady mixture of mango and pineapple. She finishes two cartons and smiles.

"I love you Kathleen."

She looks me deep in the eye, "I love you too, Suyen."

The morning Kathleen died I had been told by Keith that she was no longer eating or drinking and he would like me to stop visiting her. That perplexed me, but I decided to see her one last time before complying. A close friend was visiting that week, so I left her in the car while I popped in to see Kathleen.

As was usual by then, Kathleen lay curled in the foetus position looking as if asleep. Her skin was dry and papery, and her bones jutted out into the air as if about to tear through the flimsy covering. She really was only skin and bone. I greeted her as I always did and went through my rituals of brushing her hair and moisturising her face. Then I sat down.

I spoke to Kathleen and told her that I could see her and Roland walking through some beautiful woodland on their way to the sea. There were daffodils everywhere and she was wearing a yellow dress with a wide skirt that kept swirling as she ran laughing and turning in circles. Swirling, swirling. I told her that her two beloved dogs, Souki and Hanna were with them, and that she and Roland were laughing. Laughing and swirling. Swirling and swirling, a haze of bright yellow. I told her that her mother and brother were also there, and that they all loved her very much and wanted her to come home.

Then I kissed her on the cheek and told her how much I loved her and how very special she would always be.

Then I left.

Kathleen died that day. Keith sent me a text to say his mother had passed only a few minutes after I had left the room. I have no idea how the staff worked that out, but there it is. I don't think Keith has ever forgiven me for being the one who was there that day, but it doesn't matter. We can't choose the ones we love, no matter how nasty or unkind or dismissive they are of us. It took four years before Kathleen and Roland even bothered to remember my son's name, and equally as long for them to ever consider including either of my children at a family gathering.

I mix up the dogs' food of cooked rice, raw meat and spinach. It's a compromise between feeding them a raw diet because it's better for them, and having to because I've run low on dry food and can't afford to buy another bag until payday, which is nine days away.

We're into the third month of Covid-19 and I'm still based at home. Being isolated cuts into the income and that impacts on everything. So by the end of the month, or three quarters through it, I'm going through my shelves to see what I can make a meal out of, and that goes for the dogs sometimes too. The cats are much luckier, since their diet is far less flexible, and they have far more continuity with what's on

offer. There's a lesson in there somewhere, about how being accommodating can sometimes result in getting you the short end of the stick.

Emma is all labrador exuberance and Ellisar the Russian aristocrat, his long snout suitably raised in the air. They can smell something exciting ahead and I scan the verges manically, hoping to avoid any possible confrontations with local country wildlife.

Two nights ago, on one of our midnight wandering, a badger had been surprised by Ellisar and gone galloping off into the undergrowth. The resulting cacophony of barking dogs would have awoken the entire village had we not been a mile or so out of bounds- Ellisar had not been so lucky a couple of years ago.

That night, we were walking back from the beach at a little after one in the morning with the dogs off lead when I suddenly heard Ellisar growling and then yelping, Emma not far ahead. I started running and could see Ellisar shaking his head vigorously, trying to dislodge something. Then something flew through the air and a young badger came running towards me before disappearing under a gate into the field to my right.

When I reached the dogs, they were running backwards and forwards and covered in a mixture of blood and froth. I had a torch with me and a quick look showed me that Ellisar had blood down one side of him and a tooth that had literally been torn from his gum and was now hanging on by a loop of flesh.

To begin with I thought Ellisar had grabbed hold of the young badger, but the more I thought about what I had seen, the more I decided that Ellisar had disturbed the young Brock and had been attacked for his intrusion. The young animal had no doubt latched on to Ellisar in self-defence and then literally refused to let go- hence the head shaking I had seen.

We walked home as quickly as we could and I administered honey and Rescue Remedy to Ellisar, there was no point in calling a vet at that hour. Ellisar was subdued and very much in shock I'm sure, although not disoriented enough to give me cause to be concerned. The next day we went to my trustworthy vet and he jabbed and stitched and pulled out the tooth and Ellisar recovered very quickly.

I contacted the nearest badger rescue and they came out to see whether we could find an injured or dead cub, but there were no signs anywhere and they felt certain the cub had survived. I felt relieved, badgers get enough of a hard time as it is from some of the farming community without having to deal with injuries from passing hounds.

I no longer walk my dogs off lead.

Dogs and cats catered to, I put the kettle on to boil and reach for the instant coffee. There's a knock on the open kitchen door- love stable doors in summer- and my neighbour is standing in the sun with an old black and white photo of the houses we live in. Mine used to be a wooden potato store apparently...

David is one of those rare, kind thoughtful individuals, and I'm blessed to have him living next door. I ask him to join me for a coffee, two sugars and whatever milk I have to hand, on the patio, and he says yes.

When I was a child we used to have what my father called Sunday Breakfast Discussions. There were only the three of us, my mother, him and myself, but we would sit around the table eating a full English and put the world as we knew it to rights. Since my parents often had diametrically opposed opinions on politics and the social strata of various countries, this led to some very stimulating conversations! Throughout them all though there was a sense of mutual respect and interest for the opinion and beliefs of others- we didn't argue so much as debate- and it was a wonderful education for an only child.

David and I use our times on the patio to have a similar type of conversations.

We are discussing addictions and the core of low self-esteem that the majority come from. The men and women who never feel good enough, their insecurities often rooted in childhood and watered by adolescence to bloom into the addictions around alcohol, drugs, nicotine, sugar, suffering and self-destruction on all levels. David looks at me and nods slowly.

"You've just made me understand something I've never recognised before," he said.

I freeze, illumination can be blinding.

David, whose own history involves abuse of both alcohol and drugs to the enth degree, is now free of the Black Dog and living his life quietly in our charming corner of East Devon. He's left behind the destructive affairs- one of which left him in hospital after he saved his partner from burning himself alive- the class A drugs and the nights which disappeared into the depths of an alcoholic frenzy. Not to mention surviving Hep-C.

And here he is telling me that I have shone a light into his darkness and helped him to realise something previously intangible.

Sunday Breakfast Discussions... one never knows where the next Lesson is going to hit us... As my father used to say, it can be a burden- being so loved.

The phone rings and it's my good friend, my only female friend really in this neck of the woods. She and her mother have been totally socially isolated since the start of Covid-19 protocols several weeks ago. Neither of them has left the house and all the shopping is delivered. Cabin Fever doesn't even begin to describe the tensions and frustrations and compromises being made in that household.

The old Wartime Mentality has gripped her mother like a long lost lover, but my friend is having to escape into her bedroom if she desires any quiet time and share the bed with her dogs, on top of balancing her working at home schedule with the deliveries of food. God bless the internet, it keeps us in touch, allows us to connect with the people we love and care about.

When I stepped off the plane in Kiev all of the signs were written in the Cyrillic alphabet, not one clue as to where I should go and it was almost one in the morning. My expected arrival party was nowhere to be seen, the airport terminal was dark and looked deserted, and I had no idea as to what to do next. I was there on a mission for the Viennese animal charity Four Paws, put into action within less than a week, and I had all my worldly cash with me- £30. Where was my driver? I tried my laptop to send Four Paws a message... no signal.

One of the booths was dimly lit and walking over to find a woman sitting behind some dirty perspex who spoke some English. I managed to explain to her that I needed to get into the city (how far was it from the airport?), that I would need a taxi (oh help, how much would it cost?), and that I couldn't contact anyone in the Ukraine. She looked at me baffled, (another idiot from the West no doubt).

Eventually we managed to arrange a hotel room- not too cheap, not too expensive I said- and a ride into town- all the taxis are run by Russian mafia I'm told and so you pay a set price. The set price just happened to be the equivalent of thirty pounds. There is a God after all. The driver was a middle-aged man who drove without speaking for the best part of half an hour through total darkness. I had no idea where we were going and could only hope that I looked too poor to rob or kidnap- the British government does not negotiate with terrorists, as the British Consul told me in Cairo when I was enroute to Gaza with Four Paws a couple of years later.

Once at my hotel, yes, I survived, I was able to connect to the internet, contact both my daughter in the UK and Four Paws headquarters in Vienna and ask them to contact the office in Kiev and bring them up to speed as to my whereabouts. In the morning I received a very apologetic call from Dr. Amir- the mission leader- apparently the Girl Friday who had arranged the flight had confused the twenty-four-hour clock with the twelve hour one and they were expecting me today at noon. Igor would be over soon to collect me.

"Spasiba" I replied.

Debbie can't travel anywhere during the C-19 lockdown because of a chronic asthma diagnosis so our monthly trips to Glastonbury have had to stop. Glastonbury Tor is one of a handful of favourite historical spiritual sites that I like to connect with as often as time and finances allow. It's one of life's ironies that I lived in Tintagel for over sixteen years quite unaware of its deep spiritual connections and that I visit it nowadays with far more love and desire than I ever had during the years I was married there.

Glastonbury, Tintern Abbey, and the cliffs at Tintagel, all favourite places that Debbie and I disappear into, wandering through crystal shops and ethnic passageways, the smell of incense and essential oils, the meals plant based and organic, the people eclectic and self-absorbed in mystic journeys of their own passing. Can't help but love a good eclectic.

Francois was one such. We met in Monrovia when I was barely a teenager, and he was a foreign correspondent for the AP- Associated Press. He had a mane of white hair, a French accent and the most deplorable teeth. He also had the most profound knowledge of Oriental Art and a personal background that encompassed past diplomatic service, the wartime incarceration and death of his mother and sisters, a brother who joined the SS, and a wife who was shot in Ceylon for political gains.

He was French in all but birth right, having been born Polish, and had been married twice but had no children to inherit the wealth of worldly knowledge he had amassed over the years. Francois was a man to be admired, and we all did. He admired my mother, was completely in awe of her and never stopped loving her. My father and he were close friends, often sharing a whiskey into the wee hours of the morning after Francois had consumed one of my mother's crab omelettes- her restaurant speciality.

For me, he personified true elegance and intellectual greatness. He loved my mother but she thought more about him as a future husband for me- ever the prosaic Chinese Mother. Shallow as I was back then, I liked my men with good teeth.

After my parents died, Francois took on the role of In Locum Parentis, and every year he would leave his flat in Chiangmai to venture into Europe and update his banking and then catch a train to Devon and spend a week or so visiting me. As he grew older, my respect and admiration for him grew too, as in his eighties he would board a bus every Christmas in India and head north into the mountains or sit on the hillsides of Sagada to admire the wild lilies.

He died the year of the Tsunami. He booked himself into a hospital in Chiangmai and said that after a four day absence at home to put his affairs in order he would return to die. Unknown to any of his friends, he had been battling leukaemia for years. Except for me, everyone received a letter of farewell from him, and since we corresponded frequently, I have always wondered where my letter went. I like to think that in the confusion which followed the tsunami just days after his death that my letter was lost, but I cannot ever know.

His letters to me over the years were great treasures, full of reflection, humour and inspiration; I hang onto them and to him deep in my heart. I know I exasperated him many times when the romanticism of my father won out over the practicality of my mother- he would shake his head and sigh while making some suitably cryptic remark.

One afternoon as Francois and I were walking along the cliff tops that look out over the Atlantic at Tintagel, I stooped down and removed a large black slug that was slithering across the track in front of me.

"What are you doing?" Francois asked me.

"Putting it out of harm's way so that no one steps on it," I replied.

Francois looked at me and shook his head.

"You can't make anyone happier than they want to be," he said.

The morning has been hot and now humid due to the recent rain. The plants on the patio look like something out of the equatorial jungle that I grew up exploring from time to time in Liberia. The young hollyhocks have leaves so large that a frog could probably sit on one without bending it and the nasturtiums are taking over every vertical surface. The humidity comes with an earthy smell, not that hits-you-in-the-face heady mustiness of equatorial Africa, but of the earth nonetheless. We need the rain.

That's what we like to say in Devon after weeks of unrelenting sun and temperatures in the mid to high twenties, we need the rain. It's an euphemism for not wanting to appear ungrateful even if we are inconvenienced or disappointed. We need the rain. We do. The land is parched. Soil is cracked and the fields of grass lie burnt and light brown instead of green and lush. The crops of fodder that the farmers rely upon for winter feed are down by thirty per cent and the grain crops that provide straw as well as food are not making any height. It could be a hard winter feed wise. So, we need the rain.

The tourists won't agree. Even with Covid-19, flocks of visitors have continued to descend upon our coastal haunts like so many suicidal sheep. Cars parked any and everywhere, along the lanes and byways, wherever they can find a spot that gives the thumbed nose to locked up parking areas. People sunning themselves stretched out on the beaches of shingle, in their family groups or alone, in some areas it's been hard to tell.

In our village, otherwise normally placid and genteel folk took to leaving notes of expletives and warnings on the windscreens of cars owned by offending tourists- only sometimes the cars didn't belong to visitors, they belonged to individuals who had to drive because they were unable for personal reasons to walk to get near to the beach for exercise. The resulting uproar may well provide the storyline for the next series of Midsummer Murders.

There's been a certain unease around C-19 in Devon, a certain detachment as we go about our enforced isolation inside our private bubbles. Linear time has stopped and no one is quite sure how to respond. It's uncomfortable, like balancing on top of stones crossing a bog. No one is certain about who to trust or what to believe. We haven't had to step over bodies in the streets or sprinkle lime into our loved ones' mass graves. It's happening but not to us. It's over there somewhere, a different reality in a different world. It's not affecting how I breathe or how I manage my day. It's smoke and mirrors, and a world of inconsistencies and confusion.

And then a whole new ballgame erupts after a black man is killed by the police in America, and the mainstream media's lens swivels on its mount to hone in on news far more sensational than the latest R figure.

The mirror may well be about to crack.

Sitting in the field after feeding my two horses, I breathe in the peace and tranquillity that surrounds me. The trees are full of birdsong and the two gees are quietly munching their way across the old pasture. It's an idyllic scene. The horses are enjoying the summer, neither is being ridden- one too young and the other too old- and so they have few worries that I would know of. This is my own oasis of calm. My permitted escape from my home during lockdown, my release from my four walls. I am so blessed. The sky is cornflower blue, and there is just enough breeze to stop me from attracting the flies- which seem to find biting me irresistible. Must be the oriental blood, Chinese food and all that. There are Arab horses elsewhere not so fortunate.

Petra is one of the new World Heritage sites, one of the new Seven Wonders of the World. During the years 2010-2012 I visited Petra many times, acting as guide to overseas visitors who had come to learn from the Princess Alia Foundation. It was hardly a difficult role, and I was really blessed to spend so much time in Jordan and explore the country so widely.

For part of my time there, an American was in place helping to educate the local horse handlers and to also redesign the chariots that the horses pulled during their daily work. It was not an easy task, and he met with much resistance from the bosses in the horse syndicates, although the men on the ground all loved him. He was a true cowboy, having his own ranch in Arkansas, and had a natural and sympathetic, as well as greatly informed, way with the horses.

Every morning, before eight, there he would be, daily removing the small whips and sticks from the boys who led the donkeys and checking the horses for any ill-fitting saddles or bits. It was a sad day when he left Petra, the victim of his own success and the stringent power play between the sheiks and the American government.

The Cowboy and I shared many things, a love of horses, books, poetry and music, and a real passion for the country we both found ourselves in. After a couple of months he asked me if I would like to ride up to Aaron's Tomb- the highest point in the hills surrounding Petra. I jumped at it, longing to ride anywhere at all, since although I was working with horses every day I seldom was able to ride one.

Aaron's Tomb can only be reached on foot or on horseback, you can't drive all the way there, and even on horseback you have to dismount and leave them roughly two hundred meters below the tomb. On the designated day the Cowboy was as sick as a dog but determined to take me since he had already cancelled the ride twice previously. A friend of his provided us with two Arab stallions and we set off into the desert. Both the horses had names.

The terrain around Petra is hard stone and scree, and the way to Aaron's Tomb wasn't marked, we just headed towards the highest point, the sepulchre situated at the tomb a tiny pinprick of white in the distance. It was absolutely fabulous. The horses picked their way over the stones, a myriad of reds, oranges, pinks and yellows, and we quietly rose higher and higher up the mountain sides. Later I would be told that the Cowboy didn't know anyone else who would have had the balls to do the route with him. High praise indeed.

I cannot now remember how many hours it took us to get there, with a short pit stop next to a lone table and chair in the rocks to sip some water, but when we did reach the end of the path I dismounted and carried on up the steps alone, leaving the horses with my sick companion. The views were spectacular, the silence complete other than for the whistling winds and I just knew, I knew this was a sacred spot.

Returning homewards, we became lost in the hills as the fever began to conquer the patient, and we ended up on the wrong side of a chasm. Luckily a young boy herding goats came to our rescue and guided us up and out of the ravine and back to his village. From there we rode along the tarmac main road into Petra. We had been in the saddle for almost eight hours by the time I dismounted and took the tack off from the horses. The next morning I wasn't even stiff. Truly blessed.

Having checked on the horses, there isn't really anything else that demands my attention on any given day. Being sent home to work has impacted on my caseload as the service I am employed by navigates its way through virtual meetings and Zoom control. The families I work with don't really want to mix and mingle anyway, and who can blame them, so we are all caught up in this no man's land of exasperation and continual limbo...it's a mixed blessing of course, because it gives us Time.

We get into routines around Time, when to do this, when to do that. Routines often deeply etched into our consciousness from childhood- when to eat, when to go to bed- and suddenly thanks to Covid-19 we can now all be a Nation of Mavericks. It's an uneasy crown, and judging by the rise in mental health problems across the country, one that many would rather refuse. It suits me though, never having liked to be one of the crowd or to follow suit or any of those many other ways of being a part of the whole. Never wanted to be "normal", and everyone knows that we should be careful about what we wish for.

Growing up with mixed parental cultures never felt like a problem to me. My parents lived in places full of cosmopolitan couples, and the only brush I had with the WASP (White Anglo-Saxon Protestant) contingent as I grew up was at embassy parties or weekend soirées. I never felt inferior or targeted because of my mixed blood, in fact rather more the opposite, and I took a certain pride in my Chinese background, happy to be able to lay claim to millennia of culture, art, cuisine and traditions. Youth is so innocent.

It wasn't until I had become an adult and more informed that I began to see and query the contradictions and inconsistencies that arise within the Oriental upon close inspection. How can a culture capable of such beauty also be capable of such cruelty? How can a country that led the fight for communism now be spearheading the greatest capitalist takeover in the world? One thing I have realised, first and foremost, the Chinese are pragmatists. Francois was right.

My mother was born into a relatively poor family in Georgetown, Guyana. Her father worked hard and by the time she was a teenager he had a fleet of taxis to his name. He also had fourteen children to care for, so they were never rich. My mother's dream was to become a doctor, but her brother sabotaged that idea and so she ended up marrying well instead, until she left her marriage and did the very unChinese act of following the man who, although the man of her dreams, was without fortune or fame- my father.

My father wanted to be a writer. He had just spent two years in the Caribbean managing a sugar estate to earn some money so that he could tell the tale of his safari across Africa on a bicycle. So he and my mother rented a tiny room in Kensington and he wrote while she demonstrated Chinese cooking at Fortnums. There was no happy ending.

My father had definite talent, he was a true wordsmith, which was proved many years later, but in the late 1950's publishers didn't want gigantic volumes regardless of how interesting or adventurous they were, and my father was told to pare down the stories by two thirds. It was a blow to the gut that he never really recovered from. My mother kept working, and then one day I was born, and their lives changed forever.

It's one of the deepest gifts, to be loved, and to be loved without question, without rhyme or reason, but simply because you Are. My parents gave that to me, a deep, profound knowledge and awareness of being completely loved. It was a gift that no one nor nothing can ever take away from me. Again, I am one of the blessed ones. Not everyone is so fortunate.

When people grow up knowing that they are loved, it gives them a solid bedrock from which to build all the sandcastles they may choose, it allows them to try, to fail, to dream, to succeed, it gives them the resilience, the faith, the hope, that life will not destroy them. It helps them to believe they can survive. It allows them to risk everything, because whatever happens, they know they will be alright.

It's a different story for those who grow up without that knowledge. For those individuals who grow up constantly attacked, demoralised, criticised, excluded, ignored and made to feel totally irrelevant, life is one long chain of hurt and unsustainable recovery. There are degrees of course, degrees of damage, of relativity, but deep down the vulnerability is universal, wounded souls trying to survive in a hostile world they can never truly become a part of.

Those are the people I work with most of the time, the socioeconomic outcasts of a bright and shiny First World Order.

It's getting late, where does the time go? And I'm getting hungry. Opening the fridge just shows the reality of my own situation, with only jars of pickle, some homemade oat milk, a bedraggled stick of celery and a yellowing head of broccoli within. A week ago I ran out of cash and I've been eating my way through the kitchen ever since.

Several days of salads as I ate my way through the fresh veg and individual tapas selections, then topped up at night with miniature pancakes since I now had milk and also a few eggs left from the last shop. Looks like the week cruising down to payday will be spent eating pasta made in veggie stock cubes- organic, of course. The rice I need to keep back for the dogs, as I mix it with raw dog mince and frozen spinach- quite a good diet for them really.

Austerity is a great dietary controller.

An old friend of mine in Tintagel used to say "Nobody fat ever came out of Belsen" - cruel, but good word use, as the man said in Jurassic Park.

When I started my Hundred Days of Gratitude idea for a mini book, Day One was "Being Fat.....because only those with money can afford to buy food."

Back to David and our conversation around addictions.

Many of my women friends comment about being overweight and not wanting to be so. It started me thinking about some of the reasons that might be behind the weight- I'm a Why person.

Although commonplace psyche theory, many people still don't want to think about the original emotional trauma that results in a lifetime of eating disorders. My personal experience is mainly with female friends but I have no doubt the theory extends across gender divides.

Women love to love, they want to meet the man of their dreams who will love them and cherish them and treasure them through thick and thin. They don't always succeed. When that happens, they blame themselves for having failed in some way (especially if they carry with them a childhood full of reprisals) and never want to feel that way again, because it hurts. So they eat, and protect themselves by putting a physical barrier between themselves and the world- the deeper the hurt, the higher the barrier, the greater the amount of fat.

Women in the west think fat is unattractive, if they are really honest with themselves- the reasons for that are many and diverse- so what better way to protect yourself from the possibility of future emotional pain than to make yourself unattractive? We now know that emotional trauma also releases certain enzymes that encourage abdominal fat in women... even nature is in on the game. So we put on the weight, eat even when we are not hungry and get fat. Mission accomplished.

The irony is of course that women are pandering to women, to the ideal that women have set, not men. Men are not obsessed with our female shape and size, they have their sights otherwise centred, but women judge themselves by their own bias and that is the greatest and saddest irony of all, and I certainly haven't gone through life unscathed, because I believed in Prince Charming- I blame Disney myself- I believed in kissing frogs and living happily ever after, but no one told the frogs.

Back in Africa when I was growing up, men were men and they knew it. I grew up surrounded by men of strength and integrity, they might have drunk too much and smoked too much, but on the whole they were all men of noble character and their word. They had grit. At least, that's how I remember them- rose coloured sunglasses and all that. Life set out to prove me delusional, and kept proving it, one relationship after another.

Now in my sixties, with one divorce and far too many unbalanced relationships notched onto my bedstead, I'm finally losing weight. The past eight years have been a long and slow rewilding of my soul, a journey through despair, fury, recrimination, grief and resignation, of exhaustion, bewilderment, acceptance and hope. No wonder our bodies recoil with the shock waves of our hearts breaking, no wonder we find comfort where we can.

Then again, it could just be the lack of calorific intake.

There's a knock on the door and all the dogs go beserk- just as well I don't have a whole pack. David is standing outside with four tubs of salad that were on sale at Waitrose which he hands to me. I'm very grateful. A pity really that he doesn't kiss lady frogs or we might have eventually ended up sharing a lily pad together. Then again, maybe not. Although he does have great teeth.

Summer Solstice is only a few days away so it's still light outside although almost nine. The rain is now hammering it down and elsewhere in the country there has been flash flooding. Do I really have to walk the dogs? I fed them later than usual so I'm hoping that my midnight jaunt will be in the dry and not result in all of us looking like something out of Monster from the Black Lagoon.

Stonehenge is closed this year to the public because of the Covid-19 restrictions around public gatherings, not that any of the protestors or police present at the Black Lives Matter demonstrations seemed overly bothered about social distancing, or the wearing of masks for that matter.

Stonehenge will be transmitting the sunrise via the internet at first light, literally, to all those wanting to witness the event, and one can only hope that the software will be able to cope with what shall undoubtedly be a huge demand from followers. I can't decide yet whether I shall get up to observe the solar coming or not.

I watched the televised event last year on the internet and became sadly aware that I was happy not to be there in person. It all felt so terribly contrived, so far far away from the quiet majesty and spiritual strength of the stones themselves. Of course people want to be there, I'm being unfair, but there seemed a lack of reverence. Maybe you cannot have a sense of reverence over fibre optics when the crowds are so large, maybe you have to be there in person to feel the vibe, to breathe in the energy. Maybe, next year.

The dogs are all sleeping, walkies can wait. I pour myself another mug of mint tea and remember another time of waiting, when all we wanted to do was sleep, but were unable to do anything like it.

The Major offered us tea. Mint with lots of sugar, and hot, served in small, glass cups set in silver holders. We were on the banks of the old Suez Canal, waiting for clearance to head into Gaza.

My companions were three of the intended five workers with Four Paws International. The other two had stayed at home in South Africa, their wives refusing to sanction their departure into the hell which is now Palestine. Amir, vet and mission leader. Phillip, video cameraman with an eye for the unexpected angle. Mihai, stills photographer and artist. Me, the only woman, along for the ride and to write and assist in any way possible.

The journey of a lifetime. In 2014 the Arab Spring had sprung.

We are there to rescue lions. Lions and other animals stranded for years at a zoo in Gaza and now so hungry that they are either eating one another or dying of starvation. Amir had called, I boarded the plane twenty-four hours later, proof that when something is meant to be, it happens regardless of the odds. So there we were, waiting.

Twenty minutes' drive ahead of us a car bomb had gone off earlier, killing over a dozen army personnel, hence the delay. The officer in charge was loathe to allow us to journey into bandit country and risk our lives so close to the Palestinian border. The danger to ourselves was something we never talked about, the whole situation far too surreal for profound contemplation. None of us wanted to look Death in the face and take her hand, it was far easier to simply not go down that road at all. So, we waited.

Eventually we were told that we would have to return to the nearest village and wait there. No crossing of the border today. Once in our hotel, washed and refreshed from a shower and air conditioning, the four of us sat down to eat in various stages of contemplation. Amir was disappointed and frustrated, he is Egyptian by birth and could therefore have crossed the border freely without us. His Palestinian counterpart would have been waiting for him at the checkpoint. Phillip and Mihai felt frustrated by the imposed limbo of not having anything to film, no adrenaline rushes like driving out of Libya ahead of the government troops' rifle fire. As for me, I was simply conscious of how mad we all were, of how we were all putting our lives on the line for a few animals trapped in a war zone, and would my children ever really forgive me if I ended up shot by an Israeli bullet?

On my way from the airport to Amir's apartment only a few days ago, the company mobile phone had rung. It was the British Consul who wanted to warn me about what I should expect as a woman were we to be kidnapped by Jihadists in Sinai. They informed me that we would probably be kept hidden for several months and that I would probably be raped and beaten. The British Government would not negotiate for our release, it was against their policy on terrorists. Amir took the phone and hung up.

"Four Paws will negotiate," he said, "Don't worry."

Worry didn't even begin to cover it.

We weren't successful, although Amir returned there only recently and successfully transported the surviving animals out through Palestine to Jordan. Vienna decided that it was too dangerous for us to proceed and the mission was terminated. Mihai had to return earlier than the rest of us to start organising his jazz festival and Phillip left the next day. Mihai had a stroke and died a few weeks later. Phillip returned home to South Africa to the hearts of his loving family. Amir and I stayed on in Cairo for a couple of days while we waited for our flights to be confirmed.

Waiting, under the shadows of the Pyramids and She of the famous riddle, or as we sipped mint tea on the banks of the Nile.

It's past midnight and the rain has stopped. The dogs look up at me eagerly as I grab their leads and a few plastic bags. It isn't cold and I feel wide awake so I'm thinking a walk down to the sea. One of the perks of living on the coast in a small Devonshire village- midnight walks with no one to see you.

We're only days away from a new moon so the sky is dark, no brilliant full moon to light up the fields and hedges. The owls are noisy though, and there is a lamb bleating forlornly somewhere in the darkness. The dogs are feeling lively after a day of being indoors most of the time and my Russian hound peers into the darkness ahead as if trying to conjure up a badger or two to bark at. Emma lollops along stopping frequently to sniff in the undergrowth, the rain undoubtedly has made all the scents more acute for a dog, and I wonder if she smells in technicolour or if it's just black and white.

The damp has also brought out an army of snails, and I am trying desperately not to step on any as they cross from one continent of grass to the other. I pick up the earthworms too and toss them into the verges... suppose I've thrown them in the wrong direction? What if they have spent entire lives just to cross the road and here I've come and thrown them back into a place they were trying to escape from. Too much philosophy for so late at night.

Or maybe late at night is the only time for philosophy. All those all nighters at university spent sitting on the floor or perched on a bed or stretched out on a desk as we debated the why's and wherefores of the world as we knew it to be, as we found the only possible solutions in a world seemingly going increasingly mad. The rhetoric and the passion and the certainty that bounced off the walls of the corridors, the bedrooms, the studies, the very essence of all our skins and breath until we collapsed exhausted at dawn, tired and extremely hungry. Ravenous for cold pizza.

I sit on the pebbles looking out to sea. No reflection of stars here, unlike the nights on the River Gambia when my father and I chugged along aboard a decommissioned World War Two cruiser, The Lady Wright, for five days. She was then the last one of two floating post offices in the world. The river was wide at the mouth but narrowed in three days to a point where we had to turn around. The water still and dark, the stars reflected in the stillness. We were the only non-Africans aboard, and my father's insistence that I travel with him had horrified the local Brits. No place for a young lady, no place at all. I was fourteen at the time.

There is little surf, and both dogs run unhindered in and out of the water. Emma would stay in the sea forever but Ellisar is more reticent, his genes happier with snow than water. I sit and watch them, always slightly nervous in case something distracts their attention from me and sends them galloping up the beach in hot pursuit. Rabbits and foxes both play here in the dark, but I'm feeling brave tonight and let them wander freely.

The sea calls to many of us. Some deep, primordial connection that sings to our bones and quickens our blood. The smell of the seaweed and iodine is strong, no doubt the rainfall has swelled the rivers and the sea will have been churned up at the nearby river mouths. Were it daylight the water would probably be brown with the river mud, but instead the depths are simply dark and quiet, a silky blackness that goes on forever into an even blacker sky.

Years ago my father had a near death experience on such a night by the sea. He felt his soul lift out of his body and look down upon himself from a great height. The experience terrified him and he blocked any further such happenings. He feared that were he to go so high as to rest upon the stars that he would not wish to return, and so he would float weightless forever, lost in space.

My father loved the sea, and always wanted to join the navy, but a childhood accident left him with one leg shorter than the other and so he could only join the merchant Navy, which was not what he wanted to do at all. When he died, my mother flew with his ashes back to South Africa, the country of his birth. After much soul searching, she journeyed to Cape Town and scattered his remains into the ocean. At her side stood my father's best friend Patrick, and his wife Maureen.

My father fell into infatuation with Maureen the same year my daughter was born. It destroyed my mother's world, her universe, her heart. She left him of course, as one is supposed to do, but after careful consideration decided that she really didn't want to live her life without him and so she returned. Breakfast as usual in the morning, as I now like to say.

He said, "Maybe one day the laughter will be real again."

Maureen and my father hadn't slept together, nothing so cras or simplistic, but the mere fact that he could become so obsessed with another woman shook the foundations of my mother's beliefs. It rocked her world, and not in a good way.

Grief.

At its most gentle, it comes softly, after a time of anticipation, holding relief cupped against our breast in the hands of guilt.

At the other end of the horizon lies a far more visceral emotion. It is the grief that screams as our hearts are torn jagged from their bony cages, as we thud to the ground, our knees scraped and bleeding on the shards of glass that house our passions, our hopes and dreams. Our places of peace and safety and joy.

Our screams are silent, our tears only salty stains on dried out parchment.

This is the grief of broken promises and of disappointment, the grief that drives all logic from our minds and leaves behind only anguish and despair.

It is a grief that feeds upon itself until we are either consumed and lost in the greyness of a life without meaning, or we find within ourselves a wish to cease weeping and cross the great divide.

There is no logic to it, no right time, no moving on, there is only a moment, a tiny ember that suddenly catches the breeze and is flickered into light.

May we all find the strength to fan the flames.

One day, if I am ever able to retrieve her own ashes from my half-sister Jacqueline, I shall place them into the sea here, on this beach where we both had so much laughter. In that way my father and mother can spend eternity following one another around the world. It seems a fitting finale to their story.

The nighttime temperature is dropping and I'm starting to feel cold. Emma and Ellisar have stopped playing and are now lying sprawled out beside me on the pebbles. I unfold my crossed legs and stand upright, calling the dogs to follow before slipping on their leads- can't be too careful when walking along the lanes, wee hours or not.

When we reach home all the cats are waiting for us. Yoda and Piri are playing tag on the lane outside but Bailey is just sitting on the doormat waiting to go in. It's warm inside and I never fail to feel grateful for my little corner of magic. It's one of very few rented properties that I could happily own. Potato shack it might have once been, but I'm willing to wager that it was a happy little potato shack. There's a peaceful, content energy that pervades the cottage and I have been told that the spirits of a very happy family still preside over it. Not that I can sense them, and the animals have never shown any signs of spirit presence, but I have to say that everyone comments upon how peaceful they feel here, and that's fine with me.

I say goodnight to the dogs- yes, I do talk out loud to them- and turn off the kitchen light. It's almost three. My grandmother would often be awake at this hour, George having gone to the "land of Nod" hours earlier, as she laid the table for breakfast the following day and called for her cat Mingi to come inside.

Nana would go upstairs and put her hair in paper curlers before covering them all with a nylon hairnet, a beaded one if she was feeling frivolous, before treating her face with rose water and glycerine, followed by some Vaseline. In her later years, when she felt that she could be less frugal, she would treat herself to a bottle of Oil of Ulay that she used sparingly every night. I'm not nearly so particular over my beauty regime, and neither do I read a piece from God Calling every day like Nana did, although I do own a copy that she gave me.

Upstairs the cats are now settled on my bed. They sleep with me but none of them cuddle up to me the way my old Strider did, my black feline familiar that lived into his early twenties by my side. I miss him, and the way he would pat my cheek in the morning, and always made sure that he was lying facing me. Now Strider is pushing up roses and delphiniums and calendulas, his remains placed permanently at the bottom of a large garden pot outside my house. The flowers are a living tribute to the joy he gave me.

I lie down and stretch. The bed engulfs me in a deep memory foam heaven covered with duvets and heavy brocade. I turn off the salt lamp and breathe. All my family come to mind, from past and present and untold futures, with thoughts of beginnings and endings and unexpected beginnings. Life is not a circle, but a series of spirals, and we go round and around them, rising and falling like the waves in the sea.

Life, like the sea, fathomless. Calling all of us in.

I take a deep breath, and dive.

"Adventure is a path. Real adventure – self-determined, self-motivated,

often risky – forces you to have firsthand encounters with the world. The world the way it is, not the way you imagine it. Your body will collide with the earth and you will bear witness. In this way you will be compelled to grapple with the limitless kindness and bottomless cruelty of humankind – and perhaps realize that you yourself are capable of both. This will change you. Nothing will ever again be black-and-white."

Mark Jenkins

DAY THREE
One Hundred Days

I'm lying in bed listening to the sound of rainfall. The sky outside is overcast and although not quite four, the birds already cover the feeders. In the corner the easel stands with its resident canvas covered by a piece of lacy curtain material. The easel stands in silent mocking, admonishing me for the unfinished work leaning against its upright frame, the painting which my son asked me to do for him three- or is it four?- years ago. Chesil Beach, his once favourite fishing place, when times were happier.

The easel, taller than me, is a silent rebuke. A reminder that I didn't keep my word, that I allowed myself to be distracted and that I still haven't completed the work. So easy to find excuses- the lights not right, the paints not what I'd normally use, I don't have the necessary hours to concentrate.... all excuses really for simply being too distracted to create a piece of art. The end result is guilt, and now even if I do complete the request set so many lifetimes ago, I know that the moment has passed and that my gesture will be meaningless, an empty resolution of intent buried under the insurmountable weight of time.

I can remember the first time I wielded a proper sable paintbrush, I was nine years old, and my parents' good friend Yanis Democopoulis had gifted me all of his painting materials. A thick roll of canvas, turps and linseed oil, dozens of Reeves oil paints, palette knives and brushes of every size. No easel.

Yanis was a huge Hagrid of a man, a Greek architect who would lose hundreds of pounds whenever he decided to diet, married to a fiery, volatile Haitian beauty called Yolanda. She was tall, svelte and exuded sensuality which even at my tender age I could recognise. They had a son named Neil, after the landing on the moon.

Yanis was larger than life in more ways than met the eye, and his Christmas revels were legendary in Monrovia, when he would have trestle tables set up outside his bungalow under the black starlit sky. He would serve roasted suckling pig and poultry that had been turned on a spit by a cloth clad Nubian, oiled to reflect the flames. Close to a hundred guests were present at the party I can still remember, his pack of Alsatian hounds padding around the compound looking for scraps; alcohol and cigarettes in gay abundance at every table.

When the meat was cooked one of the servants would stagger to a table with a six-foot spit covered in roasted fowl and stab the end of the spit into the end of the table before the weight of the birds brought the blackened metal crashing down between the seated guests. The suckling pig was carved off the bone as it cooked. As the night wore on and the levels of drunkenness increased, the scene resembled a Fellini photo shoot, all bulging eyes and grease covered faces, leering eyes and manic laughter.

On one such night the air was suddenly wrent with the sound of a gunshot. Yanis dashed into the house certain that Yolanda had shot someone in a fit of pique. He found her undressed in their bedroom, lying on the bed beside a stack of his favourite opera records, gun smoking, with a bullet hole neatly through all of his collection. Outside, the guests were jumping into the pool in various stages of undress. I think for a moment Democopoulis would have rathered the bullet was in Yolanda.

I had a colourful childhood, one way or another, in the White Man's Grave that was West Africa.

The rain starts to fall more heavily, and although not in a thatched cottage, the vaulted roof of my bedroom means that the rain falls directly onto the other side of my ceiling and is loud. It starts to drum with a lashing persistence that reminds me of the monsoon rains of Liberia. Six months wet, six months dry, equatorial seasons, with six weeks of dry that we called the mid-rains amidst all of the wet.

Outside I notice that the birds are still all eating, even in the rain. How do they know, I wonder, how do they know just how wet they can get before they can no longer fly to safety? How do they gauge when the time is right to leave the sustenance behind and return to the safety of somewhere dry? What is the force that makes them risk becoming water-logged in exchange for easy food? How long do they endure the discomfort and relative risk before abandoning their easy breakfast......what makes them decide to fly? What makes us take the first leap of faith?

I'm lying in bed propped up on pillows, like one of those Hollywood divas of black and white films, where the heroine is dressed in a frilly negligee and surrounded with lacy cushions while she spends her morning chatting on the phone, putting the world to rights. We don't do that anymore of course, now we spend the time scrolling through social media posts, or catching up on emails, the personal connection more often than not exchanged for a virtual one. I try to call a friend using a video call but she cuts it off and sends me a message-

"I was horrified to see you were requesting a video call.......Can't talk, I look dreadful."

We have become a world of imaging and surface appearances. Who gives a fuck what someone looks like when all you want to do is connect with them and ask how they are? Have them ask how you are?

Easel looks at me reprovingly- I mustn't judge; appearances are by definition only that.

When my father was crossing Africa on his bicycle with Ray, they ended up stopping at Anne and Pat Putnam's camp in the Congo. The Putnams worked closely with the Mbuti Pigmies and also with a nearby leper colony. Ray and my father stayed with them for a few days, deep in the forest, and it was here that my father learnt that leprosy is not contagious. I did a Google search for the Putnams a while ago and discovered that Anne had written a book about their time in the Congo, which I must find.

On their second night in camp, a group of Pygmies arrived with a very heavily pregnant woman. She was in great pain and apparently unable to birth the child in the village. They had reluctantly come to ask Pat for his help.

The camp was in the bush, there was no electricity and no running water. The heat would have been palpable and the humidity suffocating. Anne was not happy at the idea of interfering with village business.

"If you help the mother and she dies, we will all be held responsible," she warned Pat, "We could all die."

The mother lay on her back on a wooden table in a tent while Ray held up a solitary kerosene lantern for Pat to see by and my father took notes. Pat, who was in a wheelchair, didn't have any surgical instruments, so after doing an internal exam of the mother he improvised with two wooden spoons. There was no anaesthetic. The child was already dead and needed to be removed as quickly as possible if the mother was to have any chance of avoiding septicaemia.

Everyone there knew how risky it was to interfere with the villagers at all, but they also knew that without intervention the mother would be dead by morning. She already had a raging fever. Pat removed the baby, wrapped it in a cloth and gave the body to the other women who had accompanied the mother. Everyone left the tent and retired to their own rooms.

In the morning the place was empty except for the Putnams and Ray and my father.

The mother survived.

My father shook hands in farewell with the lepers and continued on his way.

Some decades later, my father wrote up the story for CBC in Canada. They refused to air the story saying that it was "too raw" for the Canadian audience. One could be excused for thinking that a country which can stomach the clubbing of baby seals and the skinning of those cubs alive would be able to handle the blood and guts of dark Africa, but apparently not.

Ray Crisp, my father's travel companion and dear friend, would slash his wrists many years later in the cold loneliness of his bathtub in Wales, and lie there in the gradually cooling water to finally be discovered by his wife.

I have no doubt that had they known, CBC would have happily aired that story.

I close the windows on the latch to stop Piri and Yoda escaping too early. Even with the rain, the birds will be fair game if they don't concentrate on the feline stalkers. It's far too early to deal with Death among the bean-poles.

The first time I saw Death my parents' close friend and business partner lay dying in the biggest bed I had ever seen. I was eight years old. The room seemed huge too, and empty, the walls white and the sheets draped over his body like so much icing. He was dying of liver failure, hepatitis wrongly diagnosed as something less malevolent and only eventually discovered when it became apparent that there would be no recovery.

Forest Farrar was one of those handsome, Californian men that combine wealth and kindness and charm in a heady mix of masculine empowerment. His wife was a tall, statuesque, blonde Dutch beauty whose catchphrase, "Stand back, I'm coming through!" would echo around our garden at weekends as she battled through groups of friends enjoying one of my mother's curry parties. The parties would run from Friday evening to Monday morning, and my mother would provide a selection of curries and a massive array of side-dishes to go with them. Any less than two dozen was considered a poor effort.

When Forest died, President Tubman ordered that he should be given a State funeral. I stood on our balcony under the blasting sun next to my father, who hated funerals, and watched with him as his best friend was paraded through the streets of Monrovia to the sound of three brass bands. He made me promise him that day that I would try and ensure that his own death would have no such fanfare, and I kept my promise to him many years later, even though it lost me forever the love of my grandmother.

After Forest died, my father's heart was no longer into setting up a company in Monrovia and so we left Liberia to go on what we thought would be a farewell road trip through France, Spain and Morocco. The journey, in a red Jaguar XK150, took us four months, and at the end of it, once again unable to settle into the grey confines of English society, we returned to Africa again after a two week voyage aboard a cargo vessel that set us down in Monrovia with nothing to call our own other than the car.

A Jaguar XK150 is really made for two. There is a back seat in theory but it's little more than a ledge, and upon this ledge I used to sit on top of our three sleeping bags, surrounded by my Barbie dolls and chosen teddy bears. Behind me there was a small recess that my mother used to store her Chinese condiments in, so that whenever we stopped she was able to conjure up something cheap and tasty on the tiny Primus stove. My mother shared the small pup tent with the stove and my father and I slept outside under the stars- I can't remember it raining but if it had I'm certain we'd have slept outside regardless.

Crossing the Pyrenees after a heavy rainfall earlier in the day, we came to a section of the road that was under water. The roads themselves coil around the mountains hugging the edges tightly, like a snake wrapped around its victim's throat. The views were stupendous, vast arid landscapes and wide-open skies. The heat in August was stupendous too.

The road disappeared in front of the car and instead there was an unending river of water that came gushing down from the right-hand side and disappeared over the side to our left into the depths below. We had no way to guess how deep or how wide the water was, so my mother took the wheel and my father rolled up his trousers and stepped out. He quickly was knee deep in water and fighting the force of the current. Inch by inch we crept forward following him through the torrent to dry tarmac. Once on the other side, he jumped back into the car.

"Look at that view!" he exclaimed, "I need a drink!"

"Look at the road!" my mother would shout back. Happy days.

Following on from Spain we crossed over Gibraltar and landed in Tangier. I remember more of Morocco than anywhere else along the route. I can still see the fabulous mixture of colours and textures that were everywhere, the aromatic piles of spices in ochre and red and yellow and blue, the aromas of strong freshly brewed coffee and charcoal grilled lamb and mint tea, the sounds of the donkeys braying and the camels trotting over the earth.

My world became a magical land of sand coloured fortress walls and the velvety blue skies at night studded with a dozen constellations and a bright moon, my days spent wandering through the casbahs of Casablanca and Fez and Marrakech, the beaches of the west coast and the sands of the Sahara at the foot of the Atlas Mountains.

As we drove into the Atlas, the scent of cedar filled the air from the forests that swept up the hillsides and filled the horizon. We camped beside a snow-filled lake and my father and I slept under the stars. In the morning, which was crisp and chill, my mother busied herself cooking breakfast while my father decided to have a swim in the lake; naturally I wanted to do whatever he did, so I jumped off from the wooden jetty into the black blue water.

The water welcomed me like a sheet of ice, the cold so intense that I could barely breathe and had to keep swimming just to feel my limbs move. My father laughed, but even he only stayed in long enough to swim a small circle before we both clambered out and threw ourselves onto the nearest sleeping bag and towel.

"Absolutely bloody freezing!" he said to my mother.

"Snow fed," she replied quietly, "Eat."

Not too many days later found us cruising on the road between Fez and Marrakesh doing a hundred and twenty mph., it was a straight road. The hood was down, and the wind whipped across us in a frenzy of long hair and hot air. Every day my parents would have a discussion about whether to leave the hood up or take it down. It was August and the temperatures next to the Sahara were soaring. My mother wanted the hood up to act as a sunscreen. My father wanted it down so that we could experience the desert up close and personal. I sided with him in my heart although I wisely stayed quiet.

One such afternoon, after a couple of hours driving, we pulled into a campsite so that we could use their showers. The air was heavy with that dense stillness one can only feel in extreme heat. Although the heat was dry, and beads of perspiration soon disappeared from our skin, it was still overwhelmingly intense.

My mother was showing signs of heatstroke, so my father insisted that she lie in the shade of the tent while he covered her with his dressing gown which he totally saturated with water. When she asked him where the water had come from- the showers were locked- he eventually had to tell her that he had found a small stream at the edge of the site where the local goats were drinking, and the water had come from there.

Some decades later I myself would feel that heat again when I visited Luxor in August with my daughter. The heat was climbing up to fifty degrees Celsius some afternoons, and I could feel it penetrating my arms and reaching into my bones. No one visits the desert in August save mad dogs and Englishmen.

I can only remember a few vignettes from that family trip in 1967, and I grieve over that. It would have been good to have travelled when I was older and more able to take notes of my own, but I was only eight. It's been a while.

The rain is really hammering now, the trees outside are swaying from side to side in the strong wind. The bird feeders swing from side to side, and only the most intrepid of chaffinches and sparrows cling on tightly, determined to fill their beaks and take back the spoils to the chicks still nest bound. It can be a tiring business, raising one's young.

It's not yet midnight and I'm in bed, so it's an early night for me. There's a knock on the door downstairs and the dogs start barking at the intrusion. I am becoming accustomed to late night visits from the local constabulary, so I'm not completely surprised, although curious. Sure enough, two officers stand in the dark, a man and a woman, asking me if I know where my son is. I point to the car and tell them that he is home, and asleep upstairs. They express concerns over his mental state, and do I know whether he is okay?

I look at them biting my tongue and choosing my words carefully.

I want to say, "Of course he's not bloody alright, his world and his life have been turned upside down and inside out by the woman he loves and he can't see his children until God knows when, and none of the bloody police have supported him in any way whatsoever when he's needed them to," but instead I just look at them without saying anything for a while. A long while.

"Isn't it rather late for a visit?"

They insist that I go upstairs and make sure that he is home, in his room, asleep.

I do so.

"Yes, he is upstairs, sound asleep."

"So sorry for disturbing you."

I close the door.

In the morning I tentatively reach out through a text to see if my son is sound; I receive a barrage of invective and condemnation instead- a compendium of all the many wrongs I have credited to my name, all the years of shortcomings and disappointments and current embarrassments that I have caused him. All of his fury and anger and frustration and hatred wrapped up in the pain and hurt he currently feels neatly packaged and delivered to my inbox. I send no reply.

We lash out at those nearest to us, we score the bulls eye when shooting at those we know best, because we know where to aim and we know that it's safe to do so. We know that the people who truly love us will forgive us our trespasses, our sins, our foibles and our failings because that is what love does, it forgives.

Still hurts though.

Still makes me think and question myself, makes me wonder where I screwed up so deeply as to have to bear witness to my son in so much pain. I know it is his path, that these are his times of learning, and I know that he may leave me behind in his quest; me, the personification of all his lost dreams and hopes, and that hurts. Deeply, hurts.

It can be a tiring business, raising one's young.

Bailey is tapping on the window glass so I open it and allow him out. He looks at the falling rain and then over his shoulder at me as if weighing up which is the lesser of two evils, then he casts his luck with the birds and leaps down onto the patio.

I sit on the window seat I've created by covering an Ikea wooden box with linens and gaze out at the rain. The water has formed small orbs of light along the edges of the purple twisted hazel, so that the tree looks as if lit by fairy lights. Each drop of rain is a perfect sphere of reflected beauty, and then it falls, unhinged by its own weight to crash onto the stone paving below.

As I look out at those drops they make me think of all the times we hang on as individuals, hang on to our hopes and dreams despite the storms and tempests that rage around us, hang on determined regardless of the trials and tribulations, hang on with all the strength given to us until we fall. And I find myself weeping, weeping for all the sadnesses, all the hurts, all the griefs, the disappointments and the sorrows that tear our world apart. My sadness wells up through my chest and sobs out of my mouth uncontrolled. A dam cracked by the constant hammering of resilience.

It's day one hundred of Covid-19. A hundred days of solitude, with a nod to Gabriel Garcia Marquez.

Easel doesn't move at all.

It's time to feed the dogs.

I look through the wire mesh, there are over four hundred animals on the other side of it, dogs of all shapes and sizes, divided into small pens with packs of two or three dozen in each. I am in the Ukraine, and standing outside one of the many rescue centres run by volunteers.

I am based in Kiev, working with Four Paws on a sterilisation program for feral cats and dogs. The project is in its last and seventh month, and thousands of animals have been treated in a neuter and release program. The animals are caught, neutered and released back into their own territory within twenty-four hours. This prevents the territories from being invaded by new dogs or cats. It's a marvel of veterinary science, with the head vet being able to sterilise a male dog in less than sixty seconds. Revolutionary. Our domestic vets could do with a taste of this reality.

The morning is dry and warm, early summer, and there is a pervading smell of boiled meat in the air, with an undercurrent of stale urine. The pens are concrete and sparse, hosed down in the early morning and then left. The dogs look fit and healthy, and live harmoniously together in their designated packs.

I walk through the gates and follow my nose. Breakfast is bubbling in three of the largest cauldrons I have ever seen, and the heat is immense as they are suspended over an open wood fire in a massive stone fireplace. I am told that the meat comes from the local slaughterhouse. The building we are in is a maze of concrete corridors and low ceilings, so the smells hang in the air I disturbed. It feels like a subterranean prison.

The volunteers are all women. Big, strong, burly women with hearts of gold. The meat is poured into wheelbarrows and pushed down the dark labyrinthian passageways, to be ladled into piles of metal bowls and feeding troughs. The smell pervades everywhere. So does the noise. The dogs are excited, eager to devour their first meal of the day. Four hundred dogs, all rescued from the streets.

Four Paws is there to meet with UK television celebrity Marc the Vet, famous now for his successful campaign to stop puppy farming in the UK. Marc later tells me that these dogs in the rescue centre are some of the most healthy he has ever seen.

He says it is because their diet is so natural and so basic-none of the added crap and sugar found in so many of our dog feeds here in the UK.

Ironic really.

Dog owners everywhere would be affronted to think how misguided their kindnesses often are.

I think about my friends, and about those owners who pamper their pets and dress them in human outfits and recreate their animals in their own image. It's such a travesty, what we do to animals while proclaiming our love for them, so long as they don't inconvenience us in any way. We dragged the wolf out of the forest, declawed it and muzzled it, and called that progress, and we never recognise our own culpability when the wolf bites back.

My own wolves are wagging their tails and waiting for me to unwrap the defrosted beef. Ellisar waits with his aristocratic nonchalance, but Emma is all enthusiasm and impatience while MJ is snuffling through her grey foggy sight to find her bowl. This is meat in a sanitised plastic wrapper, not just hewn off the still warm carcass of a suspended cow.

We are all guilty in some way. Even the most ardent vegan will be condoning insufferable torture if they own a carnivore as a pet.

I can hear Easel chuckling.

All over the world, people yearn to see the pyramids, and desire to walk the avenues of Petra, in a bid to touch history with their own breath.

When I was in Petra, I quickly realised that the horses and donkeys used for the tourist trade needed help to improve their daily lives, and Egypt was no different.

In Petra, I had a baptism of fire as I slowly unravelled the hypocrisies- a polite term for lies- around the Brooke foundation, the horse owners association that leased the rights to the Petra carriage-drivers and the politics that ensnared everybody. PAF- the Princess Alia Foundation - struggled valiantly while I was there to introduce a modicum of fairness and humanity, but it was only a few years later that the situation improved when PAF was able to have Four Paws assist with the logistics around horse and donkey welfare on a day to day effort in Petra.

I stepped out of our taxi at Giza and looked up. You have to look up, it cannot be helped, because you automatically want to see how high the pyramids are. I was disappointed.

It was the days of the Arab Spring, and the tourists had stopped visiting Egypt, fearful for their lives and their wallets, so the car park was empty and only two cars were waiting outside the information building.

Camels and horse drawn carriages stood in long rows, the animals with heads down and tails swishing away the flies, unwanted by absent tourists and looking as dejected and depressed as their slowly impoverished owners. The lack of tourists to Egypt has had a massive impact on the population's economic wellbeing to this day, with the domino effect meaning that many horses and donkeys have slowly starved.

Walking in the summer heat, I watched as a paltry handful of visitors climbed the great stones and sat eating sandwiches and drinking cans of pop. I felt detached. Here among the tombs of the Pharaohs, my steps leaving imprints in the same sand that had been crushed under the soles of thousands of workers and their managers millennia ago, I gazed out across the desert boundaries and turned my back on the apartments of Cairo.

I wandered down the empty slope to She of the lion body and human head, to the mesmerising gaze from the face with the shattered nose. In the air around me I could hear the call to prayer echoing around the city from mosque to mosque. I also heard a horse's squeal, I turned.

Behind me, up the slope a few yards away, a horse was down on the concrete, its hind legs splayed out from its body, and its owner standing over it beating the horse with a whip. The horse was struggling to rise but the weight of the carriage attached to it and the gradient of the slope meant that he couldn't get any purchase on the smooth surface- his owner kept beating him.

As I turned to run up the distance between us my good intentions were thwarted by the arrival of a family of tourists. They started shouting at the horse owner and helped the horse to get up, gesticulating with their arms and making their anger plain. The horse owner looked at them and shrugged. His command of English no better than their use of Arabic.

He took hold of the horses reins, jumped into the carriage and trotted up the hill. The tourists looked aghast. I turned to continue down the slope and stopped in front of the Sphinx...

She, like Easel, said nothing, having seen it all before a million times.

Back in Devon, I chop up three bags of carrots and take them with me to the car. Carrots are my modus operandi for bribing Darcy towards affection and acceptance.

Horses are phenomenal creatures. They stir within us profound links to our psyches and reflect back to us our primordial thoughts and fears. For this reason, horses are now the new Philosopher's Stone, promising a magic mix of enlightenment and salvation. Horses are the animal of the moment, the key to all of our dis-ease and disease, the Holy Grail in our world of chaos and confusion. Poor poor horses, to be so saddled with the burdens of our hopes and fears.

When I set up Growing Together in Amman, equine behavioural therapy was a phrase that hasn't been coined yet, while now it slips off the tongue worldwide with the ease of overuse and familiarity. The reason for that is simple, equine therapy works.

I'm sitting on the grass with my legs crossed, watching as Darcy and Sparkle eat their way through the chopped carrots. Darcy will allow me to investigate his legs for lumps and bumps while so distracted, and I have checked the deep cut he sustained while I was away visiting my daughter recently. That visit cost me one of my best friends as she disapproved of my travelling during Covid-19 restrictions.

The wound is healing well; the friendship is mortally damaged.

I listen to the chomping, it's a slow and comforting sound. There's a rhythm to it that relaxes and slows the breath. The horses are inches away from my feet, trusting as I trust them that we are mutually safe. I gaze up at the shining blackness that is Sparkle's coat, black hammer marks a sign of her healthy condition, and marvel at how truly beautiful she is.

Nearby someone is using a chainsaw. The neighbouring property is removing several trees and there is a group of young men that I observed earlier on my way in who were laughing and talking in the distance. The noise is like a demented giant wasp on speed.

Darcy raises his head so that he can look at me directly in the eye, he still has a hint of anxiety lying deep within that gazes back at me, and I feel that it will be some time before that expression goes. I can smell the scent of horses when I lay my cheek against his neck, and I breathe in deeply. My horse loving friends tell me that this is one of the things they miss most when no longer sharing their lives with an equine- the smell of the horse. That warm recollection of shared moments and deepest intimacies. It's like breathing in the scent of your lover as you drift into sleep.

I stay seated for a while after the horses have drifted away in search of natural fodder. It's a peaceful spot, here in this Devonshire field under the sun, the grass slightly wet from the earlier rain. I close my eyes and concentrate on breathing deeply, recognising the sweetness of grass and wild honeysuckle growing in the hedges. The damp is seeping through my trousers but I don't care, the tranquillity is infectious, and I can feel myself spreading out in all directions, as if my very essence is stretching forth to join with the air and bond with the trees and clouds.

Birdsong and the occasional hum of an insect punctuate the silence, and for a brief nanosecond God is in his Heaven, and all is right with the world. Sometimes you just have to ignore the chainsaws and concentrate on the birds.

Equine Therapy. You can't beat it.

By the time I return home my son's car is gone. The house is quiet and all the animals are dozing in various positions that look like a group yoga class. I'm still reeling from the hate-laden texts and I feel far too flat to do anything creative.

Easel laughs quietly. I retreat into that bastion of the British Empire, and make myself a cup of tea.

The phone rings- my friend can talk now, having applied her makeup and styled her hair. I keep the call on audio only.

When my father died, I sat and told my mother that he was feeling more peaceful now and suggested she go back to bed. It was fourteen minutes past two in the morning. I didn't tell her that he was dead, knowing that were I to do so my mother wouldn't get any sleep at all for the rest of the night. Mummy, bless her, heard what she needed to hear and never for a moment thought that I would be so calm if my father had just died. So she did as I suggested and went back to bed. Champers, my psychic shadow, an American cocker spaniel, looked at me and climbed onto my lap. Neither of us moved again for several hours.

Somewhere, in my house of no doors, a key lies hidden. I walk through passageways of time and glimpse memories playing in dusty sunbeams, laughter hiding behind skirting boards and quiet footsteps drumming on the moss in moonlight. I hear the rolling thunder of your voice, and the laughter in your eyes. I can sense it, the room, the one behind the closed door that does not exist- the vague mists of past years when I could feel the pulse of your heart within mine.

My steps stride with purpose as I stride through the corridors of our past, and through the tall, lonely windows I catch a glimpse of you fading into the future, as our paths no longer entwine. In my mind, my arm stretches out, my fingers grasping for the shadows, but instead I can only clutch at the emptiness from your passing.

There is an empty room now in the house of my soul. It gasps with the enormity of your death and the chasm filled with impossible futures no longer able to take their first breath.

My grandmother was furious with me.

She was angry at me vetoing a funeral for my father since he had always hated funerals. My mother agreed with me. My grandmother wanted to hold a ceremony that would celebrate her grief and her loss in the village, she wanted to be The Grieving Mother. In my self-righteousness, I was appalled.

Now I wonder if I was right to deny her those moments of adulation, but it seemed so unfair for the village folk to be focusing upon my grandmother while at the same time paying no heed to the heartbreak that was his wife's.

In my certainty, I sent my father's body to be cremated and his ashes were sent to us afterwards. From that moment my grandmother turned her back on my mother and disinherited me from my share of her estate. It was a real lesson in the duplicity of love. When my mother died two years later, Nana openly grieved over the loss of her "Beloved Lucille".

When my father died, I didn't cry.

Nowadays, I cry easily. Looking at the drops of water falling from a leaf, I weep.

We hit stone and we explode, a thousand thousand splinters of shattered light, shooting out in all directions like so many lightning bolts, landing in a drop of our own making, a pool for the gods.

Had I had one back then, Easel would have roared.

The rain has refreshed the plants on the patio and I am spuddling amid the pots, still in slow motion response to my son's vitriol. I know that I should be writing, or painting, or reading, but I can't quieten my thoughts, or soothe the emotions that are poking at my subconscious with needles of recrimination and doubt. So I spuddle, softly treading between the lilies and the calendula, deadheading the roses and picking off the yellowed leaves on the honeysuckle. I need to ground my centre to have any hope of spontaneous creation.

The bees are busy. They disappear into the foxgloves and sit appeased on the sunflower heads, their tiny bodies dusted with pollen. Many years ago I had hives in Tintagel, three of them, until I learnt that bees and horses are not a happy mix.

Tom Parkin was a poacher of the old school and a master Beekeeper. He couldn't have been much more than five foot eight, and his skin was deeply tanned in summer and somewhat lined with wisdom and the elements. He smoked a pipe and wore a tweed hat and a battered old Barbour most days- I was in awe. What Tom didn't know about bees and fish wasn't worth knowing, and one memorable evening he was generous enough to share some of his exploits with me over a single malt.

Tom helped me move my bees, carrying the hives up from the bottom field to his van. He never wore any protective equipment, but I hated the sound of a bee trapped in my hair, so I wore a beekeeper's hat and mask. The hives were heavy, as we were stupidly moving them in high summer and so we were lifting over seventy pounds of honey as well. Two hundred yards felt like forever. Tom took the hives and added them to his collection of a few hundred that were spread throughout Cornwall. I fantasise sometimes about keeping bees again, but it's hard bloody work and now I'd rather support someone else's efforts.

Tom had many talents, and he was a true man of the country, well versed in country lore. Eventually the River Authority made him a river warden, which was a huge irony and a very wise move on their part. His stories of moonlight walks along the riverbanks to check up on the salmon enthralled me, and his ability to cast a spinner so that it landed exactly where he wanted it to was a true art. I like to hope that there are young boys and girls growing up now out there with that same feeling of reverence and respect for Nature, while at the same time being able to be an integral part of it.

In Africa, poaching isn't anything like the slightly romantic, sentimental, nostalgic version we think of here in the UK when we imagine old timers like Tom. Nothing like Tom pottering along the hedgerows and netting himself a rabbit or tickling a trout under the belly. In Africa, poaching is blood and guts, buzzing flies and slow deaths, with mutilated limbs and missing body parts. In Africa, poaching is nothing like a lazy afternoon saunter down the riverbank on an August afternoon.

In Africa, poaching is the trickle of blood winding down across the bloody maw where the horn used to be. It's a photograph of a lone sentinel, semi-automatic cradled in his arms, standing under an acacia tree while the last survivor of a species grazes behind him. In Africa, poaching is the cry of a hungry child, its eyes covered in flies, watching its father take money so that the family can eat. It's the dust covered rusty pickup, full of laughing soldiers, bumping over the rough stone strewn track in pursuit of one their countrymen, guns loaded and fingers on the triggers.

In Africa, poaching is the slick well-heeled foreigner who pays a small fortune for pieces of bone and compressed hair that are in such high demand by the medicine men and women continents away. In Africa, poaching is not a game or an afternoon's sport, the unspeakable in pursuit of the inedible as with foxhunting and the stalking of red deer. In Africa poaching is raw, visceral, and chokes humanity with the cloying stench of putrid flesh and stagnant blood.

In Africa, our hypocrisies rise to meet us, as canned hunting and trophy kills are deemed acceptable for those wealthy enough to indulge their basest instincts. While all the time we condemn the men who have no choice but to earn what they can by whatever means they can find in order to save their families from starvation.

It isn't much fun for the rhino either, and we have already forgotten the dodo.

David knocks on the patio gate with his hands holding a big pile of spinach. Home grown and courtesy of our neighbours. Thanks to Covid-19, the entire stay at home members of the population appear to be either baking for their lives or growing their own veg. If we have to remain in isolation for another hundred days the country will either be morbidly obese or disgustingly healthy- it's all a toss up really.

David is feeling good, and so he should be. We went to a birthday gathering last night and he didn't drink any alcohol- this morning he awoke without a hangover and devoid of any self- inflicted injuries. It's a major achievement. He sits down while I come inside to make hot drinks, coffee for him and tea for me. His with two sugars. Mine black and with none.

Back on the patio David is looking at my tiny solar powered fountain- it's all of six inches wide and spills more water than it circulates but it's fun. I have it sitting in a wok, one that I bought recently but don't like using- it's too light weight- so the insects and birds get to use it instead. The sound is good though and makes up for the lack of practicality.

David is telling me how good it was to not drink last night, although being sober had an impact upon how he perceived the gathering around him. Me too. I've known a couple of very high functioning alcoholics in my time, men who wheeled and sealed their way into the top tax bracket, whiskey in hand from dawn til midnight, never showing even a small indication that their livers were working overtime and their brains quietly disintegrating.

These men could hold highly intellectual discourse, buy and sell on the stock market and charm the pants off the proverbial jackass, but they couldn't go even half a day without a drink in their hand. People accepted their alcoholism because it was integral to these men's persona, it made them who they were- charming, gregarious, kind, and attractive.

Their friends looked sideways around the issues that cause addiction and concentrated on the comfortable veneers instead, because to scratch beneath the surface would mean having to confront the pain and the damage and the self-denigrating disgust and dismay. So my friends drank, and their circle of friends brought bottles of wine to their dinner parties, and nobody called out the shovel when the spade would do the job.

Then one day, the alcoholic quits. He finds the courage to look at himself and decides to stop the self-destruction, and to really try to reinvent himself. It is not the easiest of roads, and it is made even more difficult because now none of his friends recognise him, none of them know this new person, and that makes them feel uncomfortable and out of place. Many walk away.

David picks up his mug.

"How's the gremlin?" I ask.

"He's fine, quiet today. I think he's sleeping."

"Have you asked him what he wants to be called yet?"

"No. But I remember to stroke his ears when he gets twitchy."

We laugh.

The Gremlin is the name we have given David's inner voice, the one that pesters and niggles at him when he is feeling out of balance. I have advised David to stop trying to escape his gremlin, but to engage with it instead. To ask Gremlin what it is he wants, what it is that he needs to share. This new relationship seems to be working, an improvement on the psychic parrying and hiding away that David has been used to.

I suggest trying to draw Gremlin and bring him out into the open from the shadow world. David says he will try, and knocks back his third coffee.

I warn him that the friends he has who relate to him as an alcoholic will feel out of their depth with him once he is sober all of the time; they won't know how to relate to him, and those who enjoy the feeling of moral superiority will now feel threatened. Our eyes meet, he nods in recognition and I can see the cogs turning deep within his mind as he starts to stretch his potential capacity for self-respect.

A bee lands on the wok and takes a drink, her legs heavily laden with the pollen of mallows. She takes off and starts her flight home, driven, helplessly committed to a lifetime of sterile productivity. She cannot reprogram herself to not do as she does, she spends her lifetime supporting the bees of her hive, unable to even procreate in a lifetime of service.

Were she human, we might call this behaviour a self-destructive addiction.

After David leaves I go back inside and open the fridge. I'm restless and without a cause. A hundred days of social distancing and the whole country still uncertain about what Covid-19 really means. We are all doing our own thing, in true British fashion, following whichever guidelines fit in with our own sense of rightness. It's like a game of Russian Roulette, and I cannot help but wonder just how many bullets are really spinning around in the chamber before we pull the trigger and take off our masks.

We have lost faith in our leadership and so are meandering like so many lost sheep, aimless and without focus, as we eat our way towards the slaughterhouse in full control of our ignorance. There are no shepherds anymore, instead only groups of well intentioned bystanders who wring their hands and avert their eyes as the deadbolt hits home.

The phone rings. Thank God. Saved by the bell.

It's twenty years since the phone rang and a woman's voice told me my grandmother was very ill and unlikely to survive much longer. I looked out the window of the rented farmhouse overwhelmed with incredulity.

"Why hasn't anyone contacted me?" I demanded.

"How long has she been in hospital?"

"I'll be there in an hour and a half."

Twenty minutes later my mobile rang in the car.

"Mrs. Talken-Sinclair? I'm so sorry, but your grandmother has just passed."

And with that, I was on my own. A Lesson in "letting go" doesn't even begin to touch the surface.

When I left my husband, taking with me my animals, his debts and our children, my father died barely six weeks later on the sofa in my living-room.

He died from a pulmonary embolism that had travelled up from his left ankle. I had questioned his doctor at my grandmother's house about the swelling and been told in a very condescending manner that it could not possibly be a blot clot. Less than two months later my father was dead. My grandmother would not allow me to contact the GP and read the riot act, it just was not the done thing to question the Doctor.

My mother died two years later from unsuspected metastatic liver cancer, having gone into hospital for a routine check-up while I went away for the weekend. She died two days after my return, never knowing that she had cancer. I sat with her all day and listened to her breathing heavily sedated on morphine.

With each shift change I had to explain to the new doctor that my mother would not want to be revived if it meant she was going to be in pain. We couldn't implement a DNR (Do not resuscitate) because we couldn't get a biopsy done because she couldn't survive the procedure and so there was no way to prove she had cancer and so we could not request a DNR. Life is full of irony.

Just short of midnight I decided to go home to rest. I never even thought that she was going to die anytime soon, but she died in the early hours of the morning, never regaining consciousness.

As I left her room, I kissed her and said,

"Night Mummy, I'll be back in the morning. Love you."

"Good-night Darling," she replied.

My grandmother, alienated from me after my father's death, died after another two years had gone by of intermittent abdominal pain the cause of which was never diagnosed. My aunt and cousins in Canada never thought that it might be useful if I were kept apprised of her situation, and so she died in hospital all alone, because no one cared enough to let me know that she had been admitted.

It wasn't the first time the Canadians had let me down, and it proved to not be the last.

I didn't attend Nana's funeral, somehow it felt hypocritical to do so, and there seemed little point in going to see her now that she was dead when I hadn't been there when she was alive. Instead I helped her daughter Eunice sort through the cupboards and drawers and boxes, filtering out the memories of ninety-four years and keeping those that were precious.

Eunice and her son Mark packed up what furniture and assorted items they wanted and shipped them back to the land of maple syrup and seal hunts. I pruned the lavender and dug up a rose and loaded the old kitchen table into a friend's trailer. I also rescued the dinner service used by Nana's grandparents, a painting done by her step father, pieces of linen hand worked by three generations of women in South Africa, and boxes of memorabilia dating back to the 1920's.

I was also gifted a ring that my grandfather had supposedly won in one of his manu poker games. Nana used to talk about it often, offering it as a reward at some point in the future for good behaviour, but never once allowing me to see it. The ring came paired with a brooch, which had two stones, and the two pieces were made of gold with half carat amber diamonds.

When Nana died, Eunice kept the brooch- I suggested splitting the stones and giving one each to her two children- and I finally had a chance to see my ring. It was exquisite, the stone a deep dark honey colour set high in a band of rose gold.

I wasn't able to keep the ring forever, one day my financial situation made me decide that I was better off selling it to a local jeweller, and although I changed my mind and went to retrieve it only three days later, the ring was gone.

Many years later, more recently, Eunice scowled at me on Skype and told me that Nana was very very angry and disappointed with me for selling her ring. I commented that had any of the family offered to help me at the time I would not have had to part with it. In her now semi- demented state, Eunice could not now understand my comments.

Sentimentality is insidious. It catches us off guard when we are lost in the fields of what might have been, and drags us to places best left behind.

I open the fridge and take out some milk. I like to keep it in an antique jug that used to hang from a hook on the old kitchen dresser in Nana's Cottage. The jug is off white with age and has a pleasantly round plump body topped with an ornate ribbon of dark blue interspersed with tiny red and pink roses. Crown something or other. Somehow the cold china makes the milk taste different, and the jug is far more aesthetically pleasing than the plastic containers or cardboard boxes that milk is packaged in today.

I slip the collars over the dogs heads and open the kitchen door being careful not to let the cats out. The night is very dark, with thick cloud cover, and hot and humid. Although the full moon was only a few days ago, there is little ambient light, and the village seems submerged in a deep sleep. It's almost one in the morning.

I feel awake and I want to walk for more than a few minutes, so I decide to take the hounds down to the beach. There isn't any traffic, and no one else is wandering about at this hour to disturb the quiet solitude. I leave my torch switched off, even though it is darker than usual, and trust the dogs to warn me of any approaching danger. Emma is already panting going up the hills, and I'm wishing that I had left my jumper behind.

As we crest the brow of the last hill before the road drops down to the sea I can feel the wind start to pick up and the sound of the surf greets me. It's pounding, smashing onto the shingle in the darkness below. I haven't heard the sea crashing in for some time. Arriving at the public car park, the security lights remove all of my night vision and I walk blinded, barely able to see where the lane leads over the bridge and onto the beach. I'm scanning for foxes and rabbits, hoping that they will run before my dogs pick up their scent and try to give pursuit, but there is nothing. Walking across the small strip of grass, I duck out of the light and into the shadows and my sight returns.

All is irony.

The sea is far out but the waves are breaking in a long white line of surf that stretches away from us down the beach. I can smell seaweed and iodine in the air. I sit down on the pebbles, feeling the water left by a high tide slowly creep through my jeans. The dogs lie next to me, cooling themselves in the moisture. Everywhere is dark. The sky is covered in dark clouds and there are very few stars to be found overhead.

The sea itself stretches away from me in a slow moving rumble. It's so completely, profoundly, totally dark.

The darkness draws me in, until everything is a part of the wind, and the salt air, and the deep deep nothingness that is forever. The wind is rising and with it the waves grow higher, their strength and purpose lashing the sand and shingle with power brought up from the depths. I sit entranced. Sit and see this water, this water that has come from countries and continents that I have not seen, that has run down mountainsides and coursed through valleys and disappeared into deserts, water that has fallen onto the faces of laughing children and washed the dead in the Holy River Ganges.

I look ahead and see the light starting to change, the darkness starting to thin, and with the light comes a slow dawning of definition as the black wholeness starts to take shape. And the sea becomes one thick black brushstroke under a lightening sky across the canvas of my sight.

Easel looks at me and says nothing.

I take off the covers. It's time to paint.

The world needs people

Who cannot be bought;

Whose word is their bond;

Who put character above wealth;

Who possess opinions and a will;

Who are larger than their vocations;

Who do not hesitate to take chances;

Who will not lose their individuality in a crowd;

Who will be as honest in small things as in great things;

Who will make no compromise with wrong;

Whose ambitions are not confined to their own selfish desires;

Who will not say they do it "because everybody else does it;"

Who are true to their friends through good report and evil report, in adversity as well as prosperity;

Who do not believe that shrewdness, cunning, and hardheadedness are the best qualities for winning success;

Who are not ashamed or afraid to stand for the truth when it is unpopular;

Who can say "no" with emphasis, although all the rest of the world says "yes".

Ted W. Engstrom

DAY FOUR
Thursday's Children

MJ's staccato barking infiltrates my dream and nudges me awake. I reluctantly sit up and reach for a red cotton shirt that lies thrown onto a chair beside the bed. No point in ignoring her, she will continue barking in some imaginary dilemma for hours. And I'm also aware that her barking will become irritating very quickly if left unstopped, particularly for my son, who is still sleeping at six o' clock in the morning. Wish I could recapture the dream, but I've never been any good at that.

Downstairs I find MJ standing looking at a blank wall intently and barking.

Woof....woof....woof. Small utterances of defiance at the monster who arrests her attention. Ellisar and Emma lie stretched out sound asleep. Oh to be so lucky. I open the kitchen door and the sunlight shoots in, a glorious positive energy that lights up the slumbering room with the scent of honeysuckle and the sound of birdsong from outside. I fill the kettle and put some lemon verbena tea in a mug before taking MJ outside; it's another bloody beautiful day in Paradise.

Once all the dogs have relieved themselves, I take my tea and pad bare footed up onto the patio. The sun is already warm, and it looks as if summer is all around me. Restrictions are easing up around Covid-19 and so people are starting to venture out more and to travel across the country. There is no doubt that the weekend will see a major increase in the number of tourists coming to share the seashore, and with that an increased number of locals who resent the visiting drivers who are apparently incapable of reversing or knowing the precise width of their cars. One can become quite proprietorial over one's little kingdom in God's Own Country.

I mix up the dog food and divide it between the steel bowls. My mind is going in circles, trying to balance the tedium of imposed repetition due to our social lockdown rules and the tick-tick of my internal clock, nagging me to sort out all of my unfinished chores and hopeful ambitions. We won't be in lockdown forever- one assumes- and the paths ahead lie swathed in a grey gauze of hope and trepidation. Can we be the force for a brave new world, or will Orwell's 1984 become the standard upon which we both measure ourselves and die beneath? It is definitely the time to ponder which reality we will become a part of.

Emma barks. She's impatient, and thrashes her tail from side to side as she stands waiting.

In the journey towards Gaza in the autumn of 2014, there had been a lot of waiting. The start had been hectic enough, an email from the leader of the mission, a hectic rearranging of my life and some cursory soul-searching, my manager saying I had annual leave due, my son giving me a lift to the coach station and then me getting onto a plane less than twenty four hours later heading for Egypt. Who says life begins at forty? I was fifty-five and not a day more sensible than when twenty.

We land in Cairo airport at five a.m. and by ten are in our van heading for Gaza. The hotel we have booked into to regroup and catch up on the mission plan is one of emptied opulence, with the longest drive and a beautiful ceiling that looks like Wedgewood- reminds me of the buildings in Kiev, with their pastel walls and light coloured brick edges- and massive bronzes that celebrated the glories of the British Empire on horseback. As we leave the compound and start to drive through the city, Phillip is busy with his camera.

"Poverty makes such pretty pictures."

The van is air conditioned, thank God. It is 37 degrees outside and the day is about to get a great deal hotter.

Several hours later we approach Freedom Bridge, eight hundred and fifty meters of it span the Suez Canal and in all it stretches across three kilometres of desert, but it stands empty now, devoid of cars or trucks or people. Not even a goat or donkey tread warily across its arc.

Waiting.

The bridge has been closed for a year due to security issues and there are very few to admire this marvel of modern engineering. The locals cross using a ferry- we are stopped from enjoying such mundanity and searched. The guards take exception to Amir's satellite phone and order us to wait, and wait, and wait, and then to go with them.

The van and the driver stay behind. They will wait for us.

We spend five hours in the military outpost offices next to Suez, and drink Tang- the American instant orange drink that I have not tasted since my last visit to the Middle East. The occasional fly buzzes around the room before falling into a somnolent torpor, coming to rest against the screened window.

Numerous officials come and go, trying to facilitate our crossing into Gaza, but in the end we are sent to spend the night at Ismalia, the nearest coastal town, while the military and the Egyptian Secret Service try to find a way to keep us safe as we cross the 400 km this side of the border with Palestine through Sinai.

It's pronounced Rhaa-ghza, at least to the people who belong there, but the world calls it Gaza, and so even in this small detail the countries of the world dispossess the very people who live there. In Ismalia we are turned away from the headquarters of the military and told to return in the morning, or we could return to Cairo.

We stay, and wait.

Ismalia is a coastal town and at night the streets are hectic and alive with people and market stalls. There are huge mounds of fish- what do they do with those not sold?- and on one stand I see the sad carcass of a leatherback turtle. We cannot save it, its eyes stare lifelessly and it makes no effort to move its flippers- the fact that it rests on its front is the giveaway. Passers-by stop and caress the shell, as if wistful to see such gentleness reduced to death. Or maybe they just want to feel a turtle shell.

We eat out of hunger and find a bed in a very welcome hotel after a long search. Our driver seems to find following directions challenging- or maybe the directions are at fault- we cannot tell. Thank God for air-conditioning and good water pressure.

Such are the things that become treasures.

On Saturday we rise early and eat a quick breakfast.

Back in the van to the Secret Service Headquarters, where after more waiting we are told that we need to return to Cairo. As we drive back towards Cairo I see a monument with the words "Asmorality to the Egyptians who dug out the Suez Canal with their bare hands." I think they meant immortality, but who really knows?

The New Suez Canal will be 50m deep and 45Km long- I doubt very much it will be dug out by anyone's bare hands.

Amir explains that the strong military presence in Ismalia is to engender confidence for its population, as anarchy soon followed in the wake of the Arab Spring, bringing with it a creeping wish to have Mubarak reinstated. The armed guards on the street help people to sleep at night, and wake in the morning.

We drink sweet strong Arabic coffee and I watch a woman walking with chickens in a crate on her head. They peer upwards and flutter to keep their balance. Moments later I hear them squawking in a small shop behind where we wait. Has Death found them? It has to be better this way. Quick, and unexpected- doesn't it?

I think back to a scene I observed yesterday on the drive- a young boy was holding onto a shaggy goat by the scruff and I have no doubt that the goat was soon to be dispatched. It made me think about how we judge and how we slaughter our own livestock in the so called civilised Western countries. How people claim the moral high ground from behind their sanitised packaging and organic food labels.

The reality is that we don't stop to think, to look, we forget about the miles in lorries destined for markets and slaughter-houses, the hours spent waiting, stomach deep in the smells of urine, blood, guts and faeces, the sounds of pain and anguish, we do not think about the jollity from the men who have long ago stopped feeling any empathy or compassion for the animals they manhandle and kill. We dare to judge that our way is better simply because at the end, at the very end, we stun the animal, after tying it securely so that it can't move, can't escape, can't look at us with its last glare, or spit in our faces with its last drops of blood and saliva, as we cut its throat.

How dare we judge our way is better?

It must be better for the animal, surely, to stand there grazing, with the earth beneath its feet and the sun on its back, and the fresh air all around, only seconds before its very life blood stains the dust?

What would you choose, if you had to? How would any of us prefer to die?

We return to Cairo. We return to wait.

132

The road to Cairo is divided with well watered flowering trees- oleander, flamboyant, and a beautiful pink star-shaped flower that festoons the branches as they fall towards the dust. There are four and then five lanes for the traffic but they lie empty, testament to a better economy and braver tourists. In the desert we see huge ventilation shafts that rear their heads above the sandy plains- all the way to Cairo we see signs of military activity.

In the afternoon, the Pyramids at Giza. Only one letter away from a world apart.

And She, that enigma of the three legs, she turns her back on us as we walk down the ramp from the temples behind, and casts her eye over Cairo instead. In the end, her heart is made of stone.

That evening we discuss the world of animal welfare. It's depressing. Animal Rescue seems to have gone the way of all good causes and become nothing more or less than political expediency. I feel sick.

The good people of the world have no idea, no idea at all. I think of Kipling- twisted by knaves to make a trap for fools- and drink another whiskey. It is no longer about rescuing animals, or just moving them to a better place, it is about making a point, being seen to be making a point and through that gleaning funding—but for what I wonder, if not to rescue the animals?

It has become a self-perpetuating industry, and I despair quietly at the loss of integrity that awaits all of us, the quiet beast lying in the darkest of corners, licking its lips as we sacrifice our redemption.

Amir tells me later that early in the New Year, perhaps in January, Four Paws is set to become the consultancy arm of the UN in animal crisis situations.

He asks me, "What do you want, Suyen?"

I cannot answer him. I do not know.

The intention is to leave the flat in Cairo, courtesy of Amir, by 7am, but our driver does not arrive until an hour and a half later, having decided to take a shower somewhat later than we all did. He says he and his wife argued- about crossing into Gaza I wonder?

This means that our first appointment of the day- with the Department of Foreign Affairs- will be late as the Cairo traffic doesn't allow for a quick dash anywhere.

Outside the building there are trucks armoured with weld mesh and barbed wire- I am told this is a defence against petrol bombs. I cannot imagine how that works. We wait in the heat, cooking slowly beneath the glaring sun.

Our eventual meeting with the relevant official informs us that first we need to go to the Austrian Embassy in order to obtain their agreement to allow us into Gaza- we drive through the crowded streets and wait patiently seated on leather armchairs, but sanction of our mission is not forthcoming.

We return to see the Minister for Palestinian Affairs and are told that we should have followed protocol and waited for the necessary permits before coming to Egypt expecting to travel into Gaza. We now pose a problem to everyone concerned since our respective governments cannot sanction our mission when they are currently evacuating nationals out of Gaza. However, she will attempt to help us and obtain the necessary permits needed to drive across Sinai.

By the end of the afternoon we have her assurances that the permit will be forthcoming, and will allow us access to the Gaza border, albeit after what will be a very dangerous and challenging drive.

But, we still have to wait.

The Jihadists have captured anti-aircraft weapons so there is no air traffic out of Ismalia- we cannot fly, so we must drive.

We hope to leave early Tuesday morning. In the meantime we drink mint tea and watch the fishermen on the Nile. There is a part of me that wonders, does any of this make any difference? Does anyone now even think about the Tasmanian Wolf?

The Pyramids look down, rock over five thousand years old, but just rock all the same. And the BBC World News has nothing but war stories to entertain us with- will we ever stop wanting next door's greener grass?

Everyone I have ever known, in the end, wants only to love and be loved- why do we have to make it all so bloody and difficult?

We "hope"—how ironic is that?

And then it is a new month. A new week.

A day of waiting. A day of contemplation. I write. Share. Communicate.

There is a part of me that wonders if we will get to Gaza safely, but I can't dwell on that. None of us can. We can't afford to or the fear would paralyze us, dry up any altruism and leave us screaming for home. For green fields and warm breezes and the soft caress of a dog's nose and the gentle wicker of a welcoming horse.

For our children and our children's children.

So I write- write to the people I love hoping that they understand, and that if it all goes wrong that some small part of them will comprehend the truths, but they won't of course. How could they? How can anyone understand why anyone that loves you would choose to enter the fray, put themselves in danger knowingly, rather than stay at home safe and secure?

I don't even understand it myself.

And if I did, I wouldn't dare to acknowledge it.

We wait.

It's now Tuesday and three in the morning and we are waiting. For the van and our driver.

We wait, to start the journey to Suez, the Sinai, and Gaza.

We wait- the driver is late by over half an hour. Feelings of irritation, frustration- we are all ready for this next stage of the journey. Finally, he arrives- his daughter was sick, he says. I don't think many of us believe him.

We sleep for the most part as we head towards Sinai, finally I awake when we stop to join the queue for the ferry across the Canal. The sun has just risen. We wait.

I watch a dog and a donkey play together in a field of young mango trees. I think they are playing, but the dog might be tormenting the hobbled donkey.

Things are seldom as they appear.

I need to find an obliging bush but any cover seems totally exposed, until at last Amir points out an obliging wall between the pine trees... He and Mihai have other more urgent matters.

While I stand sentry my eye picks out two boxes of tablets that turn out to be hydro-cortisone and antibiotics, I wonder which poor soul has dropped them in the hurry to relieve themselves- they are well within date and too precious a gift to leave behind. I put them in my pocket in case we need them in Gaza.

At last the soldiers arrive to open up the roadblock and we can drive onto the ferry.

I can take no photos from this part of my journey- too much security for me to feign an interest in my iPhone screen.

We drive off the other side and onto the Sinai Peninsula, the road is flanked by the rail tracks on one side and marching lines of pylons on the other. This is desert. The smell is of heat and dust and desiccated lives.

We drive past a small oasis rich in palms and on the road ahead I see a pick-up truck with a load of camels sitting in the cab behind- I had forgotten how easily they transport animals here by road—camels, horses, cows, they all sit or stand obligingly as their lives are whipped along the tarmac to an uncertain destiny.

Like us.

A couple of hours later we are at the second military checkpoint, and we are stopped from advancing any further. The local populace drive through with barely a nod, they can go where we cannot.

So, we sit, and wait. Again.

For many hours.

During this time my colleagues Amir and Phillip help a man who is scalded from removing the radiator cap of his overheated engine- Phillip has his master-of-all-trades hat on and produces an emergency burns kit- It may well turn out that he saved the man's face.

Amir remarks later that the wife, conditioned to a life of silence, could barely bring herself to shout for help. Her voice, so long made to be silent, could not find the way to cry out, and instead her eyes implored as her tongue froze.

Irony, all is irony. It stands on the sidelines, armed crossed and feet wide apart, throwing its head back in deep raucous laughter.

For his part, Amir confesses to a moment of fear, a split second of wondering about what had happened to render the man in the car immobile and his wife so startled- a moment of realisation that we are in Sinai, a place where Death can lurk within every vehicle and behind every stone.

And so it proves. We are held immobile because up ahead, twelve kilometres from the Gaza border, there has been a Jihadist incident. In retaliation for a previous attack by the Egyptian militia the day before, the local Jihadists have attacked and killed twelve uniformed men, including officers (why is that mentioned in a different clause?)- It is unlikely we will be going anywhere eastward today.

Ahead, the Director of Gaza Zoo waits for us at the border, behind us the Minister for Palestinian Affairs asks that we wait until she has reassessed the situation with her colleagues, and all around us the men- they look scarcely more than boys, with their semi-automatics tucked under their arms on fraying pieces of rope- go on with their duties.

I think of the twelve families, the grief, the blood, the lives cut short. I can imagine the scene- the dust, the mangled iron, the bodies thrown and now quiet in their silent contortions. The sun beating down as it has forever.

Truly, battlegrounds are land laid to waste.

Five hours after we have arrived we are advised to return to Kantara for the night and to come back in the morning. We are too late now to cross into Gaza, the border closes at three in order for people to be at their destination before the four o'clock curfew.

We turn around, heavy-hearted, the inactivity taking its toll and leaving us with a mixture of boredom, frustration and mind-numbing fatigue.

Kantara is a small roadside town that has a hotel with excellent water-pressure, clean toilets and air-conditioning and polite staff- we go to our rooms to sleep for a couple of hours before deciding what our next plan of action will be.

In Gaza, will the lions sleep tonight?

By seven we are on the balcony drinking mint tea. I get bitten by a silent insect that makes my cheek bone swell up like a boxing champion's. Amir has spoken with the directors of Four Paws and they want us to abort the mission- The latest incident in Sinai has made them decide that it is too dangerous a situation for any of us to be involved with. Amir, although able to enter Sinai as an Egyptian carte blanche, is hampered by being the head of the Four Paws team and thus under the directives of the head office in Vienna.

Help from PAF in Jordan can only go so far as to provide food and medicine to the animals in Gaza, they cannot transport people across the West Bank and Israeli borders. He has to acquiesce.

We all do.

But he will not give up, i know this, he will simply find another way.

I recognise how relieved all of our families and friends will be to know we are not going into Gaza- Gaza, totally ring-fenced and cut off from foreign intervention.

Gaza, from where we hear of nothing to cause us alarm, but where we cannot reach.

It leaves all of us with a feeling of sadness and impotence, there is nothing more to be done here. After eating, we return to Cairo, arriving a mere twenty four hours after we had left.

Who knows whether those thirty minutes that we spent pacing this morning have in some way saved our lives? Who knows whether had we been that much further ahead of ourselves we too might have witnessed the carnage first hand near the border? What have we achieved by coming here at all? Did Amir and Phillip give aid to the father of a child who will one day remember the kindness of strangers from the West? Have we left an imprint in the sand, with our high hopes and blind ideals? Have I given some prepubescent girl in the desert a glimpse of a future where she does not have to cover her head? A time when she can sit with men and laugh in the open? Is this Thursday's child?

We cannot know, the effect of a butterfly's wing.

Before we sat down to eat our last meal in Sinai my friends called out, "Something spicy! Drink Whiskey! Bring meat!"

Above us the moon is a blood-red orange lying low in the sky, neatly divided in half.

She hangs suspended.

Waiting.

Once Phillip was home he posted on Face Book some updates on what we had all been up to- Four Paws took exception to this and requested that he remove some of the content. I can only guess that since I am not an employee they decided that my blog wasn't worth worrying about. As I like to ask, What price, freedom?

The worry apparently was that some of their contributors might see our time in Egypt as a waste of charity funds.

The Zoo in Gaza was in crisis- animals died and starved to death. The Director of the zoo asked for help, and Amir, in his typical way, responded. He did not wait for the bureaucrats or the diplomats or the politicians to wade their way through all of the protocols or mountains of excuses, he acted. He called together his team, and he went. We all did. He had a stack of verbal assurances that we would be able to get to Gaza, but in the way of the world, the reality once you are on the ground is very different.

It may be true that it would have been more prudent to have waited, and yes, it might have saved money, but the thing is that in times of conflict you have to be on the spot, in the right place at the right time, you can't say to a military escort- "Hey! Hang on a minute! I've just got to catch my plane and I will be with you in a couple of days." You have to be there so that when the light turns green, you run. And you can't do that from the safety of a board room.

I hope the people who donate to Four Paws understand.

I hope that they understand that what their money paid for was for a team of individuals to be there, on the spot, and that with each turn of the wheel on our van across Sinai, we took the chance of being attacked and killed. Or possibly worse, kidnapped.

As Phillip pointed out as we waited for the five hours following the bomb attack on the Egyptian Police, every car that passed us- and there were many, as many Egyptians still live in the Sinai- would have clocked the fact that there was a car soon following with Europeans in it; by stopping we were effectively earmarked to Jihadist extremists in the area.

The fact that we were not allowed to enter Gaza means that there was no fanfare, no celebratory patting of backs in Vienna, no fireworks- but the story IS the non-story, it IS the failure to get into Gaza, and why we failed to do so.

When I return to England I write the epilogue, those last few days when only Amir and I remained in Cairo, from the sanctuary of my couch- with the sun shining outside in that delicious Autumnal way it has in England, when the air is fresh but the sky is blue, and the fields are just starting to lose their green vibrancy for the mellow browns and yellows of September.

I needed to write it down before I forgot- because we do forget, we forget the urgency and the passion, the frustration and the doubt. We forget because if we didn't we would go quietly mad, as we struggle to juxtapose our vet bills and non-bio-environmentally-friendly laundry powder with the flies and the grime and the sheer scale of the problems in the Middle East.

I read the Saturday Times and see that NATO has decided that it is time to take a "stand" against ISIS- that if the West doesn't come out all guns blazing we will inevitably all end up part of a global caliphate. That it doesn't matter whether it takes one, two or three years, or ten.

The images of Gaza courtesy of the BBC drones are devastating- and I know that we are lucky not to be there, not to have succeeded with our mission, when even now there are threats to behead another well-intentioned charity worker.

I needed to write it down, before I forgot.

My plane left Cairo on time and touched down in London five hours later.

My bus wasn't scheduled to depart for several hours.

So I waited.

I am still waiting, as is the entire world, for a time when the sands of the Middle East are not splattered with the blood and tears of broken lives and shattered dreams, congealed with the phlegm of political corruption and international greed.

The memories bring tears. They crack open from deep inside my heart and stream down my face. Earlier on my iPad my timeline was burdened with stories of Israeli troops demolishing Palestinian C-19 treatment centres. There are only the dogs to witness this upwelling of sorrow, the cats lie in sunny spots sleeping and outside the quiet is disturbed only by the humm of a discordant fly.

"I think you need another water feature there, something to hide the bath."

David is giving me gardening advice. He and I are enjoying our ritualistic mid-morning coffee- well, his coffee, my tea. The bath is an old plastic baby bath which I keep hostas in, I thought it was a way of making sure their roots never dried out. It's worked too, and the upright blooms of lilac stand to attention in the shaded morning light. The purple colour is echoed by the lavender but I have recently moved from in front of the house. It's my grandmother's ancient rootstock, a piece I transplanted upon her death two decades ago. The bees are busy pollinating the fragrant blooms.

"Don't worry, I'm on it. There's a space there because I've moved all of the lilies to the front of the house. The stargazers, they're all about to open up."

David nods quietly, his thoughts already on another track. I'm busy thinking about the toxicity of lilies and whether the cats will be safe now that I've moved them. Will have to remove the stamens.

"Gremlin's behaving at the moment, he's there but not inside my head at the moment. It's better. I have to go to Dartmouth this weekend. Can't decide whether to make it one night or two. Meeting some friends for a party. I'll have to have a drink..."

"Just make sure you drink loads of water and try to remember to eat."

"I'll be fine," he says, looking at me squarely in the eye, "Don't worry, I'll be fine. Gremlin's behaving himself, I'll be fine."

It's two o' clock in the morning and I'm standing on a railway platform from a Sam Spade novel. Black and white and grey and sepia tones everywhere. Cold bare concrete and only a handful of other bodies in various states of exhaustion either lying flat out or huddled in corners with their eyes closed. Any light at all comes from naked low wattage bulbs that droop suspended from wires high high above me. There is no sound.

Three hours ago I was on a high speed express designed for the European Football Championship enthusiasts and travelling at over a hundred and fifty kilometres an hour. Now I am waiting to complete my journey to Lutsk, with only a few of the four hundred kilometres left to go, but there's a stopover of three hours before the next lap. So here I am, in Sam Spade mode, where no one speaks any English, and the liveliest thing around is a small black beetle trying to navigate its way across the cracks in the cement walls. Don't even think black coffee and a croissant.

I sit. The concrete is damp and cold, but I don't want to stand. I slip into a type of daze, lulled by the very nothingness around me, no sound, no movement, no smells. The very air itself takes on a suspended quality, as the mist from somewhere in the distant dark on the other side of the tracks creeps unnoticed towards me.

When the train does roll into view it comes with the crash and clatter of solid metal. It looks like a cattle train, a freight carrier from before the Cold War ended. It stands tall on the tracks, solid and square, with a wide flat roof and harrumphs to a standstill with a loud screeching of wheels. One or two of the windows have dull yellow light shining out of them, but the bulk of the machine is in darkness, looming over the platform with an air of menacing inevitability.

Two women officials stride purposely towards a carriage, they are almost as wide and as solid as their target, dressed in khaki uniforms with ribbons of medals displayed upon their ample bosoms. Their blonde hair is pulled back tightly into controlled buns at the back of their heads, and their shoes are black, well polished and very practical looking. They don't speak, or smile, as they walk over to the train.

Someone from inside the train opens one of the carriage doors and unfolds a metal stairway of about eight to ten steps. The coach sits high above the tracks. The women stand on either side of the steps and wait as those of us who are boarding line up with our tickets in hand. One of the women looks at me, reads my ticket and says something in Russian.

She looks at me with definite disdain when I gesticulate that I cannot understand her or make myself understood since I speak neither Russian or Ukrainian, being the typical English traveller. I can feel her disgust, and really want to just crawl away under the train where I'd probably feel more welcome.

Instead, I clamber up the rusting, shaky steps and a conductor inside the carriage points me towards the interior. I may never be seen again. Somewhere in the night a gulag awaits.

My ticket, purchased by the ever-resourceful Igor, was for an overnight sleeping cabin- what I have is the top bunk in an open carriage. Red vinyl, no sheets, and a man sleeping beneath me who is snoring almost as loudly as I can on a cold-congested night. I take off my shoes, place my feet carefully around his sleeping form and hoist myself up onto the bunk. Where the hell was I going to put my laptop and bag? I decide to rest my head on the laptop, thus keeping it safe, and place my bag in the small of my back. My case stays on the floor, luckily I travelled with only a very small one. I didn't dare fall asleep, absolutely paranoid that I would miss my stop, which was scheduled to occur at seven thirty in the morning. Seven a.m. found me standing by the door, under the baleful stare of our friendly Fat Controller.

The conductor had been disgusted to find me horizontal on his bunk bed with my shoes on, wrongly believing that I had kept them on all night. He made it quite plain, even without any English, that I was a filthy addition to his pristine carriage. As I had walked to the exit, I noticed piles of clean cotton sheets and pillowcases piled high on a seat, they leaned against the wall of the carriage in an array of alarming angles, like so many drunk ghosts. So that was where they had been, hiding in the dark. Next time I would know.

I stand by the door and watch the countryside chugging by. It had taken us five hours to cover not all that many more miles, a distance that a car would have completed in half an hour. The land stretches away from the train, green and empty, with only a meandering river to keep us company. Every now and then I see a lone cow standing on the verges of the river bank, tethered with a chain as she grazes her way along the edges of the water. And where there are houses, back gardens full to bursting with rows and rows of vegetables, growing between fruit trees which at this time of year had branches fully laden with fruit. It was a quiet, simple life that I observed, with hardly any cars or satellite dishes or shops, just an occasional horse-drawn cart or bicycle.

As I step off the train in Lutsk I wonder whether there will be anyone to meet me or whether it will be another confusion like the one at Kiev airport. I follow what few people there are leaving the train and wend my way through the station and through barriers erected to protect the public from building works taking place in the car park. No one I recognise is waiting for me.

An old hand at this abandoned-in-a-foreign-place-without-a-clue persona, I sigh and flag a taxi, at least I knew the name of the hotel this time. As we pull out of the carport I see the Vier Pfoten bus coming towards me and ask the driver to stop. I feel very guilty at not using him since I doubt there are many fee-paying tourists in Lutsk, so I give him something for his help and cross the sandy car park area to the bus.

"Welcome! Welcome!" exclaims the Head of Ops in Lutsk, "How was the journey? How are you?"

"Hello! It was good, thank you. I'm fine."

With David gone, I sit for a long time in the sun. It's been a tough few days, and I'm weary.

Weary of being told to be "the Light in a world of darkness".

Weary of all the New Age memes, the jolly Good Always Overcomes, the posts and threads of sage advice and the What a Wonderful World clichés.

Weary of hearing that what doesn't kill you makes you stronger.

Weary of being understanding, compassionate, empathetic, objective, non-judgemental, patient, forgiving, wise, tolerant, resilient, supportive, courageous, faithful, positive and resolute.

Some days I just want to rip the throats out of the people who have hurt me, disappointed me, exploited me, betrayed me, pour oil all over them and watch them burn. Some days I just want to be a Viking and pull back the arrows and unleash them.Some days I want to scream and rant my fury.

I'm tired of watching people who lie, cheat, steal and swagger their way through life live their lives unrepentant and unaware of the pain and chaos around them. I'm tired of individuals profiting from their lack of integrity, from their bullying of other souls, from their selfish demands and lack of conscience.

Some days I question the concepts of Divine justice, karma, and just deserts, of everything working out in the end as it should. Some days I just want to be a Dragon, and with a blast of molten ire burn the world clean. Some days I just want to curl up in a ball because I'm weary and tired and see only an oncoming train behind that light at the end of the tunnel.

And I am one of the lucky people, the much blessed, the loved.

My father once said to me, " Keep five per cent for yourself" and my mother once implored me to never be a social worker.

I should have listened. My poor mother, I know she was totally devastated when I made the decision to leave veterinary study and change to a degree in English. All of her practical Chinese genes screamed out at the loss of a lifestyle that guaranteed financial security, but she never said that. She took the news with quiet resignation, and hoped that whatever I did would make me happy.

I pour myself another cup of tea. The phone rings inside and I hurry to answer it before it stops. My daughter's voice greets me.

"Hi, just thought I'd call you on the way to work. The traffic is insane....Don't think C-19 lockdown is happening much anymore! The roads are just like normal. Yesterday I had to stop and help a man who'd been in an accident on the motorway. We're not meant to, of course, because of insurance, but I could hardly keep on driving by."

My daughter is eight years old and looking intently at the illustration of the kidneys in Gray's Anatomy. She turns to me and says,

"Mummy, I want to be a doctor."

And now there she is, standing on a stage taking her parchment of success from the Dean of Medicine. It's been quite a road travelled. I have a wonderful photo of her taken on the day of her graduation. It shows her throwing her cap into the air and her looking upwards as she reaches out to grab it, her face alight with happiness.

Along the way we've had the failed chemistry mock GCSE, the car disappearing into a ditch to avoid a deer, countless disappointments caused by her father's broken promises, the career advisor who said that medicine was a step too far and it would be wiser to aim less high, and early love affairs. I laughed with her too, as Life delivered joys, happinesses and great achievements.

There was the daily grind of getting to a sixth form college in the next county which meant that I drove her there and collected her every day, clocking up over two hundred miles every week, so that she wouldn't have to catch a six thirty bus and return home at eight. To this day I have no idea where the money came from to pay for the petrol, but somehow it was found.

I stand at the door to her bedroom and see that she has been crying. She is sitting on her tiny bed propped up against the wall, and she looks up at me lost in a lake of despair and crushed dreams.

"I hate chemistry. I'll never be any good at it, I hate it. I can't study any harder than I did for the mocks, and I've still failed. I'll never pass my GCSE. I'll never be a doctor."

She weeps, holding her knees to her chin, rocking on the bed.

I hold her in my arms as she cries with regret, doubt, disappointment, low self-esteem and heartache. I tell her that of course she will be a doctor, that this is only a mock exam, and that by the time she sits the real GCSE's she will pass. I tell her that she must not give up, that she must decide, here and now, in this moment, how she will respond to this failure. I tell her that she has to make a decision to keep on going, to keep on trying, and to do everything that she is capable of doing in order to make the next attempt a successful one. I tell her that in the years to come, no one will even remember that she failed a mock exam. I tell her that I love her.

She was born a Star, and blesses the world continually with her grace. It's a difficult act to be a part of, an almost insurmountable obstacle for a sibling to overcome; for intense light is blinding, it burns the tips of our fingers as we grasp our way out of our own shadows, and it's sometimes easiest to close our eyes, turn around and slink away, retreating back into the comfort of our own anonymity.

I'm sitting with the cliffs behind me, resting my back against the hard granite of the North Cornwall coast. The primary schools have broken up and my two children are playing in the rock pools that lie between the tide lines. It's one of the great perks to living by the sea, the ability to spend almost every day enjoying sun, sand and salt air if we wish to. Here there aren't too many crowds, preferring as they do to gather in closer proximity to food, drink and laundromats. This strip of coast has no such luxuries, boasting only the quiet turquoise water, the sound of seabirds and a tepid breeze.

I watch in silent gratitude. Both the children love the water, and I can hear them laughing as they jump from rock to rock looking for tiny hidden treasures amidst the seaweeds. They're tanned from the sun and the wind, and their dark brown hair is gritted with grains of sand, little jewels of boulders long ago whittled down by the surge of the oceans.

I want to freeze the moment. To stop time and hold this picture forever in front of me, to see their eyes lit up with their discoveries of little crustaceans and shy anemones, to feel the wind caressing the back of my neck, to take a deep breath and smell the salt and the iodine in the air, to hear their voices calling back and forth to one another before they both come running across the sand, breathless with excitement because one of them has a small fish in the bucket.

And my heart breaks with the fullness of it all, with the love and the joy and the wonderful wonderful connection that exists between us, the bond that will glue us together throughout all the rest of Time, regardless of the distances, the difficulties, the sorrows and the pains. The bond of blood, of shared experience, of instant recognitions of one another.

I want to freeze that moment, that feeling, that certainty that this is what is real, that this is what will survive all of the trials and hurts and wounds and angst, that we will always know the Truth of one another. I want to freeze the sands of time as they cascade down through the egg timer and settle, finding their resting place in the brief moments before all becomes once again topsy turvy.

That's what I want.

But then Life happens, and the sand turns to dust, and everything is swept up in a tornado of accusations and retribution, and all of a sudden none of us is in Kansas anymore.

I'm keeping a nether eye on my son's Facebook page, just to know what's happening in his life. He's still not really speaking to me but I'm not blocked. I wonder whether this is a Freudian slip on his part. We grasp at straws in moments of desperation, particularly when it involves the people we love.

Over the years I have become a truly expert clutcher-of-straws.

There's a voice in my head nagging me to go and check on the horses. I've grown somewhat detached over the last few weeks, retreating into my cocoon of imposed social isolation and finding it to be a comfortable state of being. Some days I don't want to venture out of the house at all and have to resist the temptation to nap through the afternoon. I don't always resist. Some days just the thought of getting into the car and driving to the nearest shop is enough to guarantee I won't be eating much that evening. Sometimes, isolation becomes its own rationalised inspiration, and it's just easier to hibernate. Even in the heat of July.

Since it is summertime, there is no real urgency to visit Sparkle and Darcy daily, they have food and water, and the landowners live on site- kind, generous spirited people, who would call me if anything were amiss. It's easy to become lazy, and stay sequestered in my sunny piece of Paradise, between the sea and the rolling Devonshire hills.

The eruption of COVID-19 has pandered to my stay at home hermit tendencies. Although I do miss the spontaneity of dropping in on my friends, I live in a beautiful and peaceful bubble in paradise. Now with the lockdown rules starting to relax, it's easy to forget the global pandemic, easy to lie in the warm summer breeze with my eyes closed and fail to see the possibility of an encroaching global pandemic disaster. Fail to recognise our own role in bringing that disaster to the fore of our own lives. My overseas friend was telling me only a few days ago how refrigerated lorries had been parked along the streets of New York so that dead bodies could be stored. We have become mummified in our own personal levels of ignorance and conceit, truly unable now to intrinsically know anything factual for certain.

I look down upon the Temple of Luxor, my daughter is beside me and peers out at the view below. The temple is approximately three and a half thousand years old, and was built to celebrate the renewal of kingship, of Divine Right, of Power. Would we build such a temple now, I wonder, as we struggle with the deluge of information provided by the internet and mainstream media? Would we be better served by a benign dictatorship where no one has to bear the burdens of an informed democratic process? How many people really want to be free, and to take responsibility for the choices that they make every single moment of their lives?

In the distance below us, everything is very very tiny. The tourists, the horse drawn carriages, the buildings, the statues. We are standing at the top of a minaret, the crowning glory of one of the local mosques, and I feel extremely privileged. My daughter has treated us both to a cruise up the Nile for her twenty-first and my fiftieth birthdays. She has always felt an affinity for Egypt, and I have bought her an Eye of Horus painted on papyrus for her medical aspirations.

The mosque we are in is not one of the famous ones. Those are closed. Locked shut. This is a far more humble one, discovered in my determination to see inside a working mosque as opposed to a grand tourist attraction. The other tourists are still on board the cruiser, laid out by the intense heat and after lunch torpor. I had grabbed my daughter and skipped down the ramp onto shore, eager to explore while others slept. The majority of our cruising companions seem to be asleep most of the time anyway, even when awake, and Egypt passes us by on the river bank, a contradiction of Biblical scenes and mobile phones and satellite dishes attached to the desert homes with their small black windows.

The three guides who are with us for the duration of the cruise are all qualified Egyptologists, and every day impart some of their great knowledge to our groups of mixed metaphors. We are witness to the eons of knowledge inscribed on the walls of tombs and temples, introduced to the wide array of local merchants and their goods, frequently mobbed by crowds of young men all of whom want to marry our younger members- a million camels for my daughter- and ushered along the well-worn paths of Pharaohs and their Queens.

After the evening meal, I will frequently sit with these three wise men and ask them about modern day Egypt, about the social and economic reality now affecting the everyday people. No one else from our group seems interested in such topics. I listen intently, my daughter beside me, learning all of the time.

Up high now in this minaret, behind us the tight spiral steps lead down into the main room of the building, and the watchman who had welcomed us in when I knocked tentatively on the door, stands waiting for us many feet below. No one comes up here very often, as the dust and gravel and bits of old paint pots and brushes confirm. I am worried about whether we will be expected to leave a monetary gesture for being allowed in- I have only twenty Egyptian pounds left and that equates to about two pounds sterling. Not very much for entrance to a holy place.

As we descend, he joins us and says, "Tea, have tea," and ushers us into a small ante- room. There is a wise and venerable looking individual sitting at the wooden table reading, he looks up at us over his glasses and long grey beard, "As-salamu Alaykum," "Va-alaykum As-salaam," I respond. He returns to his book.

Years later I would be humbled by the everyday presence of the Divine in the lives of the peoples in the Middle East. God permeates their everyday language in a way long lost to the West. The daily greeting, "May Peace be with you" is far more beautiful than "Hi there," our long ago "God be with Ye" now lessened into "Goodbye." We have largely removed God from our everyday interactions and thus become far less accountable to the divine morality once imposed by religious belief.

With freedom comes responsibility, and with responsibility comes accountability. When freedom comes and delivers choice, we are all accountable for the effects those choices impose upon our worlds... no small wonder so many individuals in our world now find it easier to simply look the other way and fall into line behind the noisiest tambourine.

The gentleman who answered my knock and allowed us to enter appears with tea, mint tea served hot in small glass cups full of fresh mint leaves and heavy with sugar. For a moment I panic inwardly thinking of waterborne diseases and unwashed glasses, but then I cast caution behind me and welcome the tea with gratitude. I'm still worried about payment though, since I am very aware that tourists are expected to donate freely to the local economy.

As we rise to leave I place my twenty Egyptian pounds on a plate and bow slightly, trying to explain my lack of funds but knowing they cannot and probably would not understand me. I hope they can see and inwardly recognise my genuine admiration and respect for their traditions and their culture, but who knows, they may just think that I've been a huge waste of time. We put our shoes back on and walk out into the blinding, blistering sunlight.

The saying goes that if you drink of the waters of the Nile you will return, and I did of course, a few years later, but now I'm looking out of my window at the green woods opposite my cottage. A butterfly flaps its wings. It rises gently upwards and disappears into a stand of lilac buddleia trees, and a bumblebee zigzags through the lavender with its Turkish pantaloons covered with amber pollen.

Is that one of the cats lying hidden in the shade, it's tail twitching casually from side to side, every muscle taut, before it pounces in a deadly flash of playful exuberance? As flies to wanton boys are we to the Gods, they kill us for their sport.

It's almost midnight and I'm chuckling to myself as I watch Bill Bryson on television. Emma starts to bark and not long afterwards I hear someone walking into the kitchen. My son appears and goes upstairs.

"Hi..." I venture.

No answer.

I sigh inside and return to Bill and the Appalachian Trail.

Waiting.

Since last year I've found myself wanting to walk a great distance too. I've thought about the Camino, and the North Western Highway in Scotland. I don't want loads of kit though, just a pair or three of comfortable lightweight shoes and a staff, like the pilgrims in Chaucer's time. Credit card and iPhone too of course, after all, I'm not totally idiotic. Small bag slung over my shoulder.. will definitely need a very healthy bank balance in case of emergencies. One foot in front of the other, day after day, just like the pilgrims.

It must still be possible somewhere, somewhere remote, since the ever increasing popularity of famous routes puts me off. Climate will be the killer.

It needs to be done.

A few minutes later my son comes back downstairs and goes into the kitchen.

I hear the fridge door open and close.

"Do we have any eggs?"

And there it is. The olive branch. The outstretched hand, the pipe of peace. It is the chip in the shell that the young chick makes as it breaks through the weeks of calcified imprisonment in its first tentative bid for a changed reality.

"No, but I'll get some tomorrow."

He walks into the living- room and stands there, my Man-Cub, all six foot three of him, tanned like dark coffee in a white tee-shirt and baseball cap.

"Went river swimming last night, it was amazing." He smiles.

"I'm going to bed, I'm absolutely knackered."

Bill is falling into a river with his pal, his best mate, overburdened with hiking gear and the expectations of middle age.

I sit.

I am overwhelmed with gratitude and relief. My son, safe, under my roof, and finding reasons to be happy. It's a corner turned, a step into a more positive future. The chick will emerge and flesh out its wings, stretch its legs and walk.

It's something worth crowing about in the wee hours of this Friday morning.

We've come a long way.

"After a while you learn the subtle difference

Between holding a hand and chaining a soul,
  And you learn that love doesn't mean leaning
  And company doesn't mean security.
  And you begin to learn that kisses aren't contracts
  And presents aren't promises,
  And you begin to accept your defeats
  With your head up and your eyes open
  With the grace of a woman, not the grief of a child,
  And you learn to build all your roads on today
  Because tomorrow's ground is too uncertain for plans
  And futures have a way of falling down in mid-flight.
  After a while you learn...
  That even sunshine burns if you get too much.
  So you plant your garden and decorate your own soul,
  Instead of waiting for someone to bring you flowers.
  And you learn that you really can endure...
  That you really are strong
  And you really do have worth...
  And you learn and learn...
  With every good-bye you learn."
  Gorges Luis Borges

DAY FIVE
Right for The Falls

It's very quiet.

I look up into those startling blue eyes and I can feel myself starting to melt around my edges. I reach up with my hands and entwine my fingers through his hair as I stroke his temples with my thumbs. I stretch my neck upwards and look into his face, the long aqua line nose that goes slightly off to one side, and the strong jaw beneath the finely etched mouth. My heart is pounding within my chest, but my legs are weak and fading into a watery ripple. My hands pull him down towards me, my lips parting as his mouth seeks mine, and we kiss. A kiss that steals my mind and thoughts and leaves behind only the urge of my desires rushing upwards through my body to greet it. I lower my head and rest against the smooth bareness of his shoulder, breathing in the scent of him, hearing the drumming of his heart as it matches the rhythms of mine. I close my eyes and listen, drinking in the scent of him, the sound of him, the taste of him lingering on my tongue, and my entire body sinks into the peace that comes with the resolution of souls.

It is very quiet.

I open my eyes, and I am awake.

I lie very very still, I can still feel my dream, and the longing I feel ambushes me and makes me cry quietly in the dawn light.

We cannot choose who we fall in love with, we can only choose how we respond to Pandora and her box of tricks.

I'm sixteen and have just started a new semester at university. Trans-Atlantic differences in education have resulted in my being accepted into a pre Vet program while not yet being old enough to vote. I have no idea what to expect but am happy to be on one of the smallest and most beautiful campuses in Canada. Sixteen, with the world at my feet, and in love.

He is half Indian, as in of the Plains, not the Ganges, with the blue-black raven hair of westerns and brilliant grey blue eyes. His skin, pale to a fault, must come from his paternal gene pool as I have seen a sepia photograph of his maternal grandmother sitting on a painted pony, and he's barely five eight, so hardly tall, dark and handsome, but I'm totally lost.

The first time we have sex is totally not worthy of remembering, except that it was my first time, although I very much doubt his. I can remember him pushing my head downwards as we lay on the narrow single bed in my room, assuming that I would know what to do and what he wanted, and that I complied because I thought that was what I should do. We didn't speak at all, but I was definitely completely besotted.

How would I not be?

My childhood was filled with Romantic idealism, and that was before Disney was to be found in every shopping mall and video channel.

My mother raised me on the stories around her courtship with my father. Warm Caribbean nights spent on golden sandy beaches under velvet skies studded with shining diamonds and caressed by warm breezes. Adventures of love and passion that inspired my mother to break with the rules of society and join herself to my father, the penniless dark, handsome adventurer with integrity and a kind heart.

My grandmother, who freed herself from a husband more attached to a whiskey bottle and the poker tables than to the routines and travails of early twentieth century marriage. He was a rough diamond suffocated by an Edwardian lady. She broke the rules and walked away and found herself a man steadfast and loyal who treated her with gentleness. He would write to her every day for the many decades they were together, while she waited patiently for over a quarter of a century to become his wife.

Add to this recipe the romantic songs and films, the old school values and mores which guided me through childhood and adolescence, and you have a creation totally out of sync with her time and her peers, you have a woman destined to search for her Prince Charming, because she truly believes in his existence. I was doomed to live out a journey of expectation and disappointment on a continual loop, refusing to give up on my dreams and beliefs that true love can conquer all.

The Indian looks at me with sadness in his eyes.

He hands me a letter. In it he describes how he has a "girl squirrel waiting for him back in their hometown of North Bay." We cannot be together and live happily ever after under a glowing red maple tree. He's so sorry.

My heart breaks. I have never known such raw pain or devastating loss. I cry uncontrolled and my sobs shake my world into a million shards of emotional glass that crash and splinter against my skin. My heart hurts, physically hurts, and I am completely and utterly devastated, without meaning, without hope, without direction.

I reel under the awareness that I am not the chosen one, I am not important enough to be the top priority, I simply do not matter enough, I am not cared for enough, and the man I love does not love me enough to want to be with me.

It will take me decades of repetition of this lesson before I reach the place where none of that matters to me, where I accept that it is not my relationship with those that I love which is most important, but rather it is the relationship that I have with myself. Still kept on self-harming though, tearing my heart out and throwing it into the frying pan, still kept on going, falling in love and then being rejected, still believing that one day my prince would come.

Patrick Stewart is reading one of Shakespeare's sonnets.

During the lockdown generated by COVID-19, Sir Patrick reads a sonnet a day by the Bard.

Let me not to the marriage of true minds admit impediments...... Sonnet 116.

"The marriage of true minds", now there's a thought. I think back to my marriages of true minds, there aren't many.

After the disaster of my first love I slept with a few men in typical freshman year complacency. I can still catalogue them all, like Andi McDowell in Four Weddings and..., but although I was always sober, and liked each of them, none of them had a claim on my heart. It wasn't until I took a year off- mandatory sabbatical resulting from too many all nighters not studying and not passing enough modules- that I really loved again.

He was a copy writer for the local daily paper, and twice my age, and one of the kindest and most gentle men that I have ever known. He taught me how to make a great chilli con carne, introduced me to the lyrics of Bob Dylan, and drove me over the Rockies to the glories of British Columbia. We stayed up watching the Northern Lights, drank cheap red wine and curled up under blankets reading our own escapes. He loved me with a passion and depth and constancy that is a rare gift, and eventually insisted that I travel my own path to heights he felt he could not climb. With the arrogance of youth, I never truly recognised his worth, and left him one morning on the platform of Saskatoon train station and headed back east.

Many years later I tracked him down and spoke with him. We corresponded for a year or two. Later I would grieve his death, the result of a brief encounter with a motorbike in a supermarket parking lot, that left him in a coma and damaged beyond reprieve. I discovered that he had reached out to me earlier over the years but that his letters, his wonderful, funny letters, had been thrown away by my husband. I do not know whether they were opened first.

My mother used to say to me that when I left and returned to Guelph, I left a broken man behind me, and in his sorrow he moved to the west coast and found himself a Japanese girlfriend. I hope she gave him joy. He was a totally selfless man, and when I think of him now I cannot help but feel that my loss was much greater than his in the long run.

"O no! It is an ever fixed-mark, that looks on tempests, and is never shaken."

Is a wife a tempest? Should affairs be shaken?

I fell in love, or, as the saying goes, I dove straight in. Only I didn't, I slipped quietly and softly, until one day I realised that I had submerged myself without even realising what was happening, and I was drowning with lungs devoid of air.

A true marriage of minds: minds, bodies and souls. Just not a marriage.

And he fell too, all the time trying so hard not to give in, not to succumb, not to be in love.

Eventually he left her. Left the warm, kind, Mother Earth figure that replaced his own dead parent, and travelled halfway across the continent to lie by my side. He promised to join me later in the land of my birth, and so I boarded yet another train and then flew East without him. Months later, seated at my desk in a busy London office, I received his letter. His letter telling me that his father was demanding repayment, that he could not now join me. I offered to return immediately but he asked me not to do so. And so, once again, the man I loved did not choose to have me, but chose another woman instead to share his life with. I looked down at one of the pair of opal earrings he had given me before my departure and watched the fire within flash. I wondered if I would ever retrieve its mate.

Decades later, he is Deputy Attorney General and the father of five daughters. He is still married to the woman who put him through grad school and welcomed him back to her ample bosom. He writes to me, saying that he truly believes that if he had been brave enough to join me that we would have been happy. That I am the part of him that he keeps deep down within his soul, secret, the part he will not share with anyone.

I am so angry that I want to slap him. Slap him for the wasted years and his comfortable, ordinary life. Slap him for not daring to take what he desired, for choosing the road more travelled. For not wanting me above all else. For not daring to follow his heart.

"Love is not love...

...which bends with the remover to remove."

The next time I fall in love, it was not with the man I married, but after I had divorced him, seventeen years later. In the years which followed my divorce, I fall in love five times, and each time I lose the man I would happily die for to someone else. You would be forgiven for thinking that I must be really stupid.

171

The first man reminded me of everything my marriage had never contained, and I revelled in the newfound closeness of spirit. In humour, and raw, visceral desire. He said I had the strongest vaginal muscles he'd ever known. I took that as a compliment. He left, scared of the intensity of it all, and married a meat and two veg type of woman, as his sister described her.

The second man was married and working on a divorce. I left after seven years and he was still married. I can remember sinking to the ground onto my knees and weeping my tears of heartbreak as he walked away to work. He left his wife two years later. I've never heard more from him.

The third man was a soul mate. We understood each other in every way, recognised the nuances of our behaviours and had our roots in the same soil. We would talk on the phone for hours every day, float away on jazz and thrill with the delight of a perfect salad dressing. My best friend slept with him. She became pregnant. They married.

The fourth man was separated from his wife for three years, he wore no ring when I met him. He sang to me and recited poetry, rode with me under the stars and made me feel unique. He waved goodbye to me and went back to be near to his grandchildren, the scandal of a divorce too frightening a prospect for a big fish in a small pond.

The fifth man, the fifth man broke me.

He slept with my friend and walked away from a decade of shared dreams and shared breath. He taught me how it feels to believe that I meant absolutely nothing, that I had no worth, that what I wanted did not matter, that he did not care how I felt, or wept, or argued, and that everything is transient.

He taught me humility. And as I choked on my ego and my expectations and my grief and my fury and my assumptions, I realised that we are all mirrors of each other, that we are that which we most love and most hate, and that what we see as flaws are simply the weaknesses within our own selves.

It is a hard reflection to own, through the glass darkly we peer into the abyss.

Love is "the star to every wand'ring bark,

Whose worth's unknown, although his height be taken."

Single women are a threat. Single middle-aged women like myself are a big threat, particularly to other middle aged women who are not single. Single women who are attractive, amusing, intelligent and self-sufficient are the biggest threat of all. It's been twenty-four years since my move to Devon, the natives are getting wary.

David is sitting opposite me looking uncomfortable. I have asked him whether I have in some way upset our neighbours who live at the bottom of the hill. Whether my antennae are correct or I am imagining a certain coolness between them and me lately. He fidgets and searches for his reply. Eventually he concedes that there is a problem, but he cannot tell me what it is. I start to delve into my memories, searching for something I may have said or down to upset two people that I think of as friends. Unsuccessfully.

I find myself starting to cry, tears welling up from some place deep, tears of bewilderment and sadness. What have I done? David looks away, assuring me that it's nothing really, really nothing. I am perplexed, and cannot imagine how I might have caused my friends to feel annoyed by me. Only a week ago we were all eating outside- socially distanced because of the Covid virus- celebrating the wife's birthday.

"Ah yes, well........" David's voice drifts off.

I look at him askance. What the hell?

Later I am told that the wife feels threatened by me, and thinks I am making a play for her husband. My choice of wine, a rich Californian red that is one of my favourites and that I rarely give away, simply confirmed it for her. The wine is called Midnight, and the vineyard label is Ménage a Trois.

I am furious.

Furious and hurt.

Furious, hurt and incredulous.

Just as well I hadn't taken a bottle of Loveage with me, or a cask of Sheepsdip.

David's revelation has flattened my mood and I retreat out of the garden and into the safety of my home. I close the door and leave the vagaries of the world outside. I'm still feeling shell-shocked, and terribly terribly alone.

I'm tired. Tired of being resilient, understanding, independent and just downright bloody wonderful. I want to be like all those other women, the ones who curl up and die, who feel unable to do anything to change their situations, who talk about what they would do if only they could, the would haves, should haves, could haves, the victims bound by their own hesitancy, by their own fear, the women who have to have a man, who have to have a shoulder to lean on, cry on, stand on. Those women. The women who want to be Scarlet O'Hara but won't scramble in the dirt for radishes.

Only of course I don't want to be one of them at all.

I'm just tired, in this moment, of having to listen to them all, day in and day out, bleat about how awful their lives are, how hard done by they are, as their husbands pay the bills and sign the credit deals. Listen to their thwarted dreams, their impotent desires for changes, their settling for less than truth and their eternal weeping over their miserable lives. For fucks sake, I want to shout, JUST DO IT! Do whatever it is you want to do, and pay the bloody price, or shut up. Stop revelling in your own victim hood, stop blaming life for your choices, grab the bloody nettle and make the goddamn tea.

Don't think it would go over very well with my friends, most of whom are women. Need to soften my approach. Most people don't help who they are, who they have become; most people allow the rivers of life to carry them along like so much flotsam, never realising that if they did but drop their feet downwards they might stand up tall, and walk a different way.

The phone rings. I take a deep breath and centre myself before speaking,

"Hi, how're you doing? How's Mother today? Behaving?"

"Love's not Time's fool, though rosy lips and cheeks
Within his bending sickle's compass come,
Love alters not with his brief hours and weeks,
But bears it out even to the edge of doom."

The man I married was many years my senior.

He was a charismatic bastard without sense nor scruples, but the people loved him. He harangued me into promising to marry him and was too much of a cad to release me from my vow. It took me sixteen years to liberate myself. Nowadays the story beggars belief, in these days when one's word is not often one's bond, but back then I felt that a promise was a promise, and I trapped myself in a cage of integrity forged by my own hands.

I was never in love with him, although there were times when I felt love towards him, but as time went on I realised that I couldn't like him very much. Our base lines were at right angles to one another, our core beliefs rested on different plateaus, but we muddled through until the time when I realised that I no longer wanted to be there, colluding by my presence with all the many ways he abused the world and the people around us.

My father used to say that had my husband been born onto a large continent instead of into a minute coastal village in Cornwall, he would have grown into an amazing Man. Instead, he became an overgrown child, spoiled and totally self-obsessed, never having to answer to anybody or take responsibility for the hurts he caused. Only once did we glimpse the person he might have become, had he not had the life of total privilege he was born into.

It's early evening and we are looking for a hotel to have dinner. We are in Francistown, on our way south to the Botswana border, and also very low on petrol. We need to make the border before the end of tomorrow, when the curfew kicks in and will strand us on the wrong side of the frontier and prevent my father from getting to his office in Mafikeng. There are no petrol stations anywhere to be found that are open.

We finally find a small hotel and park the car. It's an old Dodge Charger, dust covered and somewhat the worse for wear after the sprint southwards from the Falls.

The four of us unfold our bodies out of the car and go up the few steps into the foyer of a dimly lit reception area. The air is thick, it is the rainy season, which is why we were stopped from entering the Wanke Game Reserve the day before by a zealous warden. We drove through anyway, and slept beside the red dirt road to wake up surrounded by leopard spoor and the news on the radio that terrorists had once again ambushed people in the reserve.

A lone ceiling fan spins to its own lazy tune. Through an archway I can see the tables in the dining room set for tomorrow's breakfast. White linen napkins stand stiffly to attention on the cloth covered tables, the silver cutlery highly polished and shining under the electric candelabra. There are small posies in ceramic vases.

It's very Casablanca.

Dinner is over we are told, but we can have drinks and a light snack on the verandah.

While ordering drinks at the bar, a local resident overhears our description of the past twelve hours through Rhodesia- sorry, Zimbabwe- and offers to put us up for the night, albeit on his floor. We are grateful. My husband downs his beer and disappears, he doesn't tell any of us where he is going.

Less than an hour later he returns looking very smug. He has managed to barter for petrol with one of the locals and is now carrying two Jerry cans full of fuel. This is no small achievement, and my father is full of high praise for the initiative and its successful outcome. We all are. My husband is justifiably pleased at his own success, and entertains us with his tale of the jungle and how obliging everyone was.

Fortunately, his newfound business partners had no idea that he was carrying close to five thousand pounds sterling in the top of his socks.

The next morning finds us racing southwards again. I've never learnt to drive but I take my turn behind the wheel, hoping that I make the right call when it comes to creeping through a ditch as opposed to flooring it over one. It's a delicate balance.

Hours later we cross the border into South Africa, only four days after my father had suggested getting lunch across the border in Pelapye, an hour's drive away. After lunch he had said,

"A beer in Lobatse?" and five hundred miles later we were looking at a fork in the road.

"West to The Swamps, or right, to The Falls?"

Life is made of such moments. A fork in the road, a turn to the left or a turn to the right. A choice between the sluggish quiet of the deep mud, watching the stately elephants of the Okavango and the green iridescent starlings, or the crashing exuberance of the Smoke That Thunders through the mists, surrounded by African Violets growing wild.

Always, I have turned right. Right, for The Falls.

Days spent in lockdown due to a global pandemic have a certain Groundhog Day feel to them.

Covid-19 means that people are no longer free to wander as they might choose, no longer able to just jump in the car for a quick jolly to the shops for retail therapy or go to the pub for some light relief. Families are forced to endure artificial amounts of time together, forced to tolerate behaviours and personal traits that they might otherwise escape from by leaving the house. As the global pandemic spreads, it is ironic that the focus narrows, honing in more and more on the individual, and the ways in which what is happening outside in the world around us impacts upon the worlds at home within us.

I am listening, with increasing amounts of concern, as a friend tells me about her reality. I use the term friend, but I don't really know her all that well. We share an interest in Arabian horses and have met once or twice at horse shows or stables belonging to mutual contacts. I listen to her voice on the phone, as her world is opened up, to the way in which C-19 has changed her life, has completely destroyed her day to day experience, has totally reduced her to a quivering wreck. My mind is working very very quickly, I need to find a way to flip what she is saying to me and find something positive within it, some message of hope. A lifeline in the darkness to pull her out from the grey.

It's a tough shout. I listen and remember. Remember my own travels into greyness.

I've just flown back from Jordan, taken two weeks leave from the project I've created, to try and rescue my relationship. I have failed. I'm lying curled on the wet grass as the sun starts to set, looking up the hill at his house now lit with his daylight bulb in the dining room as they no doubt sit down to supper. My heart is anguished, and I look blindly into the darkest tunnel of despair. Beside me is a bucket with some water in it, and at the bottom of the water are turquoise coloured grains of wheat, strychnine coated, rat poison.

I incorrectly believe that the poison is in the colouring, and so the gods have their belly laugh, as I drink deeply thinking that my life is simply not worth living without him. I wait. Throw the wheat into the river- poor fish I will think later, possibly condemned by my ignorance to toxic water. Nothing happens. I simply get cold as the night air creeps over the land, and eventually I have to accept that I am not going to expire after all. Like flies to the Gods indeed.

Suicide is a strange thing. As a mother, I always thought maternal instinct would prevent a woman from killing herself, but it doesn't. In those moments of deep despair, nothing and no one matters more than the imagined release from heartache. No one matters, not your friends, your family or your children. It is an act of total selfness, not selfishness but selfness, where you act knowing no one will agree with you, but it does not matter, because dying is what you want, you want an end to feeling, to being. Absolutely terrifying moments of Power.

My friends will be appalled, surprised, stunned. My children will most probably feel deeply hurt and saddened. As for me, years later, I know how it feels to dive into the abyss without a parachute and to truly not care about the effect your actions will have on those you love. I can now talk from my soul with others who are poised to jump with credibility, because I too have stood on that spot, and jumped. Life had other plans for me however, and I survived my beau geste. I had to stand up, shivering, trudge with weary steps up the long grass of the eight-acre field in the darkened light, climb into my car and drive.

I had to straighten my veneer and pretend to have been caught in traffic on my way home. Had to make small talk on the phone. Had to wake up the next morning and breathe. Had to listen to the deep roaring laughs of the gods as I cooked breakfast for my son and fed the furries their food. Had to endure the waves of sharpest acidic guilt that splashed all over me every time I thought about my darling daughter. Had to face the nihilistic aspect of myself that would allow me to prioritise nothingness over the people I love and who love me. Had to keep on feeling, every goddam minute of the rest of my life.

I realise now, years later, that as I lay curled up in the damp grass in that field on the side of a hill, that he was already worlds away from me. He was already in another place and time, sitting down to eat his dinner behind the light blue blind lit up by his newly acquired daylight bulbs.

He was eating and drinking, listening to the day's retelling by another woman, laughing at her jokes, sharing her truths. He no longer cared at all about my pain, or my grief, or my heartache, it was completely unimportant and irrelevant to his sense of well-being.

I cringe inwardly now to remember the depth of my despair, the enormity of my neediness, the agonising Truth of my shattered self, the open honesty of my soul, flayed bare with my chest cracked open, exposing all my third ribs and my crucified heart. I should have played the game if I had really wanted him back. Should have given him the chance to miss me instead of bombarding him with the immensity of my loss and passion. Should have walked off into the horizon and left him gazing after me, wondering whether he had done the right thing. Instead I played my hand openly, refusing to pretend, I allowed him to see my Royal Flush, to get to know the Inside Straight, and by so doing I lost the match altogether as his victory was assured with each flick of his wrist and my defeat became inevitable.

"I don't know what to do. I can't sleep, haven't slept for months, I'm so tired. Just so tired. And I have prophetic dreams. And I've seen my parents who are dead, with me lying dead beside them. I'm so afraid. Just so afraid. So afraid of dying. From this bloody virus. From Covid Nineteen."

How can I flip this? How?

"Your dream....." I'm scanning the horizons of my mind looking for a hook into light...."Your dream.... I don't think you should take it literally.... It's not about you being dead, it's about your parents being with you, being around you, giving you their support and their love."

It's a stretch, but she takes it and makes it her own. I'm grateful. We carry on talking, I'm able to suggest some alternative treatments for anxiety and fearfulness. I'm able to help her to see a way out of the constant mind-numbing fatigue, to recognise the positive aspects in her life, to realise that she is not alone nor the only one suffering under the black clouds of C-19... that there are support groups out there who will help her in practical ways too, all she needs to do is to ask. It's all any of us has to do, once we know the questions.

She thanks me.

I can only hope that her tomorrows are happier places.

Mine certainly were.

History repeats itself, isn't that what we say? Astrologers say that we repeat our cycles every thirty years or so- the time it takes for Saturn to circumnavigate the sun.

At just past sixty, I've done two circuits and am now working on my third. Lots of loose ends need tying off, Lessons that need to be put to bed so that I can change the sheets and sleep elsewhere. Some are easier than others to discard, like so much old linen, as we cling to the hopes and dreams that were once our anchors in earlier times, our fingers clasped tightly around the ropes that tie us to our pasts.

I'm in the car driving to the horses. Our PM has decreed that citizens on holiday in France must return by four tomorrow morning or have to go through two weeks quarantine once back on home ground. Chaos has ensued as tens of thousands of tourists scurry for a way to cross Le Manche in a bid to avoid more of the Covid-19 fallout. I listen to the interviewer on Radio Four explaining the ramifications on employment and the approaching school terms. It's not pretty.

Sparkle and Darcy are grazing quietly when I arrive. It's a timeless scene. As was the bank of the Nile as we cruised upstream. As is the sunset across the ocean when I perch on the rocks on the North Cornish coast. As are the stars at night above the Devon sands, the reflection of the moon creating a silver walkway across the sea to my feet. I dreamt once of walking along that pathway, walking beside my white stag and my lover, walking out into the darkness alight with the brightness of the moon. Walking with the sea kissing my bare feet as we felt a warm wind on our skin, and each other's fingers in our hands. Walking on water. Who needs parables?

I'm waiting at Heathrow Airport. A friend first met almost forty years ago is arriving, hoping to become a UK resident. It's been a while. We've seen one another a couple of times since my divorce, and once before that, when he visited us in Tintagel, but over the last few months communications increased. Now here he is, retired from being a department head in New Zealand, rare survivor of pancreatic cancer. In the UK, enroute with me to Devon. Deep down within me I can hear the wheels whirring, their teeth interlocking in a precise dance of destiny and fate. The first waltz ended in a flurry of mistaken identities- I'm wondering what form these steps will take now, all these years later.

Not all that many months have passed and I am once again at Heathrow, this time waiting to welcome my first lover. He is now head of his department at an American University, and he and his lady squirrel never did set up a drey together. Instead he married elsewhere, and has a son, and now a divorce. He is visiting after months of video chats between us, on a whim. His visit coincides with my daughter's thirtieth birthday. We will have to travel northwards together to join in the celebrations. I do not recognise him to begin with when he walks through the doors into the waiting area. Was he always so short? Who is this small man in a checked shirt and cloth cap? I have become used to tall men, over six foot plus, and I admit to being a shortist. I used to call my Ex a fattist- we were a perfect couple, he tall, me fat, a perfect ten.

With the excruciating determination of a Swiss watch, the wheels kept turning, putting my past before me for reappraisal. My childhood sweetheart, my first kiss at forty thousand feet, my guilty pleasure. He spends a week with me, at a hiatus in his second marriage, sharing his home with a wife suffering from PTSD after the death of her favourite cat. A house of Platonic love and empathy and some frustration.

I am tempted. I love this man. I am comfortable with him, fit happily under his arm with my head on his lap on the sofa. I know I am desired. We have similar roots, children of the East and West. We share an African childhood and boarding school memories. Our parents were close friends and are now all deceased. He waited until the deaths of his before he would divorce his first wife. He is with me on a fishing trip, wondering whether this is finally going to be our time, when all through our pasts we have never been free at the same time. He is kind, this man from my youth, kind and thoughtful, good looking, humorous, and my children like him. So do my animals, and he them.

I turn it down. I know I shall regret it at times, but I cannot allow myself to exploit his emotional vulnerability, and I tell him so. If he meant less to me I could have rampant sex with him but I know it would mean too much, and I have no desire to hurt him. Such irony. I want to sleep with him, but stop myself. I'm not in love with him, I'm still in love elsewhere. Our timing has always been off. Later, once he and his wife are once again enjoying each other, I tell him that there are times when I wish I had decided differently. He says thus was our destiny. I miss him often, when I allow myself to remember him, and allow my mind to wander down the roads of possibilities.

It's good to know you're loved.

And sometimes profoundly lonely living without it.

It was an enlightening year, and yet I still sleep and awaken alone. I would choose to sleep next to a man I loved, but the dances left me single. I would choose to share special moments with a special partner, but that is not where my paths have led me. So I sit on the grass at Darcy's feet and listen to the sounds of Nature that thrill my soul instead.

The man in the cloth cap decided that his attentions were once again needed elsewhere, and I was happy to see him leave. We didn't fit anymore, if we ever really had, and could not find a common language.

My old-time friend from forty years ago who had adopted New Zealand after South Africa and then left it to start anew in England told me one day to "Bugger off", and so I did. We haven't spoken since.

My childhood sweetheart and I remain close, and his predecessor calls me in his wee hours from Oz to occasionally say Hi. The occasion is usually the drinking of a few bottles of beer.

Self-sufficiency is a family trait. It's an expensive legacy.

This weekend I shall pack for a week away with my daughter and her family in the middle of Welsh Wales. Covid-19 restrictions forbid me to stay at her home as previously planned since she lives near Manchester, and she cannot find anywhere self-catering to rent in the entire South West for less than a King's ransom, so we are going camping. I'm taking two of the dogs, Big Nose and The Decrepit One - who I think may well expire during the holiday- while Emma stays at my friend for the week having her own holiday. My daughter will be travelling south with her two children and husband and new puppy. Their car is going to reinvent the science of spatial displacement theories. It's going to be fun.

The main difference between driving in Devon and heading across Wales is the lack of traffic. Unlike my day to day, here I go for miles hardly seeing another car, or HGVs or caravans or anything. As I continue northward the roads become smaller and the terrain wilder. I love it. Vast expanses or moorland that remind me of Cumbria only more so, North Yorkshire maybe, Dartmoor times ten. Wild, open spaces wind swept and high, with only sheep grazing from time to time. There is also artillery, signs from the MOD warning that one must stop when directed that a road is closed. Do unsuspecting tourists literally have their minds blown away by the wild places I wonder?

The week away is an exercise in escapism. Covid-19 is a spectator hovering in the wings as we play out the days driving to remote shores and child friendly locations. The roads are definitely less busy than their southern counterparts, and there is no compulsion here to wear masks in every shop, although we do out of habit. My daughter is informed that masks are only mandatory on public transport in Wales, and the next day her husband is berated for not having one when we visit underground caves and dinosaurs.

The children and the dogs are welcome at the campsite, and we share the site with only two other groups of people. One group is an Indian family, males and teenagers, no women, who are fascinated by Ellisar. On their last day I am approached and asked if they may do a photo op for their YouTube account- something to do with marketing cocktails. So if you ever see one, you heard it here first. I didn't take names. Ellisar was suitably disdainful of the whole proceedings, immune to the adoration as only a genuine Imperialist can be.

MJ survived the week, her battered physicality meandering around the tents unseeing but searching still for a bone-shaped Nirvana. She slept beside the rivers in the sunshine while the children swam and Katie the puppy jumped and bounced up at the Russian trying to rejuvenate his lofty ideals. MJ lies beside me now, back in Devon, while I measure out her remaining days in coffee spoons and tea bags. Her breathing comes out rasping as she sleeps, battling with pancreatitis, bloating, fluid retention, chronic heart disease, a heart murmur, compromised sight, partial deafness, a blocked saliva gland, intermittent D and V, and some sort of neurological condition that makes her walk in circles.

Each morning I notice the lack of her irritating "Woof, woof, woof,woof" as she sleeps more deeply with each passing day. Each day I debate whether it is a good day to die, and throw the pros and cons backwards and forwards in my mind like some demented badminton player. My friends all ask me the question, "Is she in pain?" as if being in pain is the only acceptable reason to end her life. Why do we wait until our animals are in pain before we have the strength to end their lives? Should we end their lives before they start to suffer? Do we prolong their lives at the expense of their wellbeing to pander to our own sentimentality? I am conflicted, at times resolute that she has no more desire to continue living, existing, of being tired, and then she perks up, and I'm lost in an abyss of moral contradictions, castrated by my own power to choose between life and death.

Which truly Wise Man would choose for a day to be God?

The schools are scheduled to open soon for the new academic year, in the wake of the exam fiasco and social distancing and the possibility of a vaccine and imposed government guidelines and endless research on the calamitous impact Covid-19 restrictions have had on the mental health of adults and children over the past six months.

The majority of the people I communicate with play their own version of Roulette, deciding in a totally arbitrary manner as to which guidelines they will follow. Some are more fearful than others, some more cavalier. None of us really knows who will end up paying the Piper, or how much he will extort or when the dues will be demanded.

This is a time for unanswerable questions, for invisible horizons and spiralling roads. It is a time of uncertainties and the chaos and fear that can arise from that.

The irony is that life has always been that way, but people have managed to remain convinced that they have had control when in fact at any time Fate could step in and turn your life completely upside down.

Upside down and inside out, completely arbitrarily. This is the great awakening happening all around us now, at this time, as people everywhere start to recognise that they cannot have control over every aspect of their lives during this pandemic, and that can be terrifying.

Darcy and Sparkle are standing in a corner of the field grooming one another. It's hot and I've just sprayed them with Skin So Soft to discourage the flies. Some sheep from the land next door decided to explore my landowner's garden, so I climbed over the fence to help shoo them away, Now I'm standing in the sun listening to my friend tell me that her husband has been made redundant. His job has been retitled and advertised at forty per cent of his original wage. He is now unemployed. In one morning their world has crashed.

Earlier I was talking to a friend on the phone who tells me that a mutual friend has gout and cannot get up from her chair. She has no food in the house and cannot access the internet. Her apartment is completely full from decades of hoarding and she is too embarrassed to ask social services for help. My friend, highly compromised physically herself, is trying to work out a way to get food delivered to our friend's London flat. It's not proving to be easy.

Nearer to home, one of my colleagues has been struggling with the isolation from her children and grandchildren. A well-grounded individual, C-19 has brought her to a sense of her own mortality and increasing physical incapacity due to chronic illness.

Every day I am hearing from people I know that are suffering from anxiety, depression, financial hardship, sleeplessness or all of the above. Our entire country is in a state of emergency and the government is in a mess, as MP's themselves become no more than flotsam and jetsam in this global tsunami.

I look at my friend as the sheep disappear up the road.

"I know the man who is head of HR at the company your husband once worked for years ago. I'll put them in touch via social media. Maybe he can help."

Should have exploited his emotional vulnerability. I never do see clearly.

Should have gone to Specsavers and traded in my rose-tinted model for a snazzy pair of Ray Bans. Would have matched really well with his brand-new Jag.

As I walk the hounds the night air is warm and still. The sky is covered with thick cloud and the moon rose and set long ago. There is no sound. It is very quiet. Emma and Ellisar pad softly beside me as we stride up the hill out of the village. Last evening we wended our way towards the sea but tonight I have no desire for such an exertion, so we climb steadily instead, through the arched trees and along the deserted lanes that criss cross our rural landscape. The scents of high summer have gone, turned to seed in preparation for next year's Spring, and even the night owls are silent, only one swooping low across my path on its search for food.

It already feels like Autumn.

Coming home, I relax into the prospect of a relatively early night, by which I mean getting into bed before much after midnight. My son is out fishing, his life slowly gaining a degree of order against the odds. We do not yet know whether his job is guaranteed when furlough ends.

MJ is asleep where I left her on the sofa, and all of the cats are draped in varying positions around the house, Bailey is sound asleep next to MJ while Piri and Yoda are both impersonating a cascading houseplant on the stairs, their front paws reaching downwards in a stretched supplication. Peace.

I undress and sink onto my bed. I remember my grandmother saying the words, "God bless Bed." Her's was an old chain link one that supported a thick feather mattress that needed beating every morning with two walking sticks and heating up every night with at least three sock-covered glass pop bottles. Mine is less cumbersome, a modern memory foam haven that I bought for my guest room when the man from New Zealand came to stay.

I stretch. My fingers feel along the lengths of my arms and I'm pleased that I can see the tone of my muscles under the skin. I stretch my legs up to the ceiling and feel a similar sense of gratification that they are fairly lean, and flexible. My hands search for my ribs and go lower, kneading the excess flabbiness around my stomach like so much cookie dough. My lifelong nemesis. I can accept this now, I know that I'm not too fat, just carrying the sediment of several decades of emotional baggage and too much careless food. I've managed to lose a stone in weight over the Covid-19 house arrest period, which has to be a plus. So to speak, being a minus really.

Feeling my body turns my thoughts to sex and the lovers I've survived. The only one I truly long for still is the man with the house on the hill. I still thrill at the memory of our kisses and think of us when I need a sexual release. I wish we were lovers now, now when I am less fat and more self-aware, more able to cry out with desire and less likely to believe that a man always knows what I am thinking. Now that I am no longer disappointed by the fact that men and women are different, and there is absolutely nothing women can do to change that. Now that I am happy to be alone, even if sometimes lonely, and desiring of company.

I once read somewhere that a man should use his fingers as if playing the lute when he caresses a woman, and it's a description that has stayed with me. The comment is made by an older man instructing a younger one on the art of love-making. I cannot remember the title of the book, which I think is set east of Europe, but I can see the two in conversation, as the older, wiser man tries to impress upon his young apprentice the value of expertise in all subjects. More men should avail themselves of similar instruction.

Downstairs I hear my son return home. Emma barks her greeting and Piri purrs beside me on the bed.

Outside an owl screeches and I think of Nana coming down the stairs in the old cottage one Sunday morning.

"What would you like for breakfast Mom?" my mother had asked.

"Ah yes, the owl hooted twice last night." Nana had replied, leaving both my parents and myself totally perplexed.

Were Nana still alive she would be a hundred and sixteen years old, and my parents would be ninety-seven and ninety-four. I miss them. And yet, they are still all around me, every day, in every moment, in every breath, because that is who we all are- the sum of all the minutiae of our lives from before the time we take our first cell full of oxygen. We carry within us innumerable memories of past lives and forgotten dreams, of people and places both cherished and reviled, of hopes achieved and ambitions unfulfilled. We carry within us all the mirrors of our soul, a kaleidoscope of colours and tastes and smells and feelings, which we peer at as through a glass window seeking meaning when all we need to do is give ourselves a mighty twist of the wrist- aka kick up the arse- to create a new vista, a cyclic panorama of glorious technicolour, a Dreamcoat upon which to sit and travel within ourselves as we simultaneously explore the world around us outside.

My fingers stop moving. The lute lies quiet, and I switch off the light.

The Layers

I have walked through many lives,
    some of them my own,
    and I am not who I was,
    though some principle of being
    abides, from which I struggle
    not to stray.
    When I look behind,
    as I am compelled to look
    before I can gather strength
    to proceed on my journey,
    I see the milestones dwindling
    toward the horizon
    and the slow fires trailing
    from the abandoned camp-sites,
    over which scavenger angels
    wheel on heavy wings.
    Oh, I have made myself a tribe
    out of my true affections,
    and my tribe is scattered!
    How shall the heart be reconciled
    to its feast of losses?
    In a rising wind
    the manic dust of my friends,
    those who fell along the way,
    bitterly stings my face.
    Yet I turn, I turn,
    exulting somewhat,

with my will intact to go
wherever I need to go,
and every stone on the road
precious to me.
In my darkest night,
when the moon was covered
and I roamed through wreckage,
a nimbus-clouded voice
directed me:
"Live in the layers,
not on the litter."
Though I lack the art
to decipher it,
no doubt the next chapter
in my book of transformations
is already written.
I am not done with my changes.
Stanley Kunitz

DAY SIX
A Day to Die

Some days the sun shines and you just know. It's a good day to die.

I've been awake for a while, Bailey kindly waking me up with his routine tapping on my window so that he can start his day outside. I listen but hear nothing from downstairs, all the dogs must still be asleep, which is unusual at this hour- just gone eight. The sun is already shining brightly in the sky, which is that wonderful blue summer colour that we are frequently blessed with here in Brigadoon, and I can feel the warmth in my bedroom.

I swing my legs out of bed and start the morning routine. The dogs are still quiet. At the back of my mind I am wondering, has MJ died in her sleep during the night? The guilty sense of relief that would bring is palpable. I fill up the dry cat food bowls and open up the sachets of wet food- a nod to lazy convenience and cheapness over nutrition. The cats are delighted with my fall from grace and tuck in eagerly. Still no sounds from the kitchen.

Quickly putting on some outside jeans, as opposed to staying in my PJ's, I go downstairs. The three dogs are standing at the baby gate which excludes them from the living -room, all looking at me expectantly (what exactly is an expectant look in a dog?) hoping for their breakfast. MJ is wagging her tail and snuffling around Big Nose and Emma. No easy reprieve for me then, I think with some resignation.

I quickly scoop MJ up and go outside so that she can relieve herself in the parking area, which she does quickly and without causing me any concerns. Next I take the big dogs out for a short walk down the hill before returning to feed everyone. It's the morning routine. I feed the dogs their fresh meat and dry food, refresh their water, water the plants in the window-sill, put on the kettle, make myself tea, and wash up the dishes from last night's meal.

Then I turn around and notice MJ is squatting on the carpet behind me, and passing blood, a lot of blood. I scramble for baby wipes and toilet paper. Part of me is very much aware that my son will be horrified and highly disgusted if he comes downstairs and sees blood and poo all over the kitchen floor. He already says that I care more for my animals than I have ever cared for him. I flinch inwardly at the accusation- how awful it is that he even feels that way, regardless of the truth.

A bumblebee flies over the open stable door and buzzes around before flying back to the potted rosemary outside. It's a good day to die.

I phone my vet.

I am scheduled to meet up with my granddaughters for the first time in six months this morning for two hours. The gods and that ole fashioned sense of humour again.

I explain to the vet student answering their phones that I'm hoping I will be able to meet with a vet after my visit with the children, in about three hours or so, somewhere not in the surgery. I don't want her last senses to be of the smells of a vet's surgery. I itemise all of MJ's health issues, the pancreatitis, lack of hearing, blindness, neurological symptoms, congenital heart problems, fluid retention, a blocked saliva gland, partial incontinence and haemorrhagic stools. He promises me he will have a chat with the senior partner and get back to me.

I look at MJ. She is not in pain, she seems quite robust. Having eaten, she is now walking blindly in circles happily looking for more food, and will soon climb into the basket she shares with Emma before going to sleep. My internal dialogue is in high gear, as I weigh out the realities around her existence. Today is a good day, her tail is wagging, her life force seems strong. Do I wait? Then I think, why do we always wait for pain to set in? Is it not kinder to stop the downward spiral while there is still some possibility of pleasure? And so I make up my mind, and put MJ in the back of the car, along with a bowl of cooked sausages, and accept that this will be the day.

A good day to die.

Afterwards, standing in the shade of an old pine tree, I thank my vet. We have known one another for over two decades, and he has always been the most amazing friend in the most awful of times. Today, after MJ had a walk in the sun under the pines and had eaten with gusto her normally forbidden fat-filled pork sausages, he delivered the lethal dose and she fell asleep in my arms within seconds. A good death, a kind death, at least that is how I comfort myself at this most horrible of times.

We stand there, and he tells me when asked of how C-19 has impacted upon the surgery and upon him himself. He tells me that for the first time in his professional career he no longer enjoys what he does, he is tired, tired of being strong, tired of being resilient, just tired. I can empathise, for I too feel weary, weary of being resolute, of coping, of being capable. We talk about his childhood experience of deep personal loss, and how his memories influence the ways in which he relates to his own children, now both grown men with their own families. How he has to sometimes fight the spectres of his past to remain constant and present for his family.

He shows me a photograph of his first grandson, and I think to myself of how our pasts cascade down through our present and out into the futures of those we love. I counsel him to move on to his next phase, to retire and enjoy the days with those he loves. To buy the camper and do the road trip. To escape. I remind him that I only ever asked that he stay working for as long as Tarac was alive. We laugh. Tarac was so kind to me, gifting me the easiness of finding him dead, releasing me from having to make a decision, not being ill or sickening or decrepid before his death.

We talk about the suicide of one of the young vets last year, and how it had impacted upon everyone at the surgery. A young man with young children of his own, a happy marriage and a successful career, found in his car on a lonely stretch of moorland. He looks me in the eye and we connect, because we both know, we know how that feels, and we weep within the tears of wisdom.

My vet asks me if I am okay with it all, with MJ lying on a blanket in the boot of my car, and I say yes, because I am. I will bury her at home, and plant a rose above her that will reach down into the darkness of the earth and create something beautiful from the gut and bones of my onetime little warrior of a dog. I will cry tears, many tears, and feel her absence in the rooms around me, and reminisce about the days of her life when she both irritated and annoyed me, and the days when I was filled with so much love for her that it exploded out of me and flattened all the logic and reason shouting in my ears that I didn't need another dog. I was there at her birth fifteen years ago, and with her death the circle is complete.

I look up, and see the sun filtering through the canopy. There are butterflies dancing amidst the last blooms of Rosebay Willow, and a robin is watching me hoping I will throw him something to eat. This is a popular dog walking and picnic spot, thankfully deserted today. MJ lies stilled, already on her next cosmic quest to higher places. I sigh, my heart hurts, and get into the car. The tears start to fall, and I sit for a while before turning the key and putting the car into gear to drive home. The dogs will be waiting and I will need to tell David the news, I know he may feel surprised that I didn't give him advance warning. My phone pings. It is a friend sending me a photo of her garden which is abundant with rose blooms and cottage flowers.

It's a good day to die.

I'm sitting on the kitchen floor next to Emma sitting in her bed. She is looking at me with those beautiful doleful eyes that labradors have. Suddenly she does something that she never does, she lifts up her front paw and taps me on the arm, twice. We don't do the handshake thing, but I know it's a natural dog movement. She taps my arm again. I fantasise that she is reaching out to me with a gesture of comfort, of shared grief, and I hug her and start to cry. Ellisar looks on from the other room and quietly walks over to stand beside me, leaning into my shoulder from his great height. We stay like that for several minutes, the three of us, me crying and the two dogs just being, in what I believe to be a sharing of love for the little bundle of independent, effervescent energy that now no longer joins us. She is already much missed.

And again, I am crying.

A wise man once told me that when you have livestock you will have deadstock.

He was an old school type of vet, well-spoken and always impeccably dressed in tweeds and brogues, with a hat that he lifted as a sign of greeting and respect whenever I saw him. He stood tall and lean, a man in his fifties I think at our first encounter, a large animal country practise of the All Animals Great and Small variety, only in North Cornwall and not the Yorkshire Dales. His wife was absolutely charming, a cheerful, pretty woman who radiated kindness and gentleness wherever she went. They had two sons, who the local children used to tease mercilessly at school by calling them Silage and Piss, instead of the more lofty Silas and

Pierce. I like to think that we became friends over the years that I spent in North Cornwall, because I had a genuine affection for the family, but I am more than likely flattering myself, since it is easy to presume too much when we enjoy a commonality with those whose expertise we employ.

By the time Mydas came to me, the practise had moved on and my original vet had retired. A few years earlier one of his sons had taken part in the London Marathon and suffered a fatal heart attack afterwards; I don't know how a parent ever recovers from that type of tragedy. He continued to practice, and his wife became a counsellor for Relate, the national charity that works to mend bruised relationships, both of them using their grief to inspire selflessness. We spoke only once about his loss, and then left it well alone, our hearts too full with grieving the sheer senselessness that Life sometimes punches us in the gut with as we gaze upwards smiling, blinded by the glory of the sun.

Mydas was a black leopard cub, six weeks old and listed for sale in the animal lovers' Mecca, the Cage and Aviary.. All sorts of species could be found within this cheap weekly paper, and my husband frequently poured over it dreaming of what rare and unusual animal we might acquire next. In a collection to rival Gerald Durrell during his childhood, we had to our name a variety of exotic species, all of them rescued from closed or failing small zoos around the country.

Coatimundi, raccoons, a wallaby, birds of prey including buzzards and kestrels, owls, ferrets, chinchillas, farmyard animals such as pigs, goats, sheep, ducks, geese, turkeys and chickens, aviary birds with cockatiels, budgies, lovebirds, then peacocks and pheasants and a cockatoo, hedgehogs, seagulls, a tortoise, finished off with several breeds of cats and dogs, St. Bernards and Borzois, Manx, Ragdoll, Persian and Siamese and feral felines, and an otter. Tropical fish and over a foot-long Koi carp. Then of course, the horses and the two donkeys.

Whenever I went away I used to have to employ three different people to take care of them all, one for domestics, one for exotics and one for agricultural breeds.

Hugh stands at the six-bar gate which leads into our yard and shouts out to me,

"How'd you like a black leopard?"

I stop mixing horse feeds and walk over to where he stands leaning on the gate holding a copy of Cage and Aviary.

"A leopard? Where is it?"

And with those innocent words of inquiry began one of the more illuminating experiences of my time with animal rescue. Illuminating, disheartening, and soul-destroying, because it ended in tears eventually, as so many well-intentioned and good deeds do. On that morning however, I was still wrapped up in my cocoon of ignorance, still idealistic and rose-spectacled, still a believer in the propaganda of charities and quite naive.

Less than an hour later we were in the car and driving north to Warwickshire, cat basket on the back seat.

All my life I dreamed about owning a black leopard. Growing up in Liberia, I witnessed first-hand the close relationship possible between a leopard and the person who hand rears it. Back in the 1930's, my grandfather by marriage had raised a leopard that became his military mascot in

Palestine, and even Joy Adamson had written about the successful bond with her leopard Queenie. Contrary to all the accepted wisdom on the subject, that insisted leopard are solitary animals and therefore one cannot have a close bond with them, I always knew in my heart that I would succeed if I tried. And I did.

I'm looking down into a small cardboard box placed on a rickety bamboo table in a somewhat dingey living room, nothing has been cleaned for some time. The man standing opposite me is explaining that with the onset of CITES he has had to close down his small private zoo and disperse the animals. I can hear a lone lion keening in the background outside, its solitary roars soft and low. The lion was reared by his owner and as such has also had daily fondles and romps with him, this is about to change. Like so many hundreds of animals across the country at that time, the lion will be destroyed by the local authorities if another zoo cannot offer him a home. It is highly unlikely anywhere will come forward to save him, every zoo is full to capacity and already euthanising stock that are surplus to requirements. A tiny straggly dark charcoal grey cub with almost turquoise eyes peers up at me and meews, its tiny pink tongue nestled behind a row of tiny very white teeth.

"He's yours."

I named him Mydas. For "My Daddy Says" from The Countess of Hong Kong with Sophia Loren. My father and I watched it once a long time ago in my childhood and he took the line and condensed it to become his signature whenever he wrote to me, MyDas.

Mydas was one of two cubs that his zoo owning breeder had removed at birth from the mother to hand rear. This was frequently done back then, with the imprinted cubs then sold on to promotional animal trainers such as the Chipperfield family. We were told that Mary Chipperfield had purchased both cubs but decided to return the male and keep the female, I do not know why. As it transpired, I learnt that the female cub was killed a few months later when she proved too difficult for her famous handler to train. Many big cats were kept in overseas countries like Spain, which did not have the same welfare laws as Britain to protect animals, and so unscrupulous traders and promoters could traffic more easily in animal cargo.

When I collected him, Mydas was three weeks old and being raised on Carnation milk and raw chicken. Every few hours he would happily sit on my lap and drink at least eight ounces of milk before curling up in true cat fashion to nap. With the deep affinity I have always enjoyed with all animal species, we bonded immediately, and Mydas became an integral part of our household. Those were Halcyon days, me totally ignorant of the storm which was brewing in the spaces around us, with my husband's long term enemies in local government about to have their chances at revenge for all the many times he had treated them with disdain.

It was a Sunday, and there was a local service at the Catholic Church being held by our dear friend, Brian Storey, to bless the animals. I took Mydas, he was six weeks old. Thus was the Cross of Crucifixion hewn from an innocent tree.

Looking around my living-room in Brigadoon, the cats lie asleep in various positions of repose. Ellisar and Emma lie stretched out on my dilapidated sofa, Long Nose on his back with all four legs up in the air like some contorted Yogi, and Emma curled tightly so that she can fit next to him. Bailey is snoozing on the reclining armchair, the Sex Chair's replacement, and Yoda and Piri are sleeping as the Sphinx on different levels of the open stairs. The sun is coming through the open windows, streaming on mini rainbows with the air fresh on this morning in September.

Yoda opens his eyes. My only black cat now that Strider has passed. He stands and stretches, walks down the stairs with an air of nonchalance, before collapsing in a patch of sunlight on the carpet. Piri, disturbed, also descends from her position of power, and jumps effortlessly onto my dining and working table. She settles in the warmth of the sun as it pools on the oilcloth covering and starts to wash. She moves in a totally feral manner, belying her wild ancestry, with her long lean body and athletic build. My own mini Asian Leopard.

Mydas used to pounce on the cheetah skin and hang onto its ears in a mock attack, until he progressed to jumping onto Solomon, our patient old St.Bernard, who would tolerate the attack with looks of long-suffering despair. After plaguing Solomon, Mydas would move on to the game of tag with Magic, a small black and white cat that we had rescued from a farm. Magic would race around the house only a few feet in front of Mydas until eventually dashing under our bed where she would taunt Mydas from beneath, her front paws stretching out to his, safe in the gap between floor and mattress which was too small for Mydas to fit into.

Finally, exhausted from play, the three animals would curl up in a heap of colours, and fall asleep.

It's a Sunday, but with Covid-19 the church bells are silent. I haven't rung a bell now for many months. In Tintagel we would meet once a week in the church tower, equipped with thermos flasks of coffee, and ring the changes literally for a couple of hours. To this day my daughter, who was being battered in utero by the din of my tenor bell, dislikes the sound of campanology. Ironically, here in Brigadoon, I live only a stone's throw from our Parish Church, and at night the flood-lit beauty of the ancient stones across the lane can be seen from my bedroom windows.

The Sunday I took Mydas to Mass we were captured by a local journalist and mentioned in a small by-line on community events, and so as with all great tsunamis which begin with a single drop of water, one small sentence in a give-away community paper started an avalanche of public opinion and controversy that would eventually completely destroy Mydas and everything he stood for.

My six year old granddaughter is standing at the door. We haven't seen one another in person for almost half a year, six months. She runs to me and throws her arms around my hips. She looks around the kitchen.

"Where's MJ?" she asks.

Covid-19 has disrupted lives all around the world. With remarkable swiftness, people have altered their daily routines to accommodate the guidelines and recommendations of their ruling government parties. Families have stopped touching, the elderly have stopped visiting, professionals have stopped working, friends have stopped sharing. People have sickened, people have died, questioned, argued, flaunted, wept, sneered, and resigned. All over the world, in less time than it takes to complete one cycle of the seasons, the day to day routines for everyone in the world have changed. It is quite simply unbelievable, were it not for the fact that it has indeed happened. And underneath it all, the rumble of discontent, of incredulity, of hesitancy, of disbelief. Day after day after day, now month after month after month, as the faith of the people in the motivations behind their governments starts to falter, and we are all left feeling adrift, lost on a sea of uncertainty, with our compasses whirling madly to the magnetism of popular beliefs and discarded faiths.

"Where is MJ?"

Her eyes are wide and looking up at me as I try to come up with a gentle answer. MJ was always her favourite of the dogs, being small, and the two of them would sit next to one another on the sofa or in an armchair, snuggled close, while I read stories or we wiled away Time watching a Disney film. I start my answer, explaining that MJ had been very sick, and became worse.

"Has she been put to sleep?"

I stop, shocked. Put to sleep? Where has she learnt this phrase? She goes on to tell me about a tv program she watched with another family member that showed a dog having a metal splint put into its leg. I am stunned at the level of her comprehension.

"Yes, she was very sick and the vet put her to sleep."

A look of sadness briefly crosses her face and then there's nothing. No tears, no commentary, no inquiry. No attachment.

Months of emotional upheaval and inconsistency. This is only one of the effects. I can feel my own fear rising, a slow dread as I see down the path into my granddaughter's future, one devoid of deep attachment because of the potential that it has for pain, disappointment and self- loathing. A future of potential unhappiness and heartache. She is only six years old and already her life is scarred by the casual inconsistencies that abound around us. Damaged by the careless inaccuracies and misdirected zealotry of social services and the complacencies of ancestral vices.

"Come," I say, "Let's do some drawing."

"Shall I draw MJ?"

My inner self sighs with slight relief.

"Yes," I reply, "Draw MJ. I'll get you some paper."

Maybe it's not too late after all.

My mother-in-law lies in the bed in front of me. Her breathing is shallow and she is already drifting away from me, her elderly body exhausted from nine decades of hard work and devotion to her husband and son. Her father was a footman in some great house and her mother was the cook, a marriage made below stairs in the last years of the nineteenth century. The Great War took her to Cornwall with many other children sent there for safety out of London, and so she met her husband to be, who would love and honour her for over sixty years before his death.

Now it is her turn, and although I sit at her side, she does not know that I am there. Her son is elsewhere, his daily routines do not include filial visits to his elderly mother, and so the owner of the care home had called me in to share those final moments of the mortal coil being sloughed off. I take her hand in mine, the skin like fine tissue paper and wrinkled, the bones beneath jutting into my palm, it lies motionless within my grasp. This woman, barely breathing, what a life she has had.

She and her darling Eddie returned to Cornwall when their son was eleven, and stayed in Tintagel for the rest of their lives, creating a business that is so successful that we describe it now as a license to print money. Private catering on cliff land nestled between Duchy and National Trust, prime location without any competition, serving up cream teas and Cornish pasties to the tourist hordes in search of the legend of King Arthur and his Knights of the Round Table. Fourteen acres of cliff land, bordered by the sea, overlooking Merlin's Cave and the glorious Atlantic. It made them wealthy, and her son completely irresponsible.

The Beach Cafe, as it was called, provided my husband with an easy income. He would bake mounds of biscuits and cakes two or three times a week and spend the remainder of his time having fun. In their day, his parents had both worked hard dawn to near midnight, but we would shut the cafe at six and spend the evenings at home. His mother was one of the kindest, sweetest people that I have known. I feel a deep sadness at her imminent passing, and whisper to her that it is time for her to let go, time to stop fighting, time to join Eddie and be at peace.

She was a gentle soul, and as she aged and senility began to ambush her, her son became increasingly detached and unpleasant. Eventually, after his father's death, he moved his mother into a local residential home, ironically the same building that had welcomed him into the world decades earlier. It was better that way, as he could no longer treat his mother with the contempt and sheer nastiness that can appear when one person is so much weaker than the other. He packed her clothes into an old battered case and drove her the quarter mile down the road to her new residence.

The next day he loaded her two aged labradors into his Range Rover, drove to the vet and had them destroyed. He did not bring the bodies home for burial.

Sometimes we don't deserve forgiveness. Sometimes people are just horrible and there are no excuses. I have never understood what it was that could justify such a chasm of non-compassion and contempt between a son and a mother who always adored him, never challenged him and gave him nothing but love from the day he was born. To this day the graves of his parents are unmarked, unnamed spaces in the lines of granite crosses and marble headstones at the Parish Church cemetery.

In a twist of poetic synchronicity, my husband's grave also lies unmarked, neither of his older children have done as they promised and placed a stone on the place where their father lies six feet under. Our own children, from time to time, talk about the commissioning of a grave stone but as yet the grave is still anonymous, the toughened graveyard grass bending in the winds that roar off the northern coast, the salt encrusted leaves a tasty treat for the sheep that graze there.

Mydas is pacing. He is confined in a tiny cage with an exercise area barely twice the size of a double bed and very unhappy. The owners of the wildlife park where I was eventually forced to move Mydas have changed their breeding policy, and Mydas is now surplus to their requirements. His playmate, an ordinary spotty as they are known, has already been killed and the pen where he and Mydas used to live together turned over to make an enclosure for a pair of the rare subspecies of Amur Leopards. Mydas, in theory still mine, could not be disposed of so easily but I am now fighting tooth and claw to find him a new home. I am losing the battle.

Mydas is a black leopard and so not indigenous to Africa. My father's letter to the head of his local African state has come back with a polite refusal to house Mydas in any of the national zoos.

My own supplications to UK animal centres such as the Aspinall and Durrell private collections are also unsuccessful, both full to capacity with big cats already on the pill. The Chipperfield family would take him, as he is an entire male with all his own teeth and claws- usually removed in promotional cats- and balls, perfect for breeding. I turn them down as they insist that I relinquish all ownership and responsibility for his welfare, and I cannot agree to him being used to sire more big cats in captivity at risk of exploitation and cruelty by circuses and collectors.

Mydas, already over two years old, is deemed unsuitable for reintroduction to the wild by the big cat sanctuaries in India. My overseas contact in big cat welfare in Canada has come through trumps for me so Mydas is crated and ready for shipping, when an overzealous Canadian official decides to cancel the permits and leave Mydas on the runway stranded in England. I am totally out of options and my time is running out. The facility keeping Mydas sees him as a liability and orders the manager to either move him or have him destroyed.

In the months while Mydas was on public display, I would visit him every weekend and salve my broken heart by feeding him a pint of clotted cream through the bars of his enclosure. I never once heard Mydas roar, although I was assured that he knew how, because as soon as he saw me he would revert to kitten mode and mew. After his cream he would lick whatever had escaped from the pot from my hand and then play hide and seek with me from behind a large tree trunk placed in his pen for stimulation. His spotted companion would watch us and, after a couple of months, would also avail himself of some clotted cream, albeit from the other side of the run where I placed it.

The call comes through to the kitchen on a perfectly ordinary morning. I'm sitting at the kitchen table drinking coffee before starting to feed the horses. It's the manager at the wildlife park.

"I need a decision Suyen. What do you want to do?"

What a stupid question.

I want my cat back. I want to have him back in my house, sleeping on my bed, playing chase with Magic and curled up at my feet. I want to hear his deep throated roar of a purr. I want to hold his body close to mine, wrap my arms around him and bury my face in his fur. I want to have years and years and years of time together without anyone interfering or assuming or attacking us. I want to be left in peace with this beautiful, noble creature and for us to love each other forever.

"There's nothing I can do, no one will have him. Put him down."

"Do you want to see him first?"

My heart cracks. How can I see him?

"Will you let me go into the cage with him?"

"No Suyen, they won't allow me to."

Cracks and opens like a nut smashed beneath the anvil of common sense.

"I can't. I can't come and watch you dart him, I'm sorry."

It is a mistake of course. I shall regret it long afterwards, like the regret at not holding Saracen's head when the shot came and he buckled at the knee before collapsing onto the ground. I am wiser now. I am always there, holding space and time at bay as I speak my final farewells to the animals I have shared my life with. I have held them all close to my

217

chest, sharing their heartbeats with mine, breathing in their last breaths as our two life forces synchronised for the final dance of death. There is no absolution, no forgiveness, when you truly look at yourself in the mirror, just a deeply buried longing for more innocent times.

Is there ever really a good day to die?

The birds are fed and I'm waiting. Waiting for my friend to arrive and take me away from the emptiness and loss that is two dogs now instead of three. She parks downhill from the cottage and arrives breathless at my kitchen door, having been delayed by the summer traffic which is increasing every week as C-19 restrictions lessen and tourists return to our magical village. The roads in and out of Brigadoon are notoriously narrow and winding, steep and unforgiving of drivers who neither know the widths of the vehicles or how to reverse those vehicles with any degree of competence. We are all pretty unforgiving of them to be honest, our arrogance and intolerance rooted in familiarity.

We are going for a drive, a change of scene, via the horses and then possibly to the moors where we can take deep breaths of fresh windswept air under a vast cloudless sky. Where I can blow away the cobwebs wrapped around grief and wishful thinking. She's driving for a change, so that I can sit back and mull over the incidents of the past few weeks. Family and loss really, family and loss.

As we reach the top of the hill and turn right onto the wider road we encounter a large truck coming towards us, this necessitates reversing and I am quickly reminded of why I prefer to do the driving. Hampered by a restriction in her neck movement, reversing no longer comes easily to my companion, and I feel remorse at having put her in the position of needing to reverse at all. I should have driven.

The lorry is followed by two more cars who are also finding it difficult to navigate our country roads and so we have to go even further backwards, by this time zigging and zagging along the narrowed lane like some Belle from The South as she shilly shallies her way to a barn dance.

I keep very quiet.

"Oh for God's sake! Can't they just pull in?"

Two horses suddenly appear from around the corner in front of us and start ambling up the lane. Slowly.

I keep very quiet indeed.

Dartmoor has a splendour all its own. Although not as wide reaching as the North Yorkshire Moors or as impressive as the heights of Cumbria in my mind, I still love the fact that it is relatively nearby and can be reached in an hour or so by car. Usually. Today it has taken somewhat longer thanks to the somewhat sedate pace employed by my friend when driving, but no matter, it's always good to escape reality for even a little while. She has been kind enough to occupy me during our travel with tales of her working week and the challenges brought about by living with her elderly and somewhat churlish mother. The daily continuum of frustration and regret, the world growing ever smaller as possibilities fade away and are replaced by practicality and doubt. It's such a cheerful way to wile away the time.

Autumn finds Dartmoor awash with purple splotches, heather in bloom, and stands of bracken still green about to turn bronze. The moorland ponies have young foals at foot, adding a charm to the surroundings that belies the fact that most of them are destined to end up in tins of dog food or frozen as whole carcasses in the freezers of zoos. Black-faced sheep graze the edges of the road with complacency, confident that the visiting traffic will slow down enough to avoid hitting them and their lambs before they too are loaded up for the meat market. In the road side lay-bys ice cream vans cater to passing tourists and local enthusiasts, many with rucksacks on their backs as they prepare to walk their dogs up to neighbouring tors. We disembark and choose to turn our backs on the crowds as per usual, preferring instead to wander less travelled paths among the gnarled trees and protruding granite.

My friend stops and sits on one of the half-concealed granite boulders. I lower myself into the tightly grazed turf beside her and wait. There will be a story coming, I know, because loss dredges up memories of loss that we ourselves have suffered, and when that happens we want to share our own losses, want to validate our own sorrow, want to appease our own grief. And so I wait, sit and stay silent, and nurse my own emptiness in the loneliness of my own knowing.

Back at home, upstairs taking off my outdoor sweater, I look out of the bedroom window for the reason the birds are chattering. Then I hear the shambolic frantic fluttering of wings in the hedge opposite and turn my head just in time to see a sparrowhawk lift off from the foliage. Its talons grasp tightly some smaller bird as it flaps and takes off up into the air. Then there is silence. The leaves of the hedge shudder and relax quietly back into their place.

After death, there is always the silence.

My son is sitting with his back to me. He's angry and frustrated with how the Local Authority are managing, or rather mismanaging, his case with regards to his contact with his daughters. I too am appalled by the consistent ineptitude of the processionals and the casual manner in which they are successfully destroying the lives of the people I love. His anger veers and focuses on me.

"I was nine years old and you tried to kill me. Bet you don't tell your friends that. Bet you've never told my sister. Whenever I talk about my childhood she always says it wasn't like that. You're just like every other woman, totally narcissistic and in denial."

The accusations come thick and fast, I sit side-swiped by the fury and angst and disgust. And truth.

"I never tried to kill you, tell me what you are referring to."

I know what he is thinking about, I know because the memory haunts me, but I want him to say it out loud so that there is no possible confusion, no place to hide away in the shadows of ambiguity. No rescue. No excuses. No salvation.

"I was nine and you drove down a track threatening to crash the car. I was screaming. Terrified. You know that if you had kids now Social Services would take them away from you. You didn't deserve to have children."

My gut is twisting. I'm sitting, trying not to cry but the grief and the guilt and the shame are rising through me, my heart hurting with a physical ache as I listen.

"I never have denied what you are saying, and I've shared what happened more than once. I can't change what happened and I hate that I behaved like that. So learn from me, learn from my mistakes. Don't be like I was on that day."

He turns around to face me.

"Just shut up. What is it with women that they always have to have the last word? Always have to justify themselves. Just stop talking."

I look at him and say nothing, my voice cut through like so much sinew in a neck severed from its body. My love lies bleeding in the mess of my parenting and I crawl away into silence as my son turns back to his phone and the emails he was reading from the social worker.

I leave the house and text him...

I'm so sorry, I have deep guilt about my actions back then, and carry my shame always. I hope there will come a time when you can forgive me for allowing my anger to motivate my responses, when my patience ran out.

Two days later it comes.

"Can you boil the kettle please?"

The fish looks up at me from the chopping board. Three hours earlier it was swimming in the icy salt waters off the nearby beach. Now it lies gazing sightless at the Portmeirion tableware and Royal Doulton china. Fish have faces too. It's a gift, one of several speared this very day and delivered with pride to my kitchen. I do not refuse, believing that would be ungrateful now that the creature is already dead, but there is a part of me that feels a hypocrite as I start to disembowel and descale it. It will taste amazing I know, cooked simply with butter and lots of coarsely ground black pepper, finished with a dash of lemon. Once a chef always a chef, it's like breathing.

I'm running the fruit under the cold water tap, prior to turning the raspberries, damsons and apples into various jams. It's a form of therapy, a valid way to spend time when I don't want to spend that time doing something more pedantic. Making jam is therapeutic, spell binding with each sweep of the wooden spoon. I am carried away in the words of the three witches from the Scottish Play, "Bubble bubble, toil and trouble, fire burn and cauldron- bubble!"

The heat is oppressive and I'm seated at a long table in the equatorial jungle of West Africa. Set down along the long length of the makeshift table are dishes filled with local fruit, rice and hot peppers. Every so often there is also a large enamel pot full to its brim with the main dish, a combination of meat and root vegetables, swimming in a mixture of bright orange palm nut oil and meat juices. Bottles of beer are also on the table. There are no glasses.

Beside me is my adopted Godfather, resplendent in his customary white Bermuda shorts and shirt, red and white polka dot handkerchief protruding from his chest pocket, white knee-length socks above perfectly polished Oxford brogues and monocle firmly in place. He is the guest of honour, the only white Paramount Chief in the country, and I am his guest. Fourteen years old, and expected to eat the palm nut stew in front of me. The drums are beating.

In front of us, in the centre of the circle created by the chanting villagers, is a man twelve feet tall. He dances wildly, covered from head to toe in a bleached raffia skirt with a carved mask of ebony fixed firmly in position above his head. The drums are beating. The sound of the chanting and the drums becomes more frantic, the dancing becomes more frenetic until with a roar the music crashes into silence and the world stands still. In front of me, the liquid in the enamel pot bubbles, and out of the depths of the enamel pot a small arm reaches upwards, slowly rising from the depths of palm nut oil and boiled cassava, the tiny fingers frozen in a final entreaty. I can feel the horror slowly surfacing within me- we are being served monkey stew.

Beside me, the Colonel accepts his bowl of rice with a nod of thanks and helps himself to a ladle full of the main dish. He picks up my own bowl and serves me a smaller helping. He looks at me and I know, I know, that I cannot refuse to eat at this ceremony, cannot do anything other than empty my bowl. Bubble, bubble, toil and trouble, fire burn, and cauldron bubble... Only the correct quote is "Double, double toil and trouble...." continuing with "Fillet of a fenny snake, In the cauldron boil and bake; Eye of newt, and toe of frog, Wool of bat, and tongue of dog."

My love of Shakespeare started young.

I ate the stew.

When I was in Jordan, I would sometimes spend weekends in the port of Aqaba, and often would be given access to HRH Princess Alia's private residence there. This was a huge honour, and one I treasured greatly. Not only did it give me complete privacy at weekends, but it also allowed me the joy of being able to skin-dive in the Red Sea off the private beach that is a part of the Royal Compound. Most days I was either under the water or on top of it. Watching the tropical fish every day meant that I was sometimes able to see the same fish day in and day out, and eventually I would actively seek out certain puffer fish or stands of pipe fish. I longed to see one of the rare giant mantas, but I knew I would never see one of those unless I went far offshore and used tanks. Instead, I spent every day I was in Aqaba snorkelling in the waters between Jordan and Eilat.

The sun is starting to set and the sky is a muted rose pink, the Red Sea tide on the turn. I have been on and off the jetty all day, mentally pleading for a manta ray to come close enough to be seen. I have no illusions as to the unlikeliness of this happening. As the wind starts to rise I decide that it's time for one last swim. The light is going, and deep water always feels slightly eerie in dim light, it is a primordial gut feeling, an awareness of my own increased vulnerability.

As I finish my swim I turn back towards the jetty and by chance turn my head to the side. Next to me, swimming beside my shoulder, are three cuttlefish. I have never seen them before, but now they are swimming with me on the slowly deepening water, their tentacles paving the way before them and on their faces wonderful smiles created by the line of their mouths. It's a true delight. Then I notice movement beneath me. The depth of water is greater than usual in this spot due to the incoming tide, and no doubt also due to the tidal bounty of increased food, below me swim three large rays. They aren't giant manta rays,but under water they look as if their wingspan is about six feet wide. Large enough, and they are a pale silver white. Angels under water as opposed to devils on horseback.

It's a great way to end the day.

I climb out onto the jetty and quickly wrap a large towel around me to keep out the now cold night breeze. The moon is rising and can be seen hiding shyly behind the silhouetted fronds of the date palms. To my right I can hear music blasting loudly across the water from Israel, and to my left there is laughter from the King's palace further up the beach. His wolves are silent for now.

The Phillipino housekeeper comes down to where I am standing looking out over the Red Sea and tells me that dinner is ready. She and her husband know my preferences and I have no need to suggest menu options, since all I eat when here is fish with rice, salad and fruit. The table, large enough for twenty, looks sadly empty with just my one place setting, but the room is brightly lit and the light shines brightly off the glass and chrome decor.

At the far end I can see my meal laid out, fresh fruit also on standby with a bowl of salad and a large platter of grilled fish waiting for me. I sit myself down and take a deep breath, revelling in the smell of the lemons that garnish the platter and the smokey tenor of the fish. I look down and say a silent thank you. I never stop feeling guilty. This animal was swimming only a few hours ago, going about his life quite happily in the sea until the cook threw out a line and hooked him for my meal, and in that one frozen moment it became the day.

The day to die.

David knocks on my door before leaning over the stable partition and calling out to me.

"Samphire anyone?"

Fish just stares ahead. No hope really.

I put down the phone with a sense of relief. The working day has ended. Now fully back in harness although still working from home, the time spent on case referrals has risen dramatically. Covid-19 still means that we are confined to virtual meetings but we have recently been directed to produce as many meetings as is possible in any given timeframe as we strive to excel under Special Measures. My heart is not in it. I am somewhat jaded from my own personal experiences around my family, and I do not believe that virtual meetings can deliver the necessary dynamic for families to get the most benefit from my service. It leaves me feeling tired and somewhat irritated.

My iPad trills to let me know there is someone calling me. God bless technology. It is a colleague who is hoping to collaborate with me tomorrow at a family conference. The conference will be held using the Teams app, but only one of the five couples involved have agreed to use the app and the rest prefer instead to access the meeting by phone. This is going to create several logistical challenges.

I listen as if under water. Covid-19 has caused so many issues in the workplace, totally compromising the very marrow of the principles behind Family Group Conferencing. By definition, FGC's require families to be able to attend conferences, to sit with one another in a shared space and confer around shared hopes and opinions. To discuss, to confer, to make family plans. None of this is possible when meetings are held virtually without the intimacy of the personal dynamic. So I listen carefully but there is a part of me that already thinks it is a hopeless exercise. Tomorrow will come soon enough.

I know that I am not the only person questioning their professional life in these strange times. Forced to stay at home and sometimes also forced to accept a massive cut in wages, many people have started to look at alternatives to their nine to fives, to think outside their boxes and stretch their creative minds. Others have realised that the only reason they go to work at all is to pay the bills, not because they want to go to work, and are left feeling restless and powerless. My daughter, a paediatrician, is making jewellery and baking birthday cakes around her fourteen hour shifts.

The lucky ones are those who can spend their days, every day, enjoying the freedoms provided by paid working from home, without any cuts, doing what they genuinely love. Not too many of that demographic in the world. Artists maybe, healers, carers and nurturers, those who find their joy in empowering others perhaps. The vast millions though are not so lucky, and toil ceaselessly to simply survive. It is a bleak indictment on our species' social evolution.

The phone rings again. I am popular this evening. It is a close friend of mine who lives at the other end of the country. She is unwell, very unwell, and needs help, but there is no one she can ask for help nearby. I look at the clock and calculate how long it will take me to reach her. I tell her that I will leave in the morning and be with her before tea time. In my head I am already writing the email to my manager asking to be excused from my backup role in the afternoon.

She starts to cry, relief falling with every tear from the dread within her soul. I hang up and put down the phone. She is young, not yet fifty, a chronic medical issue the wild card to tip the scales. I shall not have the chance to speak with her again, at first light tomorrow the call will come from her neighbour to tell me that I am no longer needed. Her death came and found her as she lay gasping for air, like so many flying fish stranded on the decks of small fishing boats far out at sea.

In the blink of an eye, life changes and we are gone.

The night air is cold and I am restless. The sky is clear with the almost full moon casting her silver light over the landscape, delving into hidden crevices and undiscovered passageways like so much molten light. The dogs have had a stilled day, lying in the near awake sleep that hounds possess to spin away the hours between their owners' activities. We walk now, towards the sea, which I can see through the darkened hawthorn and hedge maple overhanging the tarmac road, clad in a silver mantle cast upon it by the moon. Brigadoon at Midnight.

We reach the beach and find revellers dancing and singing around a large fire. I walk away from them into the beckoning darkness of the westward cliffs. There are fishing men also on the beach, lured no doubt by the full moon and the quiet tide. The company means that I cannot let slip my dogs, and so we walk carelessly just above the waterline, listening to the soft whisper of salt upon sand and peering into the future to see if there are any other inconveniences ahead.

In the moonlight, the large white boulders that are scattered over the beach resemble boy scout tents at a jamboree or ladies frozen into standing stones, arranged in strangely concentric circles. As we progress further along the beach an eerie calm overtakes us, the large rock pools still the incoming waves to mere ripples, the black mounds of stone and seaweed motionless beside the shore. I hesitate before releasing Emma from her lead. I know she will head for the water but I am also sure that she will not go far from me, and will return when called. I am not so sure about Big Nose.

Ellisar can cover ground at the speed of a galloping horse, and it's been a while since I allowed him his freedom on the sands. Were the beach deserted I would have no qualms, but a galloping borzoi hitting standing rods and line is a catastrophe I can do without. So it is that our fearfulness renders us impotent. I keep Ellisar on his lead until Emma has cavorted in and out of the sea to the point of being happy to pace beside me, and then I brave my fears and unclip him.

He immediately runs towards the sea, much to my surprise, and wades in. The week in Welsh Wales has obviously taught him that the sea is nothing to fear. Me leading him into the surf and then forcing him to swim out of his depth on the lead beside me. I never expected him to voluntarily enter the sea again.Now he is entranced by a plant covered rock, looking perhaps like a stilled marine creature, and stands as the small waves break against his body and wrap around his legs.

Eventually he comes out and joins Emma at my side for a few minutes before blasting up the beach in a blur of sand. I can barely see him as the moonlight bounces off the rocks and hides him in their shadows. He comes back after only a few minutes, and I feel myself relaxing as the anxiety caused by not knowing his exact position dissipates. We all sit. I relax into the magic of moonlight and sea, and the hounds relax onto the sand. We breathe.

Walking home, retracing our steps along the moonlit lanes, there are only the sounds of disturbed cattle and Emma panting uphill. As we pass the local car park I can smell stale beer and a hint of weed, residue of the Bank Holiday weekend just passed. The moon reflects off the drawn down blinds and closed shutters of houses now emptied for the winter months ahead. Owners who live in other places so that they might holiday here. The windows stare blindly across the silver lit fields, silent witnesses to the approaching longer nights and shorter days. A badger crosses our path a few yards ahead and I watch as the stumpy tail waggles the bum as it disappears around a corner.

Seeing the badger starts me thinking about the odd duplicity that allows individuals who believe themselves to be animal lovers to nonetheless condone badger culls. I think also about the selective compassion that colludes with all blood sports, soon to be resurrected with the coming Autumnal country pursuits of hunting and shooting. We no longer have to hunt for our food or kill for our clothing, but we still continue to pursue prey for our amusement in the names of tradition and sport.

It seems something of a travesty really, disrespectful of life, wasteful of the magic and wonder that abounds in the natural world around us.

And it makes no day at all a good day to die.

I am standing on a tall cliff looking out at the ocean. The day is a wild and windy one but the sun is shining, making the sea below me a glorious shade of Mediterranean turquoise, and the cries of gulls surround me as they rise and fall looking for fish.

Behind me the sound of departing cars reminds me that I am here to say farewell, to close a chapter on part of my life that helped more than most to make me into the woman I have now become. Made me strong enough to find myself and walk away from everything I knew, taking with me only that which I loved the most, my children and my freedom.

I take off my sunglasses and remove the clip that keeps my hair tamed, shaking my head to loosen the tresses and allow them to blow carelessly in the wind across my face, blinding me with each gust from the Atlantic. It's been a hard road, a road littered with pitfalls and self-discovery, with heartache and relief, with intense love, and grief, with joy and with disappointment. I look out over the ocean as the church bells start to peal behind me, the rhythmic sound repeating and repeating itself as the team starts to lower the rounds.

So it is with us, we live our lives in ever decreasing circles, spiralling closer and closer to our source until the time when, if we are really lucky, we finally understand that who we are was at the centre of our Self all the time, and that finding that true core is the only pursuit that really matters. Revolution after revolution, we circle ourselves like boxers in the ring, waiting for the moment to land the knockout punch instead of joining hands and sharing the prize.

"And the end of all our exploring...to arrive where we started...And know the place for the first time." My thanks to TSElliot.

I hear my name drifting towards me on the wind. I am wanted. Turning I see my friends and family waving at me, with their beckoning asking that I join them, return to the land of the living and cease my gentle musings that take me away and out across the horizon. I look down at my feet and see the last of the sea pinks nodding in the gusts of air, and the purple heather hugging the soil closely to avoid being swept away on the breeze.

A tiny butterfly rests for a moment on the blooms before taking flight, rising in erratic bursts, buffeted as the wind grabs hold of it and lifts it up and high above me in patterns out of its control. All around me life continues its crazy, uncontrolled, unfathomable dance. We are fools if we think, even for a moment, that we have any say in the ways we twirl, when the real challenge is simply to just keep moving our feet.

I wrap my hair around my hand and tuck it into a bun, put my glasses back on and return down the earthen path back to the church, breathing in the cool fresh salt air as I walk.

It's a great day to be alive.

"Cure yourself,
with the light of the Sun and the rays of the Moon.

With the Sound of the river and the waterfall.

With the swaying of the Sea and the fluttering of birds.

Heal yourself, with the mint and mint leaves,
with neem and eucalyptus.

Sweeten yourself with lavender, rosemary, and chamomile.

Hug yourself with the cocoa bean and a touch of cinnamon.

Put Love in tea instead of sugar

And take it looking at the Stars

Heal yourself with the kisses that the wind gives you and the hugs of the rain.

Get strong with bare feet on the ground and with everything that is born from it.

Get smarter every day by listening to your intuition, looking at the world with the Eye of your forehead.

Jump, Dance, Sing, so that you live happier.

Heal yourself, with beautiful Love,
and always remember..

You are the Medicine. "

Maria Sabina

DAY SEVEN
Tea and Cake

There's a tapping noise in the background that's coming from somewhere I can't see. I feel myself surfacing from a place that I can't quite remember and open my eyes. Bailey is sitting on the windowsill silhouetted against the dim grey light of early morning, asking for me to open the window. I reluctantly toss back the duvet and stretch my legs before getting out of bed. Piri lies still asleep, now completely covered with bedding. She's come a long way. Bailey keeps tapping on the pane with his paw, impatient to be out of the house and off for his morning ablutions. I acquiesce and undo the latch so that he can escape, watching his rotund figure casually walk down the rungs of the step ladder positioned outside my bedroom window. My impromptu fire escape should one be needed. There are no doors on the first floor of the cottage.

Outside, the patio is looking a tad jaded. With the coming of Autumn the plants have started to die back and lose their lustre. The roses are dropping petals more quickly, the honeysuckle has bloomed and the lavender that I moved looks positively decrepit. Not sure it is going to survive, which will be a sad finish to over half a century of beating the odds. Strangely, I find myself hardly caring whether the lavender lives or dies, which feels very ungracious. I just feel that the time has come to let it go, to move on from the attachment if that's what happens. There is a sadness but not really any grief. Nana will be appalled.

September is my birthday month, which also happens to coincide with the Autumn Equinox, the day of my birth, World Peace Day, and the Pagan festival of Mabon, celebrating the year's harvest. This has resulted in a lifetime full of cryptic astrological implications and inferences and welcomed synchronicities with the potential for profound interpretation. I wonder who it was that first ascribed certain personal qualities to certain star signs. Who decided that those born under Taurus were bull-headed, and those under Cancer soft-bellied, and Virgo's pretty damn near perfect in every way?

A little too much of a perfectionist at times, sometimes a little too honest, too clean and tidy, but all in all a well-grounded individual with integrity and noble aspirations. And then to also be born in the Year of the Dog- all loyalty, steadfastness and devotion. And then to be born on the Sabbath- Bonny, blithe, good and gay. The Gods must have been drunk on ambrosia the day I was born. My father certainly was a tad tipsy when he was finally allowed in to see me, arms full of flowers as he kissed his wife.

When do we become that which we are? Before or after we are brainwashed by the infinite number of minutiae which constantly accompany us through life from the moments of our first intake of air?

The birds are starting to feed again in large numbers. There has been a hiatus while the adults went through their summer moult, which left the peanuts going mouldy and the seed containers oddly full, but now the masses have returned, flitting busily from fat balls to sunflower seeds, mealworms to nuts. It's like Old Home Week for avians. The late afternoon sky is full of circling martins and swifts, preparing for their legendary autumnal migration, but as yet the telephone lines are empty, not yet encumbered by hundreds of tiny feathered sprites about to head south for the winter.

I have rigged up a convoluted web of gardening twine and brass bells to warn the birds of any stealthy ambush engineered by Piri or Yoda- it has worked for the most part, with Yoda managing to kill less than half a dozen during the summer months. Piri, if she has caught any, has not shared her guilty secrets with me at home.

I sit up in bed and slide my legs out and over the edge tentatively. Yesterday I went riding for the first time in over six years, a baptism of fire of two and a half hours in the saddle. A fabulous afternoon in sunlit dappled woodland, riding a truly beautiful Arabian. Luckily, the ibuprofen I downed like a House MD wannabe once I reached home seems to have worked and my inner thigh muscles are not yelling at me in retribution. I haven't had to wrap my legs around anything wider than the top rail of a five bar gate for some time.

Downstairs all is quiet, and I am deeply conscious of MJ's absence from the party. No incessant barking, no snuffling noises. No need for me to throw on any clothes at hand to dash downstairs in a bid to get MJ outside before she relieves herself on the kitchen carpet upon awakening. No necessity to hide her tablets, drain her saliva gland or clean her teeth in an effort to be rid of the halitosis that could whither an oak tree at twenty paces. No more watching her dithering in circles in the car parking area or attempting to tip over the dog food bin in the kitchen by scrambling up it.

Instead, I look out of the bedroom window at the large black planter on the patio wherein lies her body. The delphiniums are sending up new growth from the core that I transplanted to be MJ's marker. In time they will stand tall with long bracts of the most beautiful electric blue, the flowers attracting bees and other nectar loving insects. MJ's essence is long gone, but what remains behind will serve to nurture the growth of something beautiful, and blue. It's a fitting memorial. Besides, Piri seems to like lying on the earth on the top of the container in the sun and sleeping there. Not sure how MJ would feel about that.

This weekend I am scheduled to head North to join my daughter and her family for my birthday celebrations. Our wise PM has just decreed that we all need to limit any familial interactions to no more than six people- just as well my daughter has only two children. This latest list of government recommendations for COVID-19 has not been well received by a nation already disillusioned by months of contradictory initiatives and illogical information updates. The country is rebelling, loathe to take at face value the countless lists of statistics bandied about by government sources. There is a quiet revolution grumbling in the belly of the masses.

Going into the second half of a year, everybody suddenly has an opinion, and more often than not, an instinctual, not an intellectual, one. People are questioning the narratives, lost in a sea of unknowingness, yet certain in their positions of revolt. It is an intriguing combination- the strength of personal conviction based on nothing intrinsic, which is the essence of faith, and the strength of conviction based on what we are told by figures of authority in whom we have no faith at all- which is the essence of fearfulness.

With every new revelation presented by the leaders of the country there is a mass of counter allegations from sources pertaining to be equally as informed and aware on the intricacies of the Covid-19 virus. Social chaos and confusion are circling like predatory hyenas, waiting, waiting for the first shots of anarchy to be fired like the cannons of 1812. It's enough to send us all scurrying for the high ground, heading for the hills with self-help manuals clasped in the sweaty palms of our hands as we desperately try to master how to grow turnips and distill essential oils.

Main-stream media bombards us with images of atrocities taking place very close to home, in cultures very close to our own, as Everyman is accosted and abused by police and militia, and are filmed doing so by bystanders on their smartphones.

It concerns me, this plethora of abuse screened so easily across nations via social media. The constant bombardments of our sensibilities normalises the horror and risks making it the norm in people's minds. People will start to think that it is acceptable to behave badly because that is how so many other people are behaving. Will start to accept that it is alright to abuse and disrespect the rights of individuals because that's what the police do or that's what the army does or that's what Aunt Sally down the road would do. Mass hysteria is far more worrying once bullets replace toilet paper.

It's a slippery slope once the horror becomes commonplace and complacency arrives, just as we have become complacent about so many other horrors that exist already around this world of ours. Tibet, Myanmar, palm oil, almond milk, silk, GM, intensive farming, slavery, deforestation, trawling, paedophilia, homelessness. Outside my window I hear the sound of several horses trotting up the lane, following hounds being prepped for the fox-hunting season ahead. An illegal activity supported and encouraged and feted by thousands of individuals across the country who see themselves as decent, law-abiding, animal loving people.

Hunting has been decreed exempt from the "Rule of Six." Such a farce.

I need a drink. Time for tea.

Anthony sits opposite us, teapot raised in mid-air.

"Milk?"

He's in his early seventies and has only just inherited his family estate upon the death of his mother. The estate and his first access to the family money. Over a thousand acres and the approach to the Hall landscaped by Capability Brown. It had taken us eight hours to drive there for our noon appointment, and we had arrived five minutes late. Anthony was not at all amused.

Swinging the car around the circular flower bed I roll down my window and ask the ancient gardener if he knew where I might find the owner of the house. He straightens up with some difficulty from his bending position where he is pruning roses and replies in an extremely curt and cultured voice,

"I AM the owner of the house."

No, not amused at all.

"Deborah, milk?"

Out of the corner of my eye I see the silver tray in the middle of the large linen- covered table. The silver service sits expectantly, pink hints of old Goddard's silver cleaner caught in the creases between the fine etchings on the surfaces. The milk jug sits humbly between the sugar bowl and a stack of china plates, the milk within sporting a very generous yellow crust lightly tinged with green. I try to catch my companion's eye, to warn her of the state of the addition she is about to accept into her tea cup, but fail.

"Yes please, Anthony. That would be lovely."

And there it goes, the little silver jug lovingly caressed by silversmiths centuries ago, carrying its cargo of cow juices and penicillin.

"I'll have mine black, thank you Anthony," I quickly respond when asked.

The Hall stands in its grandiose gardens, complete with large lake and swathes of perfectly cut lawns, with an air of faded gentility. In the corridor leading from the tradesman's entrance to the reception rooms, genuine Ming plates hug the walls, slightly askew amid the heavy dusty cobwebs. The dog room, floored with red brick tiles, sports a lone bale of barley straw next to the large fireplace, which is empty and reflects the cavernous room, echoing in its loneliness. There is no sign of a dog.

We are shown into a breakfast room where a large table sits unfettered by any other furniture except for the three chairs placed there for our use. On the table there are two dinner plates, one piled high with KitKats and the other with cold pork pies. The area is famed for its pork pies we are told. The silver tea service holds court from one end of the array, waiting for its lord and master to be Mother and pour.

Tea, black or otherwise, is followed by half a pork pie and the offer of a KitKat for dessert. I am ravenous after our journey but realise that good form dictates I eat hardly anything, so I refuse the bar of chocolate and dream instead of cucumber sandwiches served on fine bone china, washed down with a sparkling white and followed by fresh strawberries and clotted cream. Did we have anything left to eat in the car?

After lunch we are taken into the living-room, a shrouded room of dusk pink and priceless antiques. Anthony tells us that he keeps the curtains drawn shut so that the sunlight does not fade the upholstery, but he draws them back so that we can see the stupendous view that stretches off into the distance through the floor to ceiling double windows. The only time the room is now used is when Anthony plays host to the local Bishop, with whom he lunches most Sundays, and to whose Church Anthony intends to bequeath his entire estate. In his seventies, he has no family.

We are there to assist with his newfound passion, Arab horses, and my companion is there to audition for the post of Stable Manager. We are both tasked with taking two of Anthony's fillies to a breed show being held the next day, using his massive Oakley Supreme lorry to travel the two hundred and forty miles after lunch. My friend can drive as she has an HGV 1, a trophy from her former marriage. I shall follow in my car as a third party shall be driving the lorry home after the show.

It's a fool's errand, showing a pair of youngsters that have had no ring training and are bonded at the hip. Still, as a way of auditioning fools with horses it has a mad rationality. Predictably, the show class is nothing more than a trial rehearsal for other shows later in the season, but Anthony is mortified at not being placed in the top six. My friend and I drive home to her house in Devon in relatively stunned silence, masquerading as exhaustion.

She will apply for the post of Manager but eventually turn it down once the level of her potential employer's demands sinks in. Nine o'clock curfews, no gentlemen callers. At all. There is a farm worker's cottage available if she chooses not to live at the Hall, but it is positioned right on a busy estate road and thus an impractical choice for her with her young son. In the weeks that followed, Anthony interviewed almost all of the top handlers and trainers of the day, and I know of at least two who were treated to the same tea service, and the same milk.

I still prefer my tea black.

Emma and Ellisar jump into the back of my silver Ford estate with alacrity, tails wagging with the excitement of a proposed car journey. The haylage has arrived for the horses and I need to start the routine of daily feeds, more so since the lack of rain all summer had left them looking too lean for my liking this close to winter. The temperatures are in the mid to high twenties, and what little grass is left in my field is fast becoming dried out. The wheat crop is down thirty per cent I have heard, which means bread prices will soar after Christmas. Mind you, with a No-Deal Brexit also on the horizon, I doubt that scarcity of our favourite loaf shall be the only dilemma at our breakfast tables.

The horses are standing expectantly on their side of the electric tape, and I carry in with me two bags of misshapen carrots, sold cheaply to cooks who don't mind their root vegetables an irregular shape or size. The horses certainly have no such prejudices and welcome the orange bounty as I spill the contents of the bags onto the ground. I call the hounds to my side and sit down in the close-cropped grass to watch Darcy and Sparkle as they crunch their way through the supermarket rejects, my morning meditation. The sun is beating onto my back and shoulders and the warmth takes me to Jordan, to desert, to Wadi Rum. To other Septembers, other birthdays.

Five in the morning and my alarm is beeping. Endurance practise today. Eighteen kilometres across sand and scree in blasting heat- it will be almost forty degrees before noon. My mount is a tall grey purebred Arabian, a gelding, and I am excited. Although I work with horses every day, I never have the opportunity to ride them in the capital, so today is special, a privilege extended by the leader of the national endurance team, an amazing Spanish woman made of sinew and muscle and nerve. She is quite amazing.

Some hours later I can hardly move. My horse decided to challenge me after our first canter, and the muscles connecting my ribs feel as if each one has been stretched and pinned onto a rack. Eighteen kilometres of opposition in the saddle. Walking is not a problem, but anything else is, each intake of breath serving to remind me that my chest really does not want to move at all, in any direction, ever. I have never known such muscular pain, and hopefully never will again. It was worth it of course, it always is, that connection with a horse, even if the connection is confrontational.

Wadi Rum is a place of magic and splendour. It captures the imagination, conquers your heart, belies your senses, and possesses your soul. Just ask Will Smith, he of Aladdin fame once freed from his lamp.

I'm driving south. To be more accurate, I'm being driven south, along the King's Highway, one of the three main routes that connect north to south Jordan. I'm being driven because the only condition I requested when agreeing to work here was that I didn't have to drive here. Not only do they drive on the wrong side of the road for us Imperialist Brits, but the number of directional combinations employed by drivers when going around the eight urban roundabouts in Amman are far beyond my own modest computations. Sitting and watching the passing landscape is far more my forte.

Jordan is a land of contrasts. In the Spring, verdant fields, abundant blooms and trees heavily laden with sweet smelling blossom. Six weeks later and it is as if someone has blasted the land with a cosmic ray gun, as the grass begins to turn pale yellow, the earth starts to crack and the temperatures start to rise. There are tall mountains, and deep ravines, vast expanses of sand and microcosms of fertile orchards, the cornucopia of the Red Sea and the paucity of the River Jordan trickling into the Dead Sea after being depleted by Syria and then Israel, many feet below sea level and too salty to sustain life as we know it.

The people however do not vary. Without exception, Jordan is a land where the native population has an inherent kindness and generosity of spirit. Where the traditional Bedu spirit of hospitality is to be found whether in the sands of Wadi Rum or on the streets of Amman. I was scheduled to return to this Land of the Black Iris early this year but Covid-19 has delayed my plans. I am eager to return and frustrated by the delay. I miss my friends there, the food, the smells, the history, the great open spaces, the sea and the sand.

I am sitting high up on a sandstone rock, our Land Cruiser parked out of sight below us, the scent of woodsmoke in my nostrils and the bright orange flames before me heating up an old dented kettle. My friend and guide, an endurance champion who is also stud manager for one of the royal stables, sits beside me, barely visible in the dark. His lean, aquiline silhouette sits perched on its haunches as he tends the fire. We are quiet. The only sound is the crackling of the branches collected earlier from the base of wild fig trees, and the wind which is slowly becoming more insistent as it wraps itself around the rocks below us after its journey across the wide open sands.

The sky above me is truly like the inverted bowl of Omar Khaiyam, a dark lapis lazuli, star studded and immense. Suddenly, from my left, a large orange-red ball of fire sweeps across my horizon, the largest meteorite I have ever seen, and blazes its trail through the air parallel to the ground. Magic. I lie back onto the hard rock, warm from the day's sun, and gaze skywards, totally at peace.

It is such a privilege to be here, far from the hustle and bustle of the city, far even from the five star camp run by my English friend for the visiting tourists and returning locals where I am staying. She arrived years ago to visit her family, then met and married the man tasked with showing her

251

the country. It is a privilege to have been brought here to this secret place so far off any beaten track, to gaze at the skies and drink tea, a privilege to share the knowledge of someone local, someone who loves the desert, whose soul truly belongs here.

The water starts to boil and steam rises out of the small spout of the kettle towards the heavens. I can hear my companion unwrapping the glass teacups from their cloths inside his saddle bags and placing them onto the hand-woven mat we are sitting on. He tears large sprigs of mint off from the bunch he has brought with him and places the mint in the glasses. Then he adds sugar, lots of sugar, before pouring the boiling water into a battered enamel teapot where he has already placed four spoons of black tea leaves. Then we wait.

After several minutes he stirs the tea and pours it onto the mint and sugar in the glass cups, the clean smell of mint cutting through the heavy smokey air. He hands me my glass cup and I curl my fingers around the heat, holding it close to my chest and breathing in the aromas of tea and mint and woodsmoke. I close my eyes. In another universe I would be sitting beside my lover and we would kiss under the night sky so festooned with stars, the cooling breeze caressing our bare skin, but instead I simply lower my head and take a sip of the hot tea, scalding my lips in the fresh night air. The fire crackles and the sparks leap into the black sky, rising high above us on travels of their own. We stay sitting in silence, gazing into the flames on our private journeys and drinking tea until the sunrise starts to tinge the sky behind the hills in the distance. Time to return to camp.

Four thirty and the alarm starts to beep. Days start early in the desert.

Today is my daughter's twenty-fourth birthday, and I have arranged a hot air balloon ride for us, a surprise from her bucket list that she thinks will be a camel ride through the vast sandy landscape. Could be a blast.

I run across the sand and jump into the battered jeep to forewarn the other clients that we are riding camels and not airstreams. They kindly agree to maintain the facade and greet my daughter with cheerful greetings of goodwill and celebration.

It's a half hour drive from the camp and we are all slightly sleepy, despite the bright glare of the desert sun. As we set off I notice everyone has donned their sunglasses and the women all have their heads covered, good cultural assimilation.

We are crossing a large expanse of flat land, the surface criss crossed with fissures in the cracked sand. Ahead of us about five minutes drive away we can see a group of people and a striped multi coloured balloon on its side.

"Wow!" My daughter exclaims, "That would be amazing!"

I look at her and put on my most apologetic face.

"I'm so sorry Darling, they were all booked up for this week."

"Oh don't be silly," she says generously, " I love camels."

The jeep pulls up a hundred yards or so from the deflated balloon and we all climb out.

"Where are the camels?" my daughter asks.

"I'm guessing they are on their way, you know nothing happens on time here."

We look over at the collapsed mound of blue, red and white canvas and follow the antics of the balloon operators as they start to inflate the balloon with the hot air from a massive gas burner.

Several minutes pass.

"Where are the camels?!" Certainly nowhere to be seen, and considering the wide open panorama we would be justifiably concerned were camels indeed on their way.

"No idea Darling. I'm sure they will get here eventually."

The balloon is now inflated enough to look like a balloon and to start moving upward away from the hot air. Below the balloon is a basket that can hold ten people, eight paying passengers and two operators. Our fellow travellers are starting to get restless, and one or two pick up their bags from the sand and start to set off towards the balloon.

"Just going to have a nosey," shouts one of them over his shoulder. He's here on loan from our MOD to share his expertise on desert warfare tactics with the local militia. He gave me his card. Do I look like MI6?

My daughter looks around worried at the empty vastness around us.

"No camels."

Another ten minutes and there's a loud whistle from the balloon, everyone looks over in its direction and we see our companion waving at us to join him. Moment of truth.

"Guess we'll have to take the balloon instead...."

"What?! But what about the camels?"

I do love this child.

"Happy birthday, Darling."

Her face lights up with genuine surprise and delight. It's one of those wonderful magical moments when one knows one is truly blessed.

"Come along, mustn't keep them waiting!"

Wadi Rum. Stretching beneath us in a deep burnt orange blanket that stretches all the way to Saudi Arabia. Miles and miles of desert sand and sandstone rock formations, their surfaces bizarre wind-carved sculptures that look like terraces of melted wax figurines. Above us not a hint of moisture. And that's just inside the basket, which is an absolute living inferno. The heat from the open flame feeding off of the gas canister bounces off the surface of a thick metal sheet and bakes us all in the reflected heat. It is horrific, a homegrown Dante's Inferno.

So much for the peace and quiet of hot air balloons. The roar of the released gas deafens us every few minutes and prevents most appreciator's gasps of amazement. Are we having fun yet? My daughter laughs, appreciating the irony. The views are breath- taking, and we watch our shadow bounce along sand dunes and stone outcrops, covering huge leaps to our few seconds. There is nothing moving below us, just an arid sea of terracotta dunes, with not even a camel to break the scene, just our lone jeep leading the charge ahead of our guy ropes hundreds of feet below.

We land and are miraculously greeted with champagne.

"Happy Birthday."

The glasses are perfectly chilled.

Darcy, once known as Dante OS, pushes me from behind and I come back down to earth with a bump. Just as well that Sparkle is not otherwise known as Sparks, too much coincidence can sometimes beggar belief.

My own twenty-first was a humble affair, celebrated a couple of months after graduating from university and before I left Canada for the UK, having decided to turn my back on pedantic practicality and embrace the foolhardiness of romantic ideals. Youth is wasted on the young. My mother had organised a small afternoon tea party which consisted of six of her closest friends and my parents and my current lover, who himself was heading to the other side of the country before joining me in England. That was the plan. It didn't work out that way of course, the gods had other ideas, and so the main memory of my twenty- first for me is an apres-tea session of sex in a wheat field, lying on a faux fur jacket that helped keep my back off of the now cool ground.

He wrote poetry about that day. I boarded a plane. We never saw each other again.

My fiftieth was far more fun. My daughter treated us both to a Nile Cruise, she twenty-one and me fifty, a fortuitous synchronicity of time.

Since she was a little girl, my daughter has felt an affinity with Egypt. I never did. When we arrived in Aswan we were greeted by a ebullient Egyptian tour guide who started smiling and laughing that afternoon and never stopped for the next ten days. He was quite remarkable, and the heart and soul of the tour. The other three guides who work for the cruise company are the qualified Egyptologists, with a profound and extensive knowledge of their subject. We are extremely lucky to be so well escorted through the millennia.

Days spent floating up the Nile impress me with the repetitive continuity of time and space. The views on either bank straight out of biblical texts, the villagers still dressed in native cotton and sailing their wooden feluccas or rowing their canoes between the deep papyrus beds along the shore. In contrast, the white-washed, flat-roofed houses with their tiny black windows and doors mostly sport satellite dishes on their walls, and the men walking behind the flocks of sheep hold mobile phones in their hands.

The women are covered head to toe in black cloth with only their eyes to be seen in the open slit above their noses, but the children all play happily in the dark earth outside, their laughter coming across the water to our open decks.

I start to subconsciously pay attention to how many camels I am offered for my daughter's hand in marriage every time we set foot off of the boat.

The alarm beeps. It is three in the morning and we have to catch our coach, one of several in an armed convoy being escorted to Abu Simbel.

Abu Simbel is witness to the remarkable ingenuity of mankind in the face of seemingly impossible odds. In 1968 the entire complex was relocated in its entirety to an artificial hill made from a domed structure, high above the Aswan High Dam reservoir. The relocation of the temples was necessary to prevent Abu Simbel being completely submerged during the creation of Lake Nasser, the massive artificial water reservoir formed after the building of the Aswan High Dam on the River Nile.

The Gods must have been feeling generous that particular day.

We stop midway to allow the army to check under all the vehicles for limpet mines. Most of us are too sleepy to care about the implications. We arrive just as the sun starts to peer around the edge of the temple, the sun god Ra himself welcoming us to the temple of Ramesses II and his queen Nefertari, built almost four thousand years ago, albeit in a different location. Although barely mid-morning the heat of the day has started, and we all carry at least one litre of bottled water with us to ward off the desert.

Inside the temple small groups of people wander past the impassive stone faces cut into relief and so painstakingly moved years ago, an ear fallen and half buried by the sand makes my daughter a Lilliputian tourist, as we gaze upwards at the huge effigies staring ahead blankly over the desert sand. The splendour of the Pharaohs is long past, truly gone with the wind, the massive stone temples and tombs now lost between the dunes. Clichés come to mind quick and fast.

The sands of time, spilling through the cracks of an egg timer inverted by the gods, unable to travel backwards, rushing down relentless, carrying us all in their path. It is a dance through Eternity, where we think we can effect a change to when the egg gets eaten when in reality all we can do is hold the spoon while Ozymandias lies sleeping in the sand. Covid-19 has yet to turn the waters of the Nile carnitine red, nor when it does will great Neptune's ocean wash the blood clean from our hands. And who ordered boiled eggs anyway?

When we return to the boat, our guides have arranged an impromptu celebration. There is a large selection of soft drinks and several very sweet confections on display, with the words Happy Birthday hanging above the tables on a glitzy red and gold banner. It is a kind gesture. In the centre of the display is a tall three-layered extravaganza in pink, decorated with many iced rosettes and flowers, and covered in a very generous layer of cream icing. Neither my daughter nor I have the heart to tell the assembled chefs that, after the exertions of the day, neither of us would choose to eat loads of cream and cake.

And there isn't a cup of tea in sight, with or without milk.

"Happy Birthday, Darling," I say, as I hand everyone a fork. I know the gods are singing, but I can't quite catch the tune.

Boris Johnson tells us that it lasts for twenty seconds and that we must wash our hands accordingly to keep the C-19 virus at bay.

When I was growing up, my mother always hoped to be able to give me a white convertible for my eighteenth birthday, wrapped up with a huge red bow. She had seen too many classic Hollywood romances, and desperately hoped to give her own daughter the gifts which she herself had gone without. As a result, my mother always made a special day out of any family occasion, going the extra mile to sew into the early morning hours making me a special outfit, or working for days on catering for family gatherings at Christmas, Easter and New Year. Her talents were an inspiration and I inherited the love of gatherings around the people we care about and love.

I look up at the man I breathe for and think how different today would be if my mother were still alive. Today I turn forty and not a candle in sight. She died just under a month ago and no one has remembered that there would have been a cause for celebration had she still been alive. It's a lonely day. Fourteen years later there is another lonely day when I walk out of hospital two days after leaving my uterus and a fibroid behind me on the operating table, while another woman receives solace from my long-term partner. No candles then either.

We had lots of candles for my daughter's eighteenth, a table surrounded by family and family friends with champagne, lobster and an effervescent Roman Candle that one of the guests used as a cigar lighter. Her brother insists on making an occasion out of the event and makes a special point of wearing a tie. No one else does. A night of vodka shots and dancing for my son's coming of age, ending with us walking the streets of Manchester in the early light of dawn diving into every open kebab shop enroute to our beds. His eighteenth celebrations are a secret honour for me, and I am humbled by being invited to join in with the activities.

Mine was a far more sober affair- dinner on the rooftop of the Sheridan Hotel overlooking the Saskatchewan River. I was home just after midnight and I know my mother was inwardly saddened that I wasn't spending the night swinging from a chandelier and dancing on tabletops. For her fiftieth my father drank champagne out of her golden shoes and placed a specially purchased gold nugget onto her stomach, her belly button the only place that she wasn't already wearing one.

Birthdays and Holy Days stretch out behind me in memory as I plan my present weekend away. Two years ago my daughter made me the most exquisite cake for my sixtieth. It would look at home on the cover of any Cordon Bleu cookbook. She has inherited my mother's gene for a love of and talent for baking, and couples it with a sense of perfection and artistic beauty. It is a heady combination. The cakes she makes for her own children's birthday parties are sumptuous creations of bright colours, tasty layers of different flavours and cartoon favourites fashioned out of edible icing. I observe with awe and wonder. My mother must be thrilled.

The dogs are getting restless. Time to move. Darcy and Sparkle barely notice our departure, far too involved with their carrots.

I am sitting on my sofa when the phone rings in the afternoon. My bags are packed for the few days away and Yoda and Piri are pouncing on the hessian Bag for Life with deadly intent. Piri trots off triumphantly with a rolled-up pair of my socks. Bailey lies curled up asleep on the armchair and the dogs are lying flat out in the kitchen after their visit to the horses earlier. The phone keeps ringing, breaking the quiet reverie before the long drive ahead.

"How are you?"

"Terrible, just terrible. Something awful has happened."

I freeze.

"What's wrong? What do you need me to do?"

House sales during this C-19 global pandemic have soared in England, due in no small part to the abolition of Sales Tax for buyers. Many sellers have benefited, my daughter included, who listed and sold her house in under five days. A close friend of mine has also sold her house recently after a long marketing exercise, and over a year of hoping to move, together with two years of gradually worsening health. It is she who is now on the phone, her sale having fallen through at the last stage a full eight weeks after the vendor committed to the purchase.

She is totally devastated, and literally shaking to her core with Essential Tremors. She has been totally shielded for weeks due to chronic health concerns and C-19 regulations, isolated on a rural property leased to the over-55's, not served by a bus or visited by any casual passers-by. It's been a lonely six months for her, and I have scheduled to see her on my way home next week. I listen as the lack of details or communication from the estate agents bewilder us, in my mind I am targeting only the exhaustion and depression in her voice, and thinking how this disappointment will impact profoundly upon my friend's life over the approaching winter months.

It comes at the same time as the government tightens up the rules governing social interaction, as everyone starts to suspect another C-19 spike coming in the weeks ahead and a total nationwide lockdown before Christmas. The wheel is turning, and the whole fiasco that is Covid-19 UK 2020 seems about to be starting all over again. Winter is coming, the geese are getting fat.

Catalina Island, playground to the stars. As in Hollywood, not Pleiades.

I have never been to California before and now, thanks to the great generosity of three university chums, here we all are to celebrate our long years of friendship and my fifty-seventh birthday. It has been anticipated now for several weeks, and I am here for a week, an hour from Los Angeles and a world away from Mexico. We are heading west across the water, basking in the early morning warmth and the spray off the sea. I wear a swimsuit beneath my dress, desperate to somehow fit in a swim in the Pacific while I am here.

My birthday surprise is a guided tour of the famed Art Deco building, the Catalina Casino, ironically situated in the town of Avalon. My birthday treat is stripping off my clothes in the afternoon heat while my companions search for a golf cart for us to move about on, and diving into the shallow water of the island marina, watching the bright orange California State Fish, the Garibaldi. The whole of the Pacific and only a tiny few square meters within easy access for swimming. I take a great photo of an English bulldog sitting on a paddle board being steered around the moored yachts.

The four of us shared freshman year together, and were sometimes described as the Charlie's Angels, more than likely because one of us drove a red and white mustang and had mastered handbrake turns at high speed. We also had a knack for clearing a room of any men shy of sexual innuendo within the first five minutes of entering it. Now we live far apart, and have grown into the other identities of wives and mothers and widows.

The sunset is spectacular. Vivid reds and oranges, a streak of gold and a backdrop curtain of deep purple and black. The air is warm, the sea crashing as the surf pounds the sand just yards from our table. Then we are ushered inside, one of us eager to stay within boundaries, and we sit in strained camaraderie as the dynamics around our table stretch and strain. It has been a long and illuminating week.

I reach into my pocket and bring out three duplicate keys for my home in the UK and give one each to my dear friends.

"You are all welcome," I say, "Just don't come all together."

We laugh, but I am deadly serious.

The imposed gathering has not worked as expected and we leave the time spent on this rendezvous with varying degrees of disappointment and regret. Our strengths and weaknesses have evolved over the last three decades, and no longer complement one another as they might once have done. Each one of my three friends has confided their frustrations and hurts to me.

I wonder what they say about me when I am absent from the room, having no doubt that their comments will reflect my lack of financial security compared to their own ample individual wealth. I am the poor country cousin come to Town, my poverty strangely comforting to them, validating their lives of sometimes less than perfect spiritual happiness.

It's a gift that I am happy to bestow. We all make our choices, we are all free to choose the consequences we feel able to live with.

I am sitting in an oasis on the edge of the Kalahari. There are small Bishop birds flitting among the bulrushes, specks of crimson in the pale desiccated landscape. Above us weaver birds have woven their colonial nests into the trees, like so many strange lampshades, and everywhere the whirl of grasshoppers underpins the birdsong. My parents have driven us to this rare place of water to celebrate my birthday with me, a basket of picnic delicacies and a chilled bottle of bubbly safely cushioned in the boot of their car. I am here having boarded a plane, a bare eighteen months after my wedding, to escape the crushing reality of my married life. I have left behind everything. Such is the confidence of Youth.

When I return to North Cornwall just over a month later I find that all of my personal belongings have been burnt in the courtyard by my husband and his two young daughters. The red Cheongsam my mother stitched for my wedding-dress is destroyed, horses are rehomed, kittens are drowned and sheep slaughtered. I reel from the horror. It takes me another fourteen years before I leave again, this time making certain that anything that breathes is safe first, and then driving away into an unknown and totally uncertain future.

Best day's work I ever did, although my children may not always agree. Such is the confidence of personal Truth.

I am looking around the table at a collection of close friends and my family. I am sixty, just ten years off our allotted time in the Bible. I am wearing a gold brocade coat that used to belong to my mother and Ben, the Chinese restauranteur, tells me that his grandmother used to wear an identical one in Hong Kong. It seems strangely fitting.

Seated beside me to my right is a friend from my early days in Mafikeng, a man my mother warned off me when I was newly engaged, something she regretted doing for the rest of her life according to one of my closest female friends. I have since told him that he should not have acquiesced so easily, not have been such a coward. My father used to call him a bean-counter. He has been extremely successful and is a very wealthy individual. It has come at a high price, but he has survived pancreatic cancer and now owns a beautiful home in a wealthy part of the local area, in which he lives surrounded by priceless antiques and high spec mod cons, and his cat.

On my other side is a handsome man who has the same ironic sense of humour as myself and whose friendship has survived the darkest nights and brightest dawns. He claims this is because we have never had any sexual frisson between us, and he may be right. My children, grown adults, join me with their own little people, and I am blessed to have my daughters from other mothers sitting around the table too.

It's a good gathering.

The Chinese delicacies are eventually followed by a beautiful cake made by my daughter. An exquisite creation in burgundy and cream, decorated with fresh figs and autumn berries. Wine flows, champagne corks pop, laughter fills the room. I am blessed. Days later I learn of how one of my guests, a very dear friend with a recurring love for alcoholic addiction, managed to insult and denigrate the guests sitting next to him. Maybe not such a good gathering after all.

My mother is sitting on a fold up canvas chair on Salcombe beach. It's a hot day in August just two weeks before my daughter's birthday and we are having a picnic with a friend and her young family. My mother is dressed in a very bright African affair in turquoise and black, very much a peacock amid the pastel colours of the English seaside.

"I like what I see and I like what I hear," she says.

"I like what I see and I like what I hear," she says again.

It is a statement of acceptance, of revelation, of coming to terms with and feeling at peace with the world around her.

Less than a month later my mother will be dead, never having suspected that her liver was under attack and that a cancer would metastasise throughout her entire body. Her death comes only four days after my children and I travel up to the middle of Shropshire to blow out candles on a home-made cat-shaped cake. A brilliant bright yellow first-time effort created by the man we have all come to love.

I am sitting at a small round table in an Italian bistro with my daughter and her husband. Having enjoyed a meal to celebrate my birthday, we are now working our way through coffee and alcoholic choices. It is a relaxed end to a busy day full of the energy of young children and the viewing of their new house. It is a happy way to bring my visit to a close, and a welcome respite from the drama that keeps unfolding back at home.

I feel quietly guilty that we are not sharing this idyll with my son and his family, that I have been unable to create a bridge of understanding between my two offspring. Life has conspired to rob my son of far too many birthday celebrations recently. I am aware that the situation is getting better for him, that the tensions and unhappiness have eased and that his daughters are once again enjoying his company. I too have been spending time with them after the restrictions imposed upon us by badly informed social workers. It has been a long and enlightening journey, and as so often happens, enlightenment has brought along its partner disillusion.

"I like what I see and I like what I hear."

A true gift.

I am walking beneath tall oak trees, the sky starting to dim and the New Moon still low on the horizon, a salmon shade of pink. Big Nose and Emma walk beside me, Ellisar trotting from time to time and Emma searching out windfalls from the apple trees which line the walkway. She is limping, a result of overenthusiastic exercise during our stay up North. I am cursing quietly inside at my own stupidity, allowing her to run off lead with a younger bundle of puppy energy in tight circles as they chased one another around garden swings. Emma's cruciate ligament is her point of weakness nowadays.

We are walking towards Glastonbury Tor, but I am wondering about the wisdom of asking Emma to climb up steps with her present injury, and decide not to continue. My loss, which is preferable to it being hers.

The Prime Minister has once again addressed the nation, daring to delay one of the same nation's favourite television shows- The Great British Bake Off - in order to spread the word. Covid-19 numbers have risen dramatically and we are once again to brace ourselves for high death figures and stricter social isolation. The response to this news on social media is one of disbelief and ridicule, with an undercurrent of irritation and resignation. Nowhere is there even a hint of admiration or allegiance for our elected representative, just a deflated sense of deja vu and despondency. Everyone is simply exhausted, and deeply worried, at the implications for the country's economic future, which will impact directly upon the wellbeing of each individual. Even the millionaires will have to tighten their Rolls Royce seatbelts eventually.

The house is in darkness and I am slightly relieved. I can unload the car and sort out the dogs without needing to worry about how much noise I am making. As I walk into the kitchen I automatically turn on the lights and the electric kettle, taking a mug from the collection stored on top of the microwave and putting three spoonfuls of Earl Grey tea into the yellow and white teapot. Sunflowers are my favourite. The dogs look at me expectantly, wanting their dinner. I feed them quickly, add boiling water to the teapot, and go back outside to finish unloading the car and bring in the collection of shopping bags and overnight cases that have travelled home with me. I start to call for the cats, always slightly anxious about their whereabouts when I've been away from home.

The air is cold and I'm sitting on piles of shingle, shaped by the tides, looking out at the night-time sea. It shines like so much onyx, the dips and troughs of the waves out from shore a moving mixture of sharp edges and softened curves. The moon is just a silvery white smudge behind the clouds, a hint of light in the darkened skies. There is a mist coming in, stretching toward me in silent menace, throwing a blanket of obscurity over the ocean depths. It appears to be solid, but in reality it is just an illusion of substance, millions of water molecules blown on the wind. It is Nature's equivalent of smoke and mirrors. A pathetic fallacy mirroring our own discombobulation over Covid-19, where fact and fiction overwhelm everyone and drown us in fable as we lie winded and gasping for truth.

My mother is sitting on the pebbles beside me, wrapped up in a quilted burgundy full-length coat to keep out the February chill, and my close friend Cat is smoothing out a red tartan rug for us to sit on in more comfort. It's my mother's birthday. All around us the air is a dull impenetrable grey, the thick sea mist engulfing us with salt air and damp cold. Brigadoon is our favourite beach, and we have driven from further inland to celebrate the occasion by the sea.

Cat sits down next to my mother and starts to unpack the plastic shopping bags, until we have a veritable smorgasbord of meats, cheeses, olives, pickles, shellfish and breads before us. I delve into the carrier bag I have beside me and take out three golden goblets, part of my wedding trousseau from years earlier in South Africa. Then I reach into another bag and remove a bottle of Heidsieck Brut, nicely chilled thanks to the cold afternoon air. The gold goblets have drops of moisture on them, glistening as they slide down the metal surface and pool at the base.

We hear muted voices from somewhere nearby and then four figures materialise out of the now thick fog, like ghosts on a theatrical stage covered in dry ice. They look at us in surprise, and then hastily carry on their way without a word, heads down, keeping themselves to themselves, not wanting to intrude, in true English fashion. We laugh, aware of how strange we must look, three women all wrapped up against the late winter weather, with only our faces showing like some lost European refugees, only we are sitting on the beach with a picnic, drinking out of golden goblets, not out on the icy ocean, hungry, lost and alone.

I light a candle and start to sing. It is many years before the tune is used to time our antiviral preventative washing of hands. My mother laughs and smiles, taking her slice of cake on the white china plate and raises a piece to her mouth on the golden fork. More wedding gifts, an entire dinner service of gold cutlery. We raise our goblets and clink them together.

"Cheers! Happy birthday, Darling."

"Thank you," says my mother, " It's been a good day."

Given the temperature, one might be forgiven for thinking that tea would have been more appropriate, hot and piping and served out of a wide mouthed flask insulated to space-station specifications. It would not have had quite the same effect of course, on those transitory passers-by, as golden goblets and champagne. As Baron von Blixen says in Out of Africa,

"It's too cold for anything else."

My own birthday coincides with the date of the French Monarchy's abolition in 1792. I have a French ancestral line going back to the Huguenots, who were only accepted fully in 1789 after the start of the French Revolution. Learning this, I can more deeply understand my father's, and my own, leanings towards socialism. It's in our family genes, blended now in me with centuries of Oriental philosophy and pragmatism.

Fated to repeat itself in close imitations down through future generations like the four nucleotides of our DNA, the double helix spiralling its way through time, twisting, repeating, evolving, revolving, time after time after time, in a near infinite number of mutations yet always confined to the basic four components.

This is the blueprint upon which all the writing of the ages will be written, the backdrop for all of the events and experiences which will shape those who come after me, the base upon which all the flavours of life will imprint themselves and make their lives their own. It is the map upon which all their lives shall cross, their choice of route the only rite of passage. The forks in the road are the only opportunity to take the path less travelled and leave their mark in stone. It is the mutation of our individual Fibonacci sequence, our product based upon the foundations of our pasts.

It might also explain our love of cake...or should that be brioche?

My father is laughing, his eyes twinkling as he holds out his arms and I run towards him with my heart full of joy.

"Happy birthday Darling."

Outside, the wheels of the tumbrils are turning, the status quo is revolving, and Madame Lafarge picks up another stitch.

I close my eyes. In the distance a dog barks and a rooster is starting to crow. How many denials will we dare? It is the best of times, it is the worst of times, and time itself is nothing but a half-remembered song from a dream long ago. There is a tapping in my head, but I cannot remember where it is coming from, or what it means.

Le Fin.

Only it isn't. Not really.

Tomorrow is just another bloody beautiful day in Paradise.

Thank God it's Friday.

The Love Song of J. Alfred Prufrock

T. S. Eliot

Let us go then, you and I,
When the evening is spread out against the sky
Like a patient etherized upon a table;
Let us go, through certain half-deserted streets,
The muttering retreats
Of restless nights in one-night cheap hotels
And sawdust restaurants with oyster-shells:
Streets that follow like a tedious argument
Of insidious intent
To lead you to an overwhelming question ...
Oh, do not ask, "What is it?"
Let us go and make our visit.

In the room the women come and go
Talking of Michelangelo.

The yellow fog that rubs its back upon the window-panes,
The yellow smoke that rubs its muzzle on the window-panes,
Licked its tongue into the corners of the evening,
Lingered upon the pools that stand in drains,
Let fall upon its back the soot that falls from chimneys,
Slipped by the terrace, made a sudden leap,
And seeing that it was a soft October night,

Curled once about the house, and fell asleep.
And indeed there will be time
For the yellow smoke that slides along the street,
Rubbing its back upon the window-panes;
There will be time, there will be time
To prepare a face to meet the faces that you meet;
There will be time to murder and create,
And time for all the works and days of hands
That lift and drop a question on your plate;
Time for you and time for me,
And time yet for a hundred indecisions,
And for a hundred visions and revisions,
Before the taking of a toast and tea.
In the room the women come and go
Talking of Michelangelo.
And indeed there will be time
To wonder, "Do I dare?" and, "Do I dare?"
Time to turn back and descend the stair,
With a bald spot in the middle of my hair —
(They will say: "How his hair is growing thin!")
My morning coat, my collar mounting firmly to the chin,
My necktie rich and modest, but asserted by a simple pin

—

(They will say: "But how his arms and legs are thin!")
Do I dare
Disturb the universe?
In a minute there is time
For decisions and revisions which a minute will reverse.
For I have known them all already, known them all:
Have known the evenings, mornings, afternoons,

I have measured out my life with coffee spoons;
I know the voices dying with a dying fall
Beneath the music from a farther room.
   So how should I presume?

And I have known the eyes already, known them all—
The eyes that fix you in a formulated phrase,
And when I am formulated, sprawling on a pin,
When I am pinned and wriggling on the wall,
Then how should I begin
To spit out all the butt-ends of my days and ways?
   And how should I presume?

And I have known the arms already, known them all—
Arms that are braceleted and white and bare
(But in the lamplight, downed with light brown hair!)
Is it perfume from a dress
That makes me so digress?
Arms that lie along a table, or wrap about a shawl.
   And should I then presume?
   And how should I begin?

Shall I say, I have gone at dusk through narrow streets
And watched the smoke that rises from the pipes
Of lonely men in shirt-sleeves, leaning out of windows?

. . .

I should have been a pair of ragged claws
Scuttling across the floors of silent seas.

And the afternoon, the evening, sleeps so peacefully!
Smoothed by long fingers,
Asleep ... tired ... or it malingers,
Stretched on the floor, here beside you and me.
Should I, after tea and cakes and ices,

Have the strength to force the moment to its crisis?
But though I have wept and fasted, wept and prayed,
Though I have seen my head (grown slightly bald)
brought in upon a platter,
I am no prophet — and here's no great matter;
I have seen the moment of my greatness flicker,
And I have seen the eternal Footman hold my coat, and
snicker,
And in short, I was afraid.

And would it have been worth it, after all,
After the cups, the marmalade, the tea,
Among the porcelain, among some talk of you and me,
Would it have been worth while,
To have bitten off the matter with a smile,
To have squeezed the universe into a ball
To roll it towards some overwhelming question,
To say: "I am Lazarus, come from the dead,
Come back to tell you all, I shall tell you all"—
If one, settling a pillow by her head
Should say: "That is not what I meant at all;
That is not it, at all."

And would it have been worth it, after all,
Would it have been worth while,
After the sunsets and the dooryards and the sprinkled
streets,
After the novels, after the teacups, after the skirts that
trail along the floor—
And this, and so much more?—
It is impossible to say just what I mean!

But as if a magic lantern threw the nerves in patterns on a screen:

Would it have been worth while
If one, settling a pillow or throwing off a shawl,
And turning toward the window, should say:
"That is not it at all,
That is not what I meant, at all."
No! I am not Prince Hamlet, nor was meant to be;
Am an attendant lord, one that will do
To swell a progress, start a scene or two,
Advise the prince; no doubt, an easy tool,
Deferential, glad to be of use,
Politic, cautious, and meticulous;
Full of high sentence, but a bit obtuse;
At times, indeed, almost ridiculous—
Almost, at times, the Fool.
I grow old ... I grow old ...
I shall wear the bottoms of my trousers rolled.

Shall I part my hair behind? Do I dare to eat a peach?
I shall wear white flannel trousers, and walk upon the beach.

I have heard the mermaids singing, each to each.
I do not think that they will sing to me.
I have seen them riding seaward on the waves
Combing the white hair of the waves blown back
When the wind blows the water white and black.
We have lingered in the chambers of the sea
By sea-girls wreathed with seaweed red and brown
Till human voices wake us, and we drown.

DAY EIGHT

Coffee spoons.

There is a soft knock on the door and the hounds explode into frenzied barking. It's very late for visitors. I walk into the kitchen and undo the top of the stable door. My Future stands before me, arms laden with sunflowers and roses. It is a smile I have not seen for a very long time. I place my coffee cup on the kitchen counter behind me and open the door. We look at one another for a lifetime in seconds, our eyes tinged with the melancholy of past moments lost and laughter unheard. Then we smile.

I take a step back.

Windmills of the Mind.

Round like a circle in a spiral, like a wheel within a wheel
  Never ending or beginning on an ever spinning reel
  Like a snowball down a mountain, or a carnival balloon
  Like a carousel that's turning running rings around the moon
  Like a clock whose hands are sweeping past the minutes of its face
  And the world is like an apple whirling silently in space
  Like the circles that you find in the windmills of your mind.
  Like a tunnel that you follow to a tunnel of its own
  Down a hollow to a cavern where the sun has never shone
  Like a door that keeps revolving in a half forgotten dream
  Or the ripples from a pebble someone tosses in a stream
  Like a clock whose hands are sweeping past the minutes of its face
  And the world is like an apple whirling silently in space
  Like the circles that you find in the windmills of your mind.
  Keys that jingle in your pocket, words that jangle in your head
  Why did summer go so quickly, was it something that you said?
  Lovers walk along a shore and leave their footprints in the sand

Is the sound of distant drumming just the fingers of your hand?

Pictures hanging in a hallway and the fragment of a song

Half remembered names and faces, but to whom do they belong?

When you knew that it was over you were suddenly aware

That the autumn leaves were turning to the color of her hair.

Like a circle in a spiral, like a wheel within a wheel

Never ending or beginning on an ever spinning reel

As the images unwind, like the circles that you find

In the windmills of your mind.

Noel Harrison

I am five years old and standing in a large candle-lit church. I am about to be christened and become an official member of the Church of England. There are other children there but they are dressed like angels, in flowing floor length white robes, holding in front of themselves a tall white candle while singing a hymn. They are walking around the outside of the pews, close to the outside wall of the building, cheeks rosy and eyes aglow, singing their hearts out to the glory of the Lord.

In the background I can hear a tap tap tap, is that the Lord knocking on my heart, waiting to come in? Tap, tap, tap.

On Nana's bedside table there is a picture called The Light of the World. It depicts Christ standing at an overgrown and long unopened cottage door, a halo of light behind his head and a lantern held in his left hand as he raises his right to knock. The door has no handle and can thus only be opened from the inside.

It is an allegory painted by William Holman Hunt and illustrates the Biblical verses of Revelation 3:20: "Behold, I stand at the door and knock; if any man hear My voice, and open the door, I will come in to him, and will sup with him, and he with Me".

I open my eyes.

Bailey is hungry, and tapping to come in. Outside, the predawn sky is still black, and there is a large chunk of white light high up in the heavens that I think is Venus. It shines like the proverbial diamond, and I wonder whether it is the celestial body or the International Space Station basking in the sun. Bailey comes in covered in moisture and settles down at his bowl on the windowsill. Piri and Yoda are still curled up into crescent moons asleep. The sky starts to lighten and as it does, Venus slowly disappears from sight, a daily reminder of all the metaphors about hidden light behind the clouds that can come with the dawn. I like to think that Venus, with her energy of Love, does truly shine out and permeate everything we do here on this small speck of blue in the immense universe. It's a comforting thought.

As outside starts to come into focus, I gaze out and watch the increased movement between the trellises and plant pots. The birds have started to return in their numbers now and my patio feeders are once again laden with many of the little beasts, coal tits and blue tits, robins, chaffinches and even the odd wren. The larger birds have not yet started to join in, the cornucopia of natural food in our hedgerows still enough to keep them all fed. Yoda almost ignores the birds now, and even Piri no longer stalks them all with malice aforethought, her youthful predatory behaviour tempered by the passage of time.

The plants seem to have acquired a new lease on life, confused by the year's irregular seasons, and are now blooming anew as if Spring had sprung. The lavender has recovered from its uprooting and the geraniums are in flower, white ones for my mother, deep blood red ones for me. Next year's delphiniums are ahead of the game, those on MJ's grave striving upwards and the ones outside the cottage drowning in leaves the size of small dinner-plates. Nasturtiums poke out of hiding places with splashes of yellow and orange. On the opposite side of the road the Virginia Creeper admonishes all of them for their idiocy with its own scarlet blaze of glory, the long tendrils festooned with leaves the colour of rich tapestries and autumnal fruit.

The moon is a bright orange sickle lying on her back, the last feature of the Cheshire Cat beaming as the sky changes partners and the sun rises.

I need to get out of bed and start the day. Lots needs doing.

Standing, looking over the gate at the peaceful Devonshire countryside. Sparkle and Darcy are grazing, the sky is blue and it is warm for mid-October. My heart is sad and happy, sad because today I say Bon Voyage to Darcy, happy because I have found him the perfect home. Two friends are going to join me in case there are problems loading the young horse into a small lorry, and I am distantly aware that time is ticking.

Darcy, aka Dante when he arrived, has grown over the past few months, changing from a baby to an adolescent, filled out and taller, paler in colour and more confident. I am going to miss him, and I know in my heart that if he stays here with me for the winter that he will then never leave me, and that wouldn't really be the right path. Instead, I have saved his life, and for that I am profoundly grateful. When he was offered to me, I felt that Tarac sent him to me so that Dante wouldn't be shot, and now we are here, with Darcy's whole future before him, and a wonderful, happy future it will be too. His new owner will keep him on the same yard that his mother now lives on, what a fairy-tale ending to the story. Still, my heart is sad for me, and I cannot help but cry silently when I think about him leaving. It's the price we pay when we part from those we love.

My friends join me and we chat while waiting for the transporter to arrive, which she does promptly on time. Darcy behaves impeccably, loading onto the small van with barely a hesitation, totally trusting. I can't stop myself from crying more, even though I know he will be much loved and treasured in his new home. I hope he knows, I hope he can sense the love I feel for him, I hope his future will be a bright one.

And then he is gone, and after waving my friends on their way, Sparkle and I stand side by side in the field, my arms around her neck under the cool autumnal sun, my face wet with tears.

I'm kneeling in the mud. It's Christmas Day and I've been here since early morning trying to get my mare Minerva to stand up. He of the Sex Chair is on his knees beside me, and my son is standing on the other side of half a tonne of horseflesh trying to rock her onto her breastbone. It's a disaster in the making, and will soon come to a tragic end.

The call came through to my mobile as we were driving to the yard to feed the horses first thing before starting the preparations for Christmas lunch. I sat in the Jeep listening with growing alarm as the landowner tells me that one of my horses has trapped herself under one side of the stables, and is lying flat out with her head and neck outside in the mud, her body on the other side of the wooden stabling. We are luckily only five minutes away when the call comes through. I call my son for backup, rousing him from his bed hours earlier than usual, and explain the situation. He joins us less than twenty minutes later.

Minerva is a quarter of a century old and came to me from a yard in Newmarket twenty-one years ago. I bought her on sight without bothering to ride her, knowing that we would be a perfect fit, and I was right. She is the most beautiful racing Thoroughbred that I have ever known, blue-black with a fine white lightning strike that runs down the centre of the head, which is why I renamed her Minerva-Goddess of Wisdom and Lightning Bolts. Today she is lying on her side, pinned down as a result of her having kicked the stable wall outwards and it closing back down onto her with a vice-like grip. We will never really know the reason for her being on the stable floor and kicking out. Tarac stands to one side watching. They have been together for over twenty years, the last fifteen sharing a field.

The Man of the Chair and my son together manage to tear the wooden partition off from its frame and Minerva drags herself out of the stable and across the concrete apron and into the mud. We roll huge plastic-covered bales of haylage to support her in what is now a kneeling position, but we can't convince her to stand. Once or twice she manages to get her front legs out in front of her body but her hind legs are completely unresponsive.

The vet comes relatively quickly for a Christmas Day callout and tells me that we need to get her onto her brisket and that she may stand up once the feeling comes back into her legs. Then he leaves us, surrounded by mud, shattered dreams and deepening despair.

It is a long day that follows, hour after hour after hour. My partner tells me that I have completely ruined what might well prove to be the last Christmas he shares with both of his aged parents. I do not reply. Eventually, as the light starts to fade and the temperatures start to plummet, I come to the realisation that I am not going to be able to convince Minerva to stand, that I am going to have to give up and ask the vet to return and put an end to the day.

Half an hour later he rattles up in his old battered Land Rover that looks as bedraggled as I feel. His two Springer Spaniels look out of the back expectantly, and he plods across the field from the gate to join us.

He looks down at Minerva and shakes his head.

"You could have saved us all a lot of trouble if you'd just had her shot this morning."

I say nothing.

The Man replies tartly, "I don't really think she needs to hear that right now, do you?"

The vet kneels in front of Minerva and reaches into his medicine case.

"Are you sending her to the hounds?"

He asks me this to know whether she should be shot or whether I want her injected with barbiturates which will render her flesh inedible and therefore it will cost more to get rid of the body.

"I don't want her shot," I reply.

He looks at me with disdain and starts to fill the syringe with liquid death.

I'm standing and then I'm not. Within minutes her heart has stopped. The vet reaches over and flicks Minerva's open eyes with his thumb and forefinger twice.

"Please don't do that!" I cry out.

He looks at me again with a hint of disgust, gets up and walks away. The sky is almost dark and there's this deep, dull ache starting to rise up from the pit of my belly, filling my chest and tightening my throat.

My son looks at me and says quietly,

"For what it's worth Mum, you did the right thing." Then he walks away into the darkness and gets into his car.

"I'll see you later," he adds. "I'm sorry."

My Beloved and I return to the Jeep and drive back to his house. It's ten o'clock on Christmas Day 2011, and we haven't eaten anything since dawn. I walk as if in a trance, numbed by the events of the day and the sadness which follows. He turns on the television and sits down on the sofa before looking at me. I am sitting on the floor at his feet with my head on his knees in a morass of grief and exhaustion.

"I think it's my turn to have some attention." He unzips his fly and looks at me,

"After all, it is Christmas and the day has been completely spoiled."

I look up at him in stunned disbelief before slowly getting to my feet and starting to walk out of the room.

"Suyen, wait."

I stop and turn around, and I can see from the expression on his face that he knows, knows that he has crossed a line, and I know that I should forgive him, but a part of me starts to die inside as I recognise how far apart we must be at this very moment. We will never again be as close or as far apart, and my world will be turned upside down in the months to follow and my heart broken and my soul betrayed. Would it all have been different if I had stopped walking?

"Thank you for all of your help today. I'm sorry if I ruined your possibly last Christmas with your parents, it really wasn't intentional.

Merry Christmas, Darling."

Outside in the cold, crisp night air I start to cry.

It's the price we pay when we part from those we love.

The sky is clear as far as the eye can see and the air is very hot and dry. The wagons rumble along the dried-out earth and scare up insects under the African sky. My grandmother's Great Grandmother is sleeping quietly in her cradle, the movement of the wagon keeping her peacefully asleep. Under the canvas awning the temperature rises as the glaring sun rises and bakes everything that lies beneath it, conversation is muted as fatigue and the constant daily hardships wear everyone down. The wagon train is heading north, searching for a place to call home. The oxen are lean and weary, like their masters.

Suddenly, out of that vast expanse that is the African Veldt, a group of African tribesmen are seen running towards the settlers. These are the Zulu Impi, a growing movement of warriors led by the now famous Shaka Zulu. The settlers raise the alarm and try quickly to form a ring with their wagons, but the dozen oxen pulling these mobile homes, laden with cloths and pans and precious crockery from the Motherland, are tired and slow and unyielding, however much they are whipped by their terrified drivers. Soon the ground is littered with the mutilated bodies of men and women and children, the dogs lie speared through their sides and the oxen gaze upwards forlornly as the light leaves their eyes.

The battle scarcely deserves the name, it is a total massacre and when the Impi leave there is only the buzzing of flies and the odd groan from a dying horse to be heard on the wind. The wheels of the burning wagons creak as they turn in ever slower circles, and the blood clots and dries beneath the bodies of the dead and dying.

Only one of the travelling Europeans survives, the tiny infant asleep in her cradle, who will later be discovered and rescued by a family from another laager that has travelled undetected. She will live with her rescuers and marry at thirteen years of age. Her husband is sixteen. Maria Johanna will live for almost another six decades.

The year is 1816.

On the other side of the world, the air is hot, heavy and humid in Whampoa, and the docks are full of people, all hustling and bustling, laden down with bundles and packages, the luckier ones carrying their worldly goods in battered leather cases. The boat lies against the wooden jetty, her hull low in the water, and the crowds of people sweat under the South China sun.

Most of the men and women are indentured to work on the sugar estates in British Guyana, and my great great grandparents are among them, destined for the Eliza and Mary Plantation in the Demerara region of Guyana. The year is 1865, and they walk up the gangplank of The Pride of the Ganges leaving behind everything and everyone they know, their family, their friends, their cultural roots and the centuries behind them. All their worldly goods are in the bags that they carry.

One hundred years later their grandson will be one of the wealthiest men in Jamaica, a self-made millionaire with land and property all over the world. His son Hugh will become a Doctor, as will his daughter also, and she will lend my son the money to carpet his home when the house he moves into has only concrete floors.

The air is hot, heavy and humid, and my mother is brushing dust off of her light pink lace cocktail suit, one she made especially for the occasion. The lace is handmade and comes from Brussels. The ship, MV Aureol, lies waiting in the harbour as the VIP guests board and make their way to the State Cabin where my parents are hosting their farewell drinks party. Fourteen years of living in Monrovia are ending as the new President Tolbert struggles to maintain the equilibrium of his predecessor.

President Tubman died over two years ago in a hospital in London, and the undercurrents of upheaval and corruption are growing stronger; my father knows that it is time to move elsewhere. Before the end of the decade a certain Sergeant Doe will stage a bloody and violent coup d'état that will leave him head of the nation. People will be beheaded on the beaches and left to rot on the sand. We will know some of the dead. My mother is having to pay over four hundred dollars a month to officials under the table just to keep her businesses open with access to water and electricity. The year is 1973.

As she leaves the Immigration Counter my mother is stopped by officials at the boarding gate and told that she cannot leave the country as she has "insulted the flag."

This is politico speak for "We want you to pay us more tax or we will put you in jail." She tells my father to board without her and welcome the friends who are now waiting expectantly on the quay, while she drives into Monrovia with our accountant and our lawyer - who also works for the Presidential Office as a financial advisor- and sorts something out. My father agrees and goes on board to pop some champagne corks.

The Captain of the vessel reminds him that once the ship has pulled out of the harbour my mother will be costing the Elder Dempster company $1500 an hour. My father pours himself another drink and refills the glasses of our friends. The aged dark oak panelling looks on at the well dressed guests and catered food. The panelling will creak for the entire Atlantic voyage, keeping both my parents from a decent night's sleep and belying the assumption that you get what you pay for.

Five hours and several hundred dollars later, my mother returns to the port. She is whisked onto a coast guard cutter and taken out to the ship lying offshore. The only way onto the Aureol is up the modern equivalent of a rope ladder, which my mother starts to climb, models' case in one hand and four-inch stilettos on her feet. The First Officer comes down the ladder to meet her and takes the case from her. To this day I cannot work out how he carried it at the same time as climbing up the ladder.

"Don't drop that!" My mother exclaims, "Let me fall if I slip, but hang onto that case! It has all of our gold inside it."

The tapestries hang from the ceiling of the Great Hall and the silver and gold threads reflect the sunlight that streams in through the leaded glass windows. Ockwells sits in its own acreage of some four hundred acres, one of the best examples in England of a classic Tudor manor, and belongs to my great-uncle, Patrick Chung. He is the self-made millionaire with estates in Jamaica and here in Royal Berkshire. It is his grandmother and grandfather who boarded the Pride of the Ganges just under a century ago. It is 1963 and I am five years old.

Ockwells is not a particularly large building, arranged in classic style around a small, rose-filled courtyard, but the imposing Great Hall dwarfs me with its singular long table and huge open fireplace. My father brings the logs into the hall with a small tractor and leaves them uncut in the hearth. The entire family eats here, Uncle Pat and his wife and several children, my parents and myself. Occasionally relatives join us and, once, a famous author came to view again the famous building he had previously seen and written about in the nineteen forties.

The gardens are sculpted and impressive, and the stables immense, with many boxes that now stand empty.

Christmas here is a delight, a traditional array of open log fires, tall Christmas trees, polished copper pans and candle-lit rooms. The year we live here it snows heavily, and the picture is complete. Not long afterwards Pat would sell Ockwells, tired of paying taxes on it in two countries. I revisit Ockwells decades later, with a set of unique seventeenth century leather wall tiles under my arm which I hope to sell to the current owner.

The story goes that the wall coverings were bought in the late 1800's by the gentleman who rebuilt and refurbished Ockwells at that time- creating a masterpiece out of a ruin- from an old woman on the quay in Paris. The tiles were said to come from the Spanish Embassy in Mexico City. Regardless, the present-day Lord of the Manor does not want them, and I leave no richer than when I arrived.

I am sitting at the top of the stairs in my home surrounded by a large collection of historic family photographs. They are mainly black and white or sepia prints and show handsome well dressed men and women looking at the camera with a smile just visibly playing on their faces. These are the faces of my father's family, that track back across time and continents, taking in the diamond mines of Kimberley, the American Civil War - fighting for The North, the Dutch Voortrekkers of South Africa, the banished Huguenots of France, WWII fighter pilots, wartime casualties and my father's own travels from Cape to Cairo by bicycle and the return trip across the Sahara escorting two land rovers for the English gentry.

My mother's family has gifted me far fewer photographic memories.

Her mother died when my mother was three years old, and other than the discoveries around her great grandparents and two pictures of herself as a child with her mother in Georgetown, there is nothing.

I look at the collection and scoop them up. I am packing them into boxes and throwing away whole suitcases full of people I cannot identify. The year is 2007. I have moved into a town after living with my children for several years in the countryside as I feel that they are now in need of a more urban environment. Living in the proverbial middle of nowhere is fine until teenagers want access to trains and city centres.

This house is next to the train station but built so that the sound of the engines float unheard over the roof slates. A local philanthropist from Victorian times built the house, placing it on top of the river that used to power the mill next door. Now we have our own private wannabe cistern under our home, and in the summer I quietly wish that I could use the underground water to swim in.

Seven years later I move again back into the rural beauty of Devon, this time living on my own with only my cats and dogs for company. It is the seventh house move in eleven years, and each time I move with dozens of plants and hundreds of books. My ex-lover, he of The Sex Chair fame, used to express his bewilderment at how much I would move from house to house, not understanding that I was moving homes, and taking the history of several generations with me.

This rural idyll has the most wonderful south-facing outdoor decking, the sun visible all year from sunrise to sunset. Ellisar has the use of a six acres field behind the house, and he explores the space independently most evenings, causing my heart rate to often speed up as I imagine the worst when he does not respond immediately to my call.

Today I am lifting boxes and packing them into my car. I live on the coast now, having finally found my haven by the sea. My home is the epitome of a witch's cottage, with low ceilings and darkened beams and tiny doors that men have to stoop down to fit through.

It is 2020 and my grandchildren are moving with their mother to another village, and I have offered to help move the small fragile objects that we decorate our lives with. My son has spent the last ten hours painting the new house, and can now barely move his right arm, but he is not yet allowed to be there with his family unsupervised. I seethe inwardly at the injustice of it all. Small steps. We can at least spend time with the children now, all allegations declared false and dropped, but Social Services are reluctant to admit to their fallibility, and so we await the final hearing several weeks hence. First we have to navigate other court appearances, each more frustrating than the last, and our self-resolve struggles against the ceaseless whittling away of security and familial life.

As I drive away from the new house, provided by the tax money of the working masses, I find myself fighting despair, as I wonder what the future holds for my son, so totally committed to this woman of his dreams who is herself so wounded by her past lives. I try hard not to panic as I conjure up the Ghosts of the Past that could so easily become the Spectres of their Future.

The children have definitely paid a heavy price and now watch bewildered as they see their father drive away with the allocated Family Practitioner after every visit. My heart weeps as the three year old cries silently into my shoulder when my son is no longer to be seen or heard, and she wakes in the night calling his name and tells me "I don't want Daddy to go to work," work being the euphemism used to forgive his absence.

When I arrive back at home, my son and I have a long discussion about the whole appalling situation that has become his daily nightmare. Seven months under the same roof and we can now talk with one another. Most days. It's a tough shout sharing a house with your mother when you are used to a home of your own and there are times when I have learnt to keep silent and just let him rant against the injustice of it all without interrupting.

Sometimes we all need the silence. As a mother I understand that he has to sort out his own problems if he is going to have self-respect, and all that I can do is offer him any support that he is happy to accept.

My daughter phones. Her house sale has fallen through with only twenty-four hours before Completion. We are both devastated by the news as she and her husband have already contracted to buy another house. I can hear the sadness and disappointment in her voice, although she tries to play it down. The would-be buyers offer no explanation other than they have decided it is a "bad time to buy." The implications around the sale falling through are huge- new schools are already sorted and the logistics around not being able to honour their commitment to the new property.

We discuss Christmas and the implications around seeing one another around the Covid-19 Rule of Six. Christmas is a time for Sharing. Will the Tory Government allow us to share time with each other?

By December we will have endured nine months of the Covid-19 virus and the restrictions it has imposed upon people and their everyday lives. Many are looking with dread at the approaching months of winter, with the dark mornings and early nightfalls. Even I have noticed that Bailey climbs out of the window each morning under a dark sky, and that the evening stars can be seen before eight at night. The stats tell us that mental health issues and rates of suicide are climbing steeply every month as despair and despondency claim the joy from people's hearts and souls. It is a difficult time, that time when all of our surfaces are stripped away to the blood and gore within. Not everyone survives.

When the doctors shout for hot water and towels in films, I always assumed it was to help with the actual birth of a child in some way. Years later I read that the hot water and towels were actually for the Doctor and the Midwife to wash their hands clean, not for the mother and child at all. I wonder if our Prime Minister realised that all along.

I am sitting on an air-conditioned coach looking out at a crowd of Egyptians that have crowded around the vehicle. Most of them are men, all holding up to the windows of our coach some local artefact or piece of food or bottle of recycled water for us to buy. My daughter sits beside me, She of The Million Camels.

At the front of the crowd, barely able to be seen, is a tiny little girl, holding a travel sized packet of tissues. I can hear her high-pitched voice shouting over the deeper rumble of the men,

"You buy? You want? Very cheap! You buy?"

She looks barely six years old, thin and covered with the grime of poverty, stunningly beautiful with her blue-grey eyes and sun-kissed burnished blond hair. She could grace the cover of Vogue in ten years if a professional photographer ever comes here. I am reminded of the Afghani green-eyed girl who featured on the cover of National Geographic, captured on cellulose by Steve McCurry in the refugee camps of Pakistan in 1985.

Her desperation reaches out beyond her own imploring arms, stretched upwards towards the windows of the coach and its relatively wealthy tourists. My daughter just looks at me, her eyes full of pain, and as she stands up to get off the coach our driver starts the engine and we move. I peer through the dirty sand and dust-blasted glass of my window and watch as she becomes smaller and disappears into the past. A packet of travel tissues we failed to buy. My heart is crying, the sun blazes down and the wheels of the bus- they go round and round, like so many lifetimes. Like so many lost chances to make a difference.

My daughter sits down beside me. We both know what we have seen. We are so blessed.

A packet of travel tissues. A meal no longer possible.

Back onboard our Nile cruiser, dinner is about to be served. In an effort to honour the foreign passengers, the chefs have created an "English Menu." As we file past the tasty delights heaped in highly polished silver serving dishes I notice that they are all labelled and that one has the words "Fish Pie" displayed in front of it.

I stop and look at the Chef standing on the other side of the table, looking quite splendid in his Chef's Whites and tall hat.

"What type of fish is in the pie?" I ask.

He looks at me and beams happily,

"No fish, Madam, no fish."

Travel. It broadens the mind.

The golden cross in my hand was a gift from my parents when I turned thirteen, a celebration as it were of my coming of age, as in puberty not voting rights. It is a beautifully crafted piece of jewellery, fashioned after a classic Agadez design, and made by one of the best Lebanese goldsmiths in Monrovia. It is also the last piece of gold jewellery that my mother handed down to me, the others all sold to keep the wolves from the door and now lost to posterity.

I am trying to decide on how I can hang onto it and keep it within the family, as my bills rise and my wages are clipped by the C-19 pandemic. Eventually I decide to swallow my pride, not for the first time, and ask one of my longest standing friends whether he will lend me the scrap metal value of the cross- just over three hundred pounds- if I hand the cross over to him as collateral. He is one of my closest friends.

I am nervous about asking him as he has made it very clear in the past that he sees me as a bad apple when it comes to how I manage my finances, even though I myself have helped him often in his past lives when he struggled with alcohol addiction and depression. Unlike myself, he has now inherited wealth, and lives comfortably at home not having worked for several years. His mother was extremely fond of me, and often alluded to what a perfect couple her son and myself would make. I sometimes wonder if he was jealous of the high regard and love she bore for me, and that this is his way of subtly getting some sort of revenge.

Nonetheless, I bite the bullet and send him the email requesting help, offering a monthly repayment plus interest. A couple of days later I receive my reply, he is happy to lend me the money- for which I am grateful- but only once I have paid him the hundred that I am currently scheduled to pay him next month.

My daughter is appalled at his behaviour, and wonders out loud about the money we used to give him when he could barely walk into the supermarket only a few years earlier. It doesn't really matter, I learnt long ago that the English have an odd attitude around money, and the lending or borrowing of it. My mother used to say that the English treat money like a dirty word, not liking to lower themselves by admitting that it is an integral part of their lives.

I think it is based in a society that is still fundamentally feudal, and all that implies. We all want to be aristocrats, who have no need to think about money or worry about their bills. When we cannot own that financial reality we feel a certain depth of shame at our lack of monetary independence, and at the same time embarrassed by friends who may themselves have failed to succeed in the capitalist world we live in.

We become embarrassed by our own relative success compared to our poor friends, while at the same time slightly disgusted by their poverty. We make a moral judgement about how people in need must not have wanted to be any other way, or have not worked and applied themselves hard enough to climb the rungs of the social ladder.

It is a harsh and ungenerous point of view, which we recognise in the deepest depths of our soul, and so we are all conflicted, filled simultaneously with self-loathing and disgust while we preen our whiskers and swallow the double cream, stepping over the cold, homeless individuals in our high street shop doorways while we order the latest smartphone without missing a single step.

I use the Royal "We" of course, because I am generalising to a fault. People have started to awaken, they do dig deep into their pockets to support the needy- donating millions to charities and good causes, brave men and women and children with special medical needs. The scale of the anonymity is a buffer, it allows good deeds without the embarrassment of a personal connection. It allows a sense of self-gratification too. Just as giving your friends and relatives the gift of your giving helps you to feel good about yourself, even if it is usually done on the assumption that the recipient wants to support your own generosity by going without themselves.

I prefer to be far more direct with my gifts, and I object strongly to anyone assuming that they know which good causes I want to support with their money. I have lost a friend or two over that.

My cross has returned to me, and now hangs with my other necklaces from the top of the oak mirror that graces the dressing-table that once belonged to my mother-in-law. It is exquisite, and despite the humiliation of having to provide collateral for a friend to lend me some money, at least it still belongs to me, and by extension, my family. There are few heirlooms left now, the diamonds and gold necklaces and bracelets all sold except for my charm bracelet which I have given to my eldest granddaughter.

We have a piece of ivory too, twenty-two kilos of exquisite African beauty that my father bought from an old man in a bar in Monrovia several decades ago. She rests for now in Canada, hidden under a bed wrapped in environmental shame, until I can find a way to liberate her and place her onto the open market. Ironically, Canada is the only country where I may still sell the sculpture legally, and so I begin to cast the crumbs onto the universal waters, waiting to see whether they can attract any serious Art collectors.

My father's stainless-steel vintage Omega is the only other piece of value, and I hope to hand it over to my son when he turns forty. His own father's watch and other gold jewelry that he wore constantly disappeared after his death, and none of the extended family can, or will, tell me where it all went.

My phone beeps. It is a text message from someone responding to an ad I posted offering a Victorian glass painting for sale. The painting is painted in reverse on the underside of the glass and is a charming depiction of a young girl with her spaniel, who is looking longingly at a piece of cake. The buyer is in her eighties and would like the painting for her elderly husband, as it reminds her of one that was given to them by her own grandmother, but which was stolen years ago.

I am thrilled to place it in such an appreciative and loving home.

My head is reeling with everything that needs to be addressed-

Christmas.

Christmas with impact from new Covid-19 restrictions... (Where do I go? Stay? So much sadness at what should be a special time filled with love and joy.)

House moves. Two of them. Both now in chaos and confusion. So much heartache all around me. So much of it undeserved.

Pep talk from publishing guru. (As if I wouldn't have already done the whole Artists and Writers Yearbook thing.... I'm so old I know what it is!.... Oh for the days when we would be writers didn't also have to be IT buffs. Oh for the money to have a PA to do it for me! Or an agent- how people like the Guru make their living.)

Catching up with social media pages... (Having to tear myself away from the things I want to do because I need to work. Hate it.)

Creating a new group page on FB around my Life Coaching. (Must get the logo design produced properly somehow. Who to ask? Cannot afford to hire anyone's services. Everything is so much easier if you can throw money at it.)

Creating a Social Media page around the actual process of trying to write a book. (Brilliant idea of Guru's)

Learn how to use Twitter. (REALLY need to do this if I want a larger presence on social media. AARGH)

Saturday on childminding duty. Most days now on duty of some sort. No one else to support my daughter-in-law.

Birthdays this month...(Where do i find the money to buy presents?)

Visit Glastonbury. (Will be good to feel the Energy there and buy some candles and oils.... Am I being frivolous?)

Ask Universe for Darcy's possible replacement. (Should I find a companion for Sparkle? Can I really afford to maintain a second horse? All the sanctuaries are full.)

The tiny room looks like a hoarder's dream, the entire floor covered with cardboard boxes of many sizes, large bags full of other bags, and a myriad of suitcases and containers. I can barely open the door to get into the room myself, and even the double bed is covered in an assortment of clothing still on hangers, piles of cuddly toys, loose books and stacks of tied together papers.

My daughter arrives in three days with her family for the Christmas season, and I have only just taken on this new tenancy. Downstairs the dogs are shut into the kitchen to try and maintain some degree of order, and the three cats are temporarily imprisoned in the bathroom so that I do not lose them to the calm outdoors. I can vaguely hear my friend saying to herself that there is no way I will ever be able to sort and fit everything in.

"Nonsense!" I counter, "Of course it will all fit in."

Everyone arrives in a couple of days and they will need to have somewhere to sleep. Including both of my own children, their partners and their children, myself and my friends, twelve of us will be sitting down for Christmas lunch.

" Hope I have enough chairs......."

The fireplace in the Old Cottage was a tiny one, now made larger with the recent renovations. The smell of woodsmoke mixed with burning coal gives the living-room a warmth that matches the temperature. Gone are the days of my childhood when we would wrap ourselves in several layers and see our breath in the kitchen before the fire was lit in the mornings. Back then there was only cold water and we washed with the lukewarm remains from inside the hot water bottles.

Now the New Cottage has all the mod cons, and the open fire is as much for the atmosphere as for heating the house.

Nana brings out a handful of silver cutlery and gives it to me. The table at which we shall all sit is darkened oak, an oval gate-leg table that no one will want years ahead when she dies. Dark wood is no longer popular by then. The table is covered with a linen tablecloth hand stitched and pulled by Nana in her childhood, helped by her mother and her grandmother.

I can see them in my mind's eye, three generations of women sitting on one of those deep wraparound verandas that were so popular in twentieth century East Africa, where families could sit and watch the rain fall while keeping dry, heads bowed as they teased out the threads to form intricate patterns in the linen. A tall pitcher of cooled juice stands on a silver tray on the coffee table around which they sit, and they are laughing, amused by the antics of a young Madeline perhaps, sharing the joy.

I place the silver in the correct positions around the family china, a deep blue Belmont service, made by JHW & Sons. in the late 1800's. It belonged to Nana's in-laws, and is used for all roast meals as it is the only porcelain in the Cottage that can accommodate a large joint with all of the trimmings. The polished silver gleams brightly and reflects the flames from the fire into the room, the sparkling lights competing with the crystal wine glasses. In the centre of the table lie branches of holly and ivy, trailing the length of the placings and bringing a breath of ancient pagan forests into the room. It is Christmas.

Behind me I can hear my two young children chattering to my parents. My father is explaining to my six-year-old son how to hold his sherry glass and my mother is telling my eight year old daughter how to fold dinner napkins. Nana is in the kitchen putting the final touches to the vegetables and finishing off the best gravy in the whole world. Leighton, her husband and one true love, is topping up everyone's sherry glasses and handing around a small glass dish of salted peanuts. The two cats are sleeping on the hearth in front of the fire and the atmosphere is one of total calm. Total magic. Tammy, the white rabbit, lies also asleep in front of the fire, her head resting on my father's leather slippers.

Across the top of the fireplace hanging from a piece of green twine, tiny Christmas stockings made out of felt and decorated to look like woodland creatures, jostle for position with a thick strand of red tinsel and baubles hanging up in groups. The mantelpiece is festooned with branches of fresh pine and small fir cones, interspersed with Christmas

314

robins and hand-blown glass animals. Christmas cards have been arranged by my father in long lengths that fall from the ceiling to just above the floor, joined by glittering red ribbon, and Nana has draped gold tinsel around the candle holders on the bookcases.

A small tree stands in the corner of the room that looks out of the wide plate glass windows, sharing its charm and beauty with the world outside. On the top of the tree is a silver star, an ancient relic from years long gone by when Nana was still wearing high heels and my father prayed before bedtime kneeling beside his bed. On the radio carols are playing and all of us start to sing along quietly, me remembering the descents from years spent singing in choirs as a child.

Nana comes out of the kitchen and puts the vegetable tureens on the table, everything glistens under a healthy layer of melted butter. Next she brings out two gravy boats brimming with sheer deliciousness, and then Leighton carries in a small turkey, roasted to perfection and surrounded on the platter with small roasted onions, roast parsnips and glazed honeyed carrots. It is a veritable feast, fit for any King.

"Yaaaay!" Shout the children, and my father puts his arm around his mother,

"Looks tremendous, Mom."

I find the bottle of champagne in the fridge and pop the cork,

"Here's to the Cook" we all cry.

"Here's to my Cooks" adds George, enveloping Nana in a huge hug. Cooks is his nickname for my grandmother.

"Merry Christmas Everyone," says my mother, and we all raise our glasses and echo the sentiment.

"May we have some?" Asks my daughter.

"Of course you may- just a sip though."

We sit down and pull at the shiny red and gold crackers, their tiny bangs making the children squeal with delight. We unfold and position the paper crowns upon our heads, turning into Royalty eating at the High Table while the peasants and the dogs scrabble for scraps on the floor beneath us. Beside the cheap plastic toy inside the now dissected crackers lies a scrap of paper with a Mot Juste typed upon it.

I pick mine up- All the world will welcome you- and am struck by how pertinent that is.

I watch as my mother pours out a tiny amount of champagne into the two tiny sherry glasses and hands them to my Little People. I am overwhelmed with love and gratitude and peace and happiness. Overwhelmed by the ability of families to pull together, to forgive indiscretions and heartache. Overwhelmed by how such simple things can mean so terribly much. Overwhelmed by our sheer ability to endure great hardship and grief and still remain unsullied by bitterness or regrets. Overwhelmed by how easy it is to find our blessings if we would but open ourselves up to accept them. I look around the table and smile.

"Merry Christmas Darlings, I love you all so much."

"And I DO know what that means," adds my father as he pulls me towards him and kisses my cheek. He and my mother reach out across the table and join hands.

"Merry Christmas Darling."

316

The rain slashes through the potted plants and the hedgerows opposite to my cottage with a vengeance. Storm Barbara I think it's been dubbed. Why do we feel we need to name our weather events? And who chooses which name? The misguided geraniums and meadowsweet buds shake from side to side as the wind gusts up the valley. On the patio my birdfeeders are dancing a maddened fanatella of their own, and any leaves stubbornly gripping tightly to the peach and hazel trees are now sodden splashes of washed out colour under the terracotta pots. The solar powered fountain lies dormant, the sky a heavy bank of indigo clouds.

Parts of the country are in a Firebreak Lockdown-seventeen days in Wales where social distancing is just the tip of the iceberg, and financial ruin is only a few weeks away as people come to the end of subsidised government pay-outs.

The sea is raging. A storm has risen up overnight and the howling wind and rampant waves crashing onto the land mirror the public responses to the latest Covid-19 Instructions from our government. Wales is leading the way and has released its dragons. Supermarkets are forbidden to sell "Non-Essential Items", this includes children's clothing but not alcohol and cigarettes. Members of Parliament have voted to stop providing children in need of Free School Meals with any food from schools over the half term holiday. Jobs are going to be lost at the end of the month when Furlough Payments come to an end.

The sky is a pale mustard, a jaundiced pall over the land. Ellisar and Emma close their eyes as they head into the wind, their steps faltering against the momentum of the natural power of the storm. I walk deep in thought beside them, wondering where this journey will eventually end.

Will I manage to publish? Will I find a path forward that does not leave me feeling emptied by the immense flaws I have seen in the service I work for?

How will I continue to survive the coming financial disaster that is always just behind the next bend in my road? This morning I woke up with a deep anxiety lying hidden beneath my breath, I could feel it creeping out of hiding and working its way surreptitiously into my heart, tightening its grip around my mind.

Also hidden away deep down is the longing I have for the man I love. I miss him, miss us. Miss being able to Share, miss being able to listen and sit in silence, miss being a part of a whole. Miss being able to relax for just a moment and not be THE person, the person who answers the phone, the person who pays the rent, the person who drives the car, the person who changes the tires, the person who sorts out the bills, cooks the food, washes the clothes, the person who walks the dogs, feeds the cats, manages the horses, the person who prunes the plants, waters the veg, dead-heads the roses and ties off the shoots, the person who does the laundry, takes out the trash, sorts the recycling, goes to the supermarket, the person who copes, every day, with the issues and concerns and worries and angst and frustrations of her many friends, her family and her clients.

There is a tapping sound. I wake up into pitch blackness and notice a light reflecting off the bedroom walls. Bailey is sitting on the windowsill looking into the dense greyness that is a November morning. I climb out from the double layers of warmth acquired from the suffering of so many geese and peer outside. Doreen can only just be seen, torch in hand, as she shuffles up the lane walking her terrier. She is intrusive even in this ordinary pursuit, shining her torch into my downstairs windows and up into the patio bird feeders that hang like so many birds on a gibbet in this pre-dawn numbness.

Tap, tap, tap. I liberate Bailey and he walks slowly out onto the sill before jumping downwards with measured calm.

As light breaks, the dahlias are in full bloom and calendula blossoms greet the day with their optimistic brightness. In the corner, almost hidden under the winter brambles, burnt orange miniature chrysanthemums cascade through the thorny arches and remind me that determination may yet win.

Lately I have awakened with a feeling of deep dread lying somewhere behind my solar plexus. It is the result of deep upheavals to both my external and internal worlds, and my battle to find resolution for them both. I am failing. I can hear my father's voice.

"This too shall pass," he assures me.

My daughter and her husband sell their house before the next full moon, and my son meets his family for breakfast every Monday before walking his daughters to school. Small steps.

I am standing high on an arid mountain top, like Moses at Mount Nebo, only beneath me the landscape is seared with the wrath of our explorations. The cities stand as blackened bones, the waterways between them thick with the green pus of greed and complacency, and the clouds overhead billow and roll on a wind of inevitability and regret. Behind me I can feel the thoughts of my ancestors, yet when I turn to find them I can see only long lines of the faceless black silhouettes of the past. As I stare unseeing into the darkness I realise that I am looking at my own reflection looking back at me, watching, waiting, all the time wondering if I can be seen.

My eyes cannot even find tears, for we knew this could be our fate, we knew and still stretched like Bailey in the summer sun, rolled over and went to sleep. We all knew. We all relied on our perfect twenty-twenty vision, our wisdom with hindsight, our blindness to the smears on the rose-tinted glasses that we all hide behind. We all knew.

Personal revolutions have begun to stir deep within the hearts and minds of Everyman in this time of ours. The entire World is holding its breath as the dice spin out their cosmic dance before rattling to a close. The year is twenty twenty, and we stand on the brink of Eternity, eyes wide shut.

My son and I are sitting in my tiny living room discussing the day's events. My daughter has messaged me to say that they have two viewings of the house booked in for next week and hopefully one of them will make an offer. Going forward it would appear that my son might soon be living back at home with his partner and their girls, all the hideous lies and allegations gone with the wind. I am happy for him.

This afternoon, with the youngest sleeping against my shoulders and the other older sisters laughing while they sat on his lap, one could almost forget all of the sadness and upset of the past few months. I tell him how impressed I was today by his calm resolve and professional approach to the legal processes playing out around him. He's come a lifetime away from the wounded warrior he was when his world and the world around everyone began to disintegrate only a few months ago.

The baby wriggles and settles back into a peaceful sleep. One of the advantages of being a buxom granny is that all of my grandchildren have fallen asleep quickly when draped across my left shoulder. There's nothing quite like a fulsome breast for resting your head on.

As we get up to leave, the Family Practitioner tells us that she is being redeployed and will no longer be able to facilitate visits between my son and his family. We are gutted. This move from the Local Authority can easily be interpreted as a maneuver to remove the one professional who has had consistent and positive interaction with all of the family members. It is simply the most recent in a long list of prejudicial behaviour and I feel nothing but contempt for the powers that be. You really couldn't make it up, no one would believe you.

This too will pass, I hear my father say. One can only hope it passes quickly.

Less than a week later our Prime Minister tells the Nation to prepare for a country wide lockdown in response to the rising numbers of Covid-19 victims. Schools will stay open, pubs and restaurants will not. The lockdown will end three weeks before Christmas. It's easy to be cynical as pensioners refuse to pay their television licensing fees and people start to hoard toilet paper for this second attempt at nationwide restrictions. One of the potential buyers pulls out from a viewing of my daughter's house. The skies lie dark and heavy on the horizon. There is a strange irony to National Lockdown starting on the very day we commemorate the aborted attempt by Guy Fawkes to blow up the Houses of Parliament. Across the Pond voters gather in the wings, and our Future lies hidden behind their scenes. Methinks there will be many long nights when we dream of a United Europe, and how we scuttled her.

It's late and I'm walking the dogs under the full moon, the moonlit mist makes a Chinese watercolour of the surrounding landscape. The ridge of woodland lies brooding ominously above the slowly moving vapours that stretch quietly up the valley and the heady scent of lavender ambushes the senses.

Rows of cottages lie tucked under the skyline, sleepily nestled between the well clipped lawns and high, well pruned hedges. Only a few windows are lit, an orange glow escaping from within, like an opened date on an Advent calendar, hinting at the lives hiding in the shadow.

We measure out our lives in coffee spoons and mugs of tea, with books on bedside tables waiting to be read and shoes no longer worn.

There is a soft knock and the hounds explode into frenzied barking. It's very late for visitors. I walk into the kitchen and undo the top of the stable door. My Future stands before me, arms laden with sunflowers and yellow roses. It is a smile I have not seen for a very very very long time. I place my coffee cup on the kitchen counter behind me. We look at one another for a lifetime in seconds, our eyes tinged with the melancholy of past moments lost and laughter unheard. Then we smile and I take a step back and open the door. The hounds go silent and curl up at my feet. The house takes a deep breath.

"Come on in."

The year is.

If you prefer smoke over fire

then get up now and leave.
    For I do not intend to perfume
    your mind's clothing
    with more sooty knowledge.
    No, I have something else in mind.
    Today I hold a flame in my left hand
    and a sword in my right.
    There will be no damage control today.
    For God is in a mood
    to plunder your riches and
    fling you nakedly
    into such breathtaking poverty
    that all that will be left of you
    will be a tendency to shine.
    So don't just sit around this flame
    choking on your mind.
    For this is no campfire song
    to mindlessly mantra yourself to sleep with.
    Jump now into the space
    between thoughts
    and exit this dream
    before I burn the damn place down.
    Adyashanti

My Law

Attributed to Ella Wheeler Wilcox

The sun may be clouded yet ever the sun
    Will sweep on it's course 'till the cycle has run
    And when into chaos the system is hurled
    Again shall the builder reshape a new world.
    Your path may be clouded and uncertain your goal,
    Move on – for your orbit is fixed to your soul
    And though it may lead into darkness of night,
    The torch of the Builder shall give it new light.
    You were, you will be! Know this while you are:
    Your spirit has traveled both long and afar.
    It came from the source, to the source it returns –
    The spark which was lighted eternally burns.
    It slept in a jewel, it leapt in a wave,
    It roamed in the forest, it rose from the grave
    It took on strange garb for long eons of years
    And Now in the soul of yourself it appears.
    From body to body your spirit speeds on
    It seeks a new form, when the old one has gone.
    And the form that it takes, is the fabric you wrought
    On the loom of the mind from the fire of thought.
    As dew is drawn upward in rays to descend,
    Your thoughts drift away and in destiny blend.
    You cannot escape them for petty or great,
    Or evil or noble, they fashion your fate.
    Somewhere on some planet, sometime and somehow,

Your life will reflect your thoughts of your now.
My law is unerring no blood can atone –
The structure you build you will live in-alone.
From cycle to cycle, through time and through space,
Your lives with your longings will ever keep pace.
And all that you ask for and all you desire
Must come at your bidding, as flame out of fire.
Once list to the voice and all tumult is done –
Your life is the life of the infinite one.
In the hurrying race you are conscious of pause.
With love for the purpose, and love for the cause.
You are your own Devil you are your own God
You fashioned the paths your footsteps have trod.
And no one can save you from error or sin,
Until you have harked to the spirit within.

Don't miss out!

Visit the website below and you can sign up to receive emails whenever Claire Suyen Grace publishes a new book. There's no charge and no obligation.

https://books2read.com/r/B-A-MJVM-OUUJB

BOOKS 2 READ

Connecting independent readers to independent writers.